JADE

THE KINGS OF GUARDIAN, BOOK 9

KRIS MICHAELS

WWW.KRISMICHAELSAUTHOR.COM

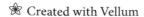 Created with Vellum

CHAPTER 1

*F*uck, *fuck, fuck!* Jade King froze and pushed back into the shadows. She sucked in a harsh breath. *Damn it!* From the darkened corner of the massive multi-purpose room, she witnessed a three hundred pound guard crush a frail woman into the cement floor of the commune's primary gathering place. He pinned her to the ground with one hand while he ripped the tattered dress from her body with the other.

The nation's largest meth manufacturing plant was hidden three stories underneath her and covered at least 10,000 square feet. As of tonight, Jade had accumulated the evidence the DEA needed. The scene she was witnessing prevented her from escaping the fucking hellhole where she'd worked alongside 150 other women, all controlled by the "Fathers". Controlled, hell... forced to work too damn hard; they were neglected, starved to keep them weak, and abused both physically and mentally.

Her DEA handlers wanted the information she had at all costs. Jade gripped her worn dress' pocket and felt the small camera where she had the evidence. Saving the woman could jeopardize their case, but god damn it! She had to live with herself, and she couldn't let the bastard rape a woman who'd already been victimized enough.

"Get away from her!" Jade stepped from safe concealment and grabbed the first thing she could convert to a weapon, an old wooden broom propped against the wall, and rushed toward the piece of shit grinding his victim into the concrete.

His head shot up at Jade's shout, and a sneer crossed his puffy, red face. The woman under him used Jade's distraction to score bloody furrows across his cheeks with her fingernails. The bastard backhanded the woman. She fell limp and still.

The man rose, and Jade drew a ragged breath. She stopped her forward movement and centered her body weight, dropping into her ready position. Cautiously she spun the handle to get a feel for the heft and length as she waited for the fucker to head toward her. Jade glanced at the door not twenty feet away. It led to freedom and hopefully to her partner and fellow agent, Garett, but there was no way she would leave the poor woman to that fucking bastard.

"You think you can take me on, missy?" Three bloody claw marks striped the bastard's face making him even more butt-ugly than usual.

"I don't think it. I know it, you fat fuck," she taunted. She baited him closer, and away from the woman on the floor. Jade choked back the overwhelming desire to whip her leg up in a roundhouse kick, knock the bastard's teeth out, and mop the floor with his face. However, she couldn't open herself up until she knew the man's capabilities. Control and determination seeped through every pore of her body as she prepared to take down a much larger opponent. The bastard finally lumbered close enough to engage. Her first strike would attempt to incapacitate the man. After years of specialized training such prioritizing was instinctive.

"Woman, I will enjoy beating you with that rod and then taking you to the Fathers. You will pay for your disobedience."

"Woman?" Jade sneered. "Is that all you see when you look at me?"

The man's sneer matched hers. "Nah, bitch, I see my evening's activities, and I like it rough."

Jade spun the broom handle and snapped it in the air. The man's eyes widened momentarily before he crouched farther and spread his stance. Jade smiled; this was what she was born to do.

"Oh baby, you have no idea how rough I can make it." Her senses hyper aware and ready for action, she heard soft footfalls behind her. Hopefully, it was the woman leaving, but she wouldn't bet on it.

"The Fathers will end you. You have no idea the pain their hired dogs can inflict. You will scream and beg. Your death could take... days. You want that, sweetheart?" He palmed his groin. "Or do you want some of this. Like it rough? Maybe that's why you didn't mind your own business. Tell ya what... spread those legs willingly, and I'll forget all about this little indiscretion."

"Put up or shut up, motherfucker." Jade shifted her weight as the man approached. He easily weighed a hundred and fifty pounds more than she did, and his bulk wasn't all fat. The man circled and Jade tracked him, always keeping him in front of her. She didn't dare glance past the bastard to see where his victim had gone. Balancing her weight on the balls of her feet, she waited. She knew how to take the man out of commission. If the son of a bitch fought as well as he talked, she'd have one hell of a fight on her hands. One she'd relish.

It had been over a month since the Fathers had escorted her from Garret's quarters to this side of the camp. She'd perfected the role of insipid mindless drone over the last year as Garett worked to become one of the inner circle. Not any longer. That persona melted away tonight when she pocketed the mini-camera that documented the evidence the Justice Department would need to take down this cult. She'd gathered enough evidence in the last month to bring the bastards who ran this camp to their knees.

The big fucker in front of her feigned a lunge to his right, and Jade followed his dance. Even this small engagement taught her about the man. He wasn't skilled; he was a bruiser. Jade hesitated on purpose. The asshole noticed and a sinister chuckle ripped from his butt-ugly face. *Welcome to my web, motherfucker*. Jade acted as if she almost missed his fake to the left, but sprang forward and effectively parried his next lunge. She hit him hard on the shoulder with her staff and backed away, centering her weight again.

Sweat rolled down his forehead. A drop hung off his mop of hair. Jade lifted an eyebrow at him and laughed. He lunged again, and she sidestepped. A set of arms clamped around her from the back, and without thought, Jade whipped the staff around and rammed the blunt end into her unseen attacker's ribs. The arms released her. She turned and swung hard and fast. A sickening crack sounded when her staff connected to the would-be rapist's forearm. Unfortunately, it wasn't the assailant's arm that broke. It was the broom handle. Jade held tight to the shorter end still in her hands. The shard of wood was as deadly as a knife, and she wielded it at her two attackers.

"Come on, honey. You're going to make your punishment worse." The new man tried to coax her with words, and he made a fatal mistake. He favored his left side where she'd driven the broom-stick into his ribs.

Jade dragged needed air into her lungs and waited. The first man lunged and the second man followed. Jade sidestepped the injured man and, with all the strength she could gather, plunged the splintered end of the wood into the fat gut of the would-be rapist. The bull rush he'd started propelled both of them toward the ground. Jade twisted so his weight would land on what remained of the broomstick. The unmistakable sound of flesh tearing filled her ears as she rolled away. She glimpsed the other half of the staff to her right, dragged herself up and pitched forward.

A hand grabbed her arm as she scrambled across the floor. Her free hand grasped for the broom handle. Jade clamped her jaw down on the wrist of the bastard who grabbed her and felt her teeth break through his skin. The tang of copper from his blood spread in her mouth. She bit down and pulled with all of her strength, trying to tear skin from bone. The son of a bitch screamed and used his other hand to try to pry her head from his wrist. Her momentum forced him backward. Jade reached out blindly and grabbed for the second half of the broken handle.

Her assailant swung his fist at her face. Grabbing the broken handle from the floor, Jade speared the shaft of jagged wood forward as the son of a bitch lunged at her. Her inability to aim didn't matter, hitting the fucker was her only goal. The man kicked her and the blow turned her as she thrust the wood upward. The shard ripped through the bottom of the man's chin, and a spray of blood splattered across her hand and arm. The son of a bitch gargled a scream and grabbed at her hand. Jade kneed the asshole and pain blazed through her leg. Instinctively she fought through the excruciating pain. With both hands, she shoved the stake up through the flesh behind his jaw and into his brain until the back of his skull stopped its forward progress. Her opponent folded in on himself; in death, his hand clenched the blood-soaked skewer.

Jade rolled away and tried to stand. Her leg crumbled beneath her. When he'd kicked her, her attacker had seriously screwed up her knee. Bad. Fuck, the bastard may have dislocated it. At least she hoped it was only a dislocation. Forced to crawl to the side of the room, she pulled herself up into a wooden chair. The fat bastard lay on the floor moaning. His victim still hadn't moved, whether alive or dead, she didn't know, but there was no way she could get herself and the woman to safety. Not now, not with the injury to her leg. She needed to get the evidence out and get help for all the people enslaved here. At least that was the plan. She winced and sucked a hard pull of air when she tried to move her leg. Her knee was three kinds of fucked up.

The room where the fight had taken place was a wide-open bay adjacent to the kitchens. It was just before dawn. As soon as someone arrived to make the crap they fed the women, they'd see the bodies. She couldn't be here. The sound of opening and closing doors in the corridor spurred her into action. She hopped across the open expanse toward the doorway. Making her way back to Garret, her partner, so they could get out and complete their mission was her only focus. She needed to find the fastest way out and put out the signal to Garret. The voices sounded nearer... *Shit.*

Jade winced at the throbbing pain radiating down her leg. She couldn't make the distance to the door, not to mention the long trek down the corridor to exit the building, in time to hide herself from whoever was coming. She regarded the window three feet away and almost laughed at her stupidity. Of course! She hopped to the window, opened it and pushed the screen out at the bottom. The drop out of the window jarred her knee again. She gave the pain time to recede while she leaned against the building. Wiping her face with the sleeve of her faded blue dress, she shivered. The threadbare garment had seen better days. The night sky was starting to lighten which meant the complex would begin to wake soon.

Jade steadied herself and used the building as a support. She made slow but steady progress. When she finally reached the fence line, she tore a strip of cloth off the bottom of her tattered skirt and tied it to the bottom rail of a fence that ran in front of the warehouse. It wasn't big enough to draw attention, but it signaled Garret to call in reinforcements. Jade surveyed the out buildings and chose the closest one. It was bigger and more frequented than the smaller structure next to it—the one she really wanted to hide in, but there wasn't time. She needed to get off her leg and find a hiding place until the cavalry arrived.

A muffled shout from the main building sent a ripple of fear up her spine. She used the fence railing as a crutch and moved as quickly as she could to the building she'd chosen. She leaned against the vinyl siding for a second to catch her breath. More shouting could be heard through the open windows of the main building. She lurched around the corner but instead of a closed door, the solid chest of a guard blocked her way. He grabbed at her, but Jade lurched back on her injured knee, falling to the ground. She crab walked backward looking for anything she could use as a weapon. He walked forward and grabbed her hair close to her skull as she writhed and fought in his hold. He drew back his arm; his hard meaty fist flew forward, and Jade closed her eyes.

The snap of air and spray of warmth across her face stilled her struggle. The man who'd caught her fell backward, taking her with him. Released from his grip, Jade lurched through the door and closed it. Someone had shot the bastard. His blood and brains spattered her dress but she had no way of knowing if the bullet was intended for him or her. She hunkered down and made herself as small as possible.

CHAPTER 2

"Jade," a low, gravelly voice rasped. Jade froze. Had she imagined the sound?

"God damn it, Jade, open the fucking door."

Jason? Jason was here? Fuck, she was hallucinating. Jade reached up and slowly turned the knob. The door creaked open a crack. She held it for a few seconds trying to see if she'd finally lost it. No, it was Jason, complete with tactical gear and an M-4. She threw the wooden door wide at the sight of her brother, not two feet in front of her. Jade lurched out of the building and Jason wrapped her in his arms. "How bad are you hurt?"

"My knee. I think it's dislocated. Are you here with the DEA?" Jade pulled away from him and took in the armed force deployed outside the building. Fuck, at least two full Guardian teams that she could see.

"No, but we'll get into that later. Let's get you out of here." Jason started to move back away from the building.

"What about the meth complex?"

"The what?" Jason shot back at her.

Jade held up a hand, her eyes opened as wide as saucers. She gestured wildly around her. "Dude, these fuckers have like a 10,000 square foot meth lab three stories below us. I have all the evidence the DEA needs, but we better get going now because I…" A long slow wail erupted from the loud speakers around the camp, and lights blinked on in every building. Jade's voice barely carried above the din of the klaxon, "… may have killed some assholes that were trying to kill me."

"Fuck." Jason's epithet rang loud and clear despite the deafening alarm. "Dixon, Drake, get her the fuck out of here. Zane, you got their six." Jason's voice rose distinctly. "Jacob, you've got operational control. Let's mop up this bitch and take the fuckers down."

Jade gaped at her brother, "Wait, all of you are here? Why?" She barely got the words out before

Drake grabbed Jade and unceremoniously tossed her over his shoulder.

"Holy Shit! Watch my fucking knee!" Jade scrambled, trying to find purchase on the man's tactical vest. "Motherfucker, install a handle on this bitch if you're going to play fireman." She finally found purchase and bent damn near in half to look at the man who hefted her as if she was a bag of flour. "Hey, big boy! Going my way?" Jade slapped the back of his bulletproof vest when he hitched her a little further over his shoulder. "Don't be like that, man. Who taught you how to treat a lady?"

"Girl, when you find a lady, let me know. Until then, shut up and hang on." A huge shit-eating grin stretched across his face.

"Oh, you smooth talker, you. I missed you, too." Jade gripped the straps of his vest. The ride wouldn't be gentle or easy, but the fastest way out of the compound for both of them was over his shoulder. He hefted her and balanced her weight, using her good knee to grab as an anchor.

The siren silenced suddenly. The voice of Jade's sister, Jewell, crackled over the comms that hung out of Drake's ear. "I have their systems under our control. There is a swarm of activity at the rear of the compound near the garage."

Damn, Jade wished she could be part of the team to take the Fathers down. She'd earned that right by giving up the last year of her life.

Jade flopped back against the foam mat of the ambulance stretcher. The twins had dumped her with the first responders and then bolted back into the compound, leaving her in the company of the bruiser who followed them out. She didn't know him, but she appreciated someone from Guardian protecting her ass. Ha! Literally. The EMTs stabilized her knee, but she refused to let them give her any drugs or take her to the hospital. She had the evidence, and she wasn't going anywhere until she handed it over to whoever was in charge of this fucked up operation.

Speaking of which, she caught the big blond's attention and motioned him over to her. Jade liked the way the man stalked; he was a damn fine looker that was for sure. He stopped at the back of the ambulance, crossed his massive arms over his chest, and peered down at her.

"Well, aren't you the strong silent type?" Jade cocked her head and blinked at him coyly, waiting for him to acknowledge her.

"Your sister was right."

Jade straightened her head and smiled. "Which one? Jasmine? Holy hell, did she finally land a keeper?" Jade was damn happy for her if she had. That woman went through hell when her fiancé knocked up the woman he was cheating with. Jade wanted to castrate the bastard, but both Jacob and Jason had threatened to release some rather embarrassing information about her to their mom if she took action. Blackmailing bastards. Fuck, she couldn't wait to have a drink or ten with them.

The man shook his head. "Jewell."

Jade's mouth literally dropped open at the comment. Seriously, she had no hinge on the damn thing and couldn't manage to close it. Jewell? Holy hell, how did her socially awkward, sweetheart of a sister bag this badass behemoth? She finally shut her mouth with an audible snap. "Really? Jewell... as in my sister, the ice-queen and work-obsessed computer nerd? Jewell, really? How the hell did you meet? When did you meet? I mean, she never leaves her fucking section."

The man chuckled and rubbed the back of his

neck with his hand. "I was assigned as her body-guard when the Bratva was threatening the family..."

"Say what now?" Jade lifted off the stretcher onto her elbows.

The man's brow furrowed. "How long have you been undercover?"

Jade lay back down and blew out a lungful of air. "Over a year."

"Then you don't know about Jasmine and her fiancé?"

"Ah... noo..." *Jasmine had a fiancé?* "That is fucking awesome!" She fist pumped and laughed.

"Joseph and Ember had a baby."

Jade squealed and lifted up to a sitting position, the pain in her knee be damned! "Joseph and Ember are having a baby?"

"Had. A boy. His name is Blake."

"B? That is so totally awesome!" Jade was happy, like a cat drinking grade A cream, happy. "Shit, I guess I missed a lot."

"Yeah, you could say that." Jason's voice came from her right.

"Hey, Jace! Did you know this guy and Jewell are an item?" Jade waved her hand at the big man standing beside her. "Isn't that awesome? I mean this guy and Jewell! Oh, and Joseph and Ember had a baby! Why didn't you say something about that?"

"Ahh... did they give her something for the pain?" Jason turned away from her and gazed at the big blond guy.

She really needed to figure out his name.

"Heeelllooo... asshat, I'm right here, and I can answer your questions. No, they haven't given me anything for the pain. I'm happy." Jade wasn't going to be marginalized. Ever again. This last year spent kowtowing to Garret and every other man in the compound sucked sweaty duck balls. Maybe she was a titch exuberant, but damn it, it was as if she pulled off a gas mask and was breathing fresh air for the first time in... fuck... almost fourteen months.

"Right. We can get you caught up with all the family news once you get to the hospital and someone looks at that knee." Jason motioned toward the EMT.

"Wait!" Jade patted her pocket and grabbed the matchbox-sized video/audio recording device the DEA had given her. "Is this our op now?"

"As of the day before yesterday. The agent you partnered with failed to make his check in and prior to that he'd lost contact with you. A hacker got through Guardian's firewalls and released your undercover information, so we had to act."

"Wait, what? Jewell's systems were hacked? Isn't that like impossible?" She shifted her stare from one man to the other. "Is Garret okay?"

"He's fine, if he survives the out brief with Jared and Jacob. The system breach was improbable, and now virtually impossible, but when a member of Guardian gives a genius a back door into the system..."

"What? Shut the fuck up! Who?" Jade's head was spinning. She had so many questions!

Jason sighed and motioned to the EMT again. The man jumped up into the back of the vehicle with her. "We'll talk about it all night long if you want, but right now you are going to the hospital. Maliki Blue will be there. He doesn't have privileges. We couldn't get them quick enough, but he'll be shepherding for you to make sure shit is done right."

"Why is Maliki stateside? Is his team here?" Jade was trying to keep up, she really was, but it seemed nothing was the same as it used to be. Holy fuck, the world had marched on without her, and it felt like she'd been dropped inside a modern version of *The Twilight Zone*.

"Later, Jade. I promise." Jason shut one half of the split rear doors to the ambulance.

"Wait! Here, here is the evidence for the DEA. The Fathers are the driving force behind the complex. I have their photos and several videos on here that implicate them in the manufacturing and distribution of the meth. There is an office off the manufacturing area. It has a floor safe. Slide the stainless steel coffee table off it. They put documents in there once a day. I don't know what, but it has to be important if they are hiding it."

Jade grabbed the rails of the stretcher and sat up again. "Oh and the lieutenants that handle the manufacturing don't arrive until about nine. I have license plate numbers, but I don't have names. I watched them pull up, park, and enter the underground facility. They'd pull on white lab coats, and they'd do shit like quality control tests or something. There is a video showing three of them making the rounds."

Jason took the device from her and smiled. "Thank you. We'll take it from here. You did well, Pogo. Now go get patched and cleaned up. I've had Jewell call and update Mom, and I'm sure she'd appreciate a call when you get released."

She flipped Jace off the second she heard him

use her nickname but was over it immediately when he mentioned their mom. "Hey! She's still married, right?"

Jace rolled his eyes and smiled a huge stupid grin.

"God, tell me she's not pregnant! Please?" Jade yelled the words at the closing doors.

Jason pounded on the outside of the vehicle signaling the driver to go.

Jade lay back and swung her attention to the EMT sitting beside her. "So, good looking, do you come here often?" A delightful shade of red started to climb up the man's neck. Jade laughed at his embarrassment. Oh, fuck, it was so damn good to be back.

CHAPTER 3

Yep, she'd had enough. Jade counted the number of tiles on the floor. Seventy-six and one half tiles. The need for that half tile took several minutes to contemplate, not that she gave a shit that the room was lopsided, but hey, it was something to think about other than how fucking long it was taking to see the doctor. She'd also memorized the anatomically correct poster of the inner ear that hung on the back of the door. The HIPAA laws were dry as dirt, but she'd still read through them three times. She'd been stuck in this tiny little room for over an hour, and she hadn't seen anyone, except the nurse that had wheeled her here from radiology and shut the door behind her on the way out. Maliki Blue was supposed to be here somewhere, but if he was, Jade hadn't seen him. And she'd definitely remember seeing him. The man was drop dead gorgeous. Tall, built, white-blonde hair and ice blue eyes. He'd make Thor feel inadequate. But nope, not a sign of anyone she knew. Five more minutes and she was taking herself out of this place. She could be on her way to the airport and back home. Ice, elevation, and rest were what her knee needed. She hoped. Yep. Four minutes and she was airport bound. No, better yet, she'd go to the airport bar. That was one hell of a goal. She hadn't had a drink in over a year and damn it, she missed it. The door to the room swung open and she glanced up. Dixon and Drake ghosted in, and Jade jumped up on her good leg. "Hey!" She hugged one and then the other before she turned and punched Drake on the arm.

"Ouch, what the fuck?" Drake grabbed his bicep and squeezed it.

Big ole baby. "Is that how you treat me after an entire year of not seeing me? Just throw me over your shoulder and then after a not-so-gentle run, you dump me on a stretcher and leave my ass in the parking lot? You are not second date material, mister." Jade hopped back to the stupid exam table, and parked her butt on the crinkly white paper that lined the top.

"Well, you must admit, you were in no shape to run, and if you remember correctly, people were shooting, darlin'. Besides, I thought you liked the Neanderthal act." Drake elbowed his brother Dixon. "Or did my memory mislead me?"

"Not going to deny it, but wasn't expecting it within two minutes of y'all showing up!" She threw back her head and laughed. It felt so good to be free of the bastards that had ruled her every breath for the last year. She'd become something less than human bending to the hypocrisy of the Bible thumping degenerates that twisted the words of God to suit their own tyrannical needs.

"The J-men are mopping up. Jacob sent us here to make sure you didn't bail without getting a doctor to look at your leg. It took us almost thirty minutes to find you. I think they hid you from us on purpose." Dixon hooked his toe around a little stool with wheels and pulled it toward him. He sat down and leaned back against the wall crossing his arms, and a smirk spread across his face.

"I think they forgot about me, period. Why would Jacob send you here? Seriously, I wasn't going to bail." Jade averted her eyes and tried not to laugh.

"Bullshit." Drake walked the two steps it took to cross the room and sat down beside her on the exam table.

"Yeah, you're right. I was down to about three minutes before I headed to the airport bar. So, what have you two been up to in the last year? Anything good? Or should I say anyone good?" She caught the quick glance between the brothers and elbowed Drake. "No shit? Who? Is it serious?" She panned her gaze back and forth between the twins.

"There are two—"

"Wait! Wait a minute! I thought you two liked to share? You admitted that, right? The last time we went out for drinks. I'm not dreaming that conversation, am I?" Jade ping-ponged her head between the two.

Identical shit-eating grins spread across their faces. "We do, but these two are... hell, I don't know, Drake, what would you call them?" Dixon peered up at his brother.

"Feisty twins with too much attitude and skittish as hell." Drake shrugged. "They've been leading us on a merry fucking dance."

Jade realized her mouth had dropped open. She

snapped it shut and blinked rapidly. "Twins, dating twins? Holy mistaken identity, Batman. Where, when, who, how and most importantly, are you happy?" Jade damn near bounced on the exam table. Her friends were actually on the hook or at least nibbling at the bait, and damn if that didn't make her happy. The twins had burrowed a lair inside her inner circle where very few people resided: her immediate family, the Twins, Chief, and Gabriel and his family. A select few and that was on purpose.

Dixon snorted. "You don't dance. Why the fuck would you use that metaphor? God, Drake, maybe you could use your imagination."

"Imagination? Really Dixon? When was the last time—"

Jade put her fingers to her mouth and blew an ear-shattering whistle. Both men stopped arguing and snapped their attention back to her.

"Thank you. Now you were saying? About these ladies?"

"Well, we met when..." The door swung open and Maliki and a man in scrubs entered the room.

Jade pointed at Maliki and the doctor and made a shooing motion toward the door. "No, do not come in here! Go back out! I need to hear this!"

"Nah, that's okay Doc, we need to get out of here anyway." Dixon stood up at the same time as Drake lifted off the table.

"Hell, no! You owe me answers!"

They smiled and sauntered out the door.

"Answers! Do you hear me?" She yelled as the door swung shut. *Damn it.* So much had happened in the past year. She studied Maliki for a moment and then scrunched her nose at him. "I'm mad at you."

He crossed his arms and chuckled. "You're mad at me? Pray tell, what did I do to earn your wrath."

"Dude, I've been in here for an hour. An hour! Do you know how much fun we could have had in that amount of time?" She gave him a huge wink and laughed at the blush that burned up his neck to his cheeks.

He shook his head and turned toward the doctor behind him. "Jade, this is Doctor Sheppard. Be nice to him. He's an orthopedic specialist, one of the best in the state. I didn't meet you at emergency because I was waiting for him to get out of surgery so I could whisk him off to see you."

Jade swiveled her attention to the surgeon behind him. Nice build, thick brown hair, and a great smile. He'd do. "Hiya doc! Are you single?"

The man chuckled and shook his head. "Sorry, taken."

"Damn it. Y'all, I'm striking out all around tonight." Jade lifted the back of her hand to her forehead and pretended to swoon. "A year undercover and nobody wants little ole me."

"Can the bullshit, Scarlett O'Hara." Both Maliki and Doctor Sheppard swung around at Jason's comment, but Jade relaxed back onto the table.

"Nope. I'm a drama queen tonight. I deserve to cut loose but nobody wants to play with me."

"Leave the doctors alone and let them examine your knee. Dixon and Drake are heading to the airfield to prep the plane and log our flight plan."

Jade popped up off the table. "No! We need to finish our conversation! Tell them to come back here!"

"Later. Now do we need to tie you down and gag you, or will you cooperate?" Jason crossed the tree trunks masquerading as arms over his chest and stared at her.

"Pa-lease tie me down! Do you have a rubber ball gag? The cloth ones get so... moist." She shivered at the word.

Jason pulled off his glasses and pinched the bridge of his nose. Oh shit, the big guy was getting serious. Jade knew when he'd reached his limit, and she was pushing him. She sighed and capitulated, "Nah, do what you need to do. I want to go home as much as you do."

Jason peered at Maliki. "Dude, patch her up enough to get her home. And a needle or two of sedative would help us all sleep on the way back."

"Hey! I can't sleep. I have too much to catch up on! Oh, did you get the lieutenants? They are probably going to be the key to unlocking the organization."

Jason nodded. "Two. The third didn't show today, so we are hunting him now. The safe under the table was a gold mine. We will be dissecting this organization for at least six months. You did well, Pogo."

Jade immediately flashed Jason the finger and got the laugh she'd been accustomed to for as long as she could remember. Joseph had started calling her Pogo when they were still young. It fit. She did bounce around, hyper and more than a little crazy at times. Hell, she'd been called much, much worse. Jade squared her shoulders and beamed at her brother. "I did do a good job, didn't I?" She huffed on her fingernails and rubbed them over the pathetic, worn dress that she longed to shed. "Hey, can you get me some clothes other than this rag? Sweats and a t-shirt? Anything?"

"I can get you a pair of scrubs." Maliki offered.

"Cool. Now let's get this show on the road because the Guardian jets have fully stocked bars. I've earned a scotch."

Doctor Sheppard cleared his throat and motioned for Jade to put her leg up on the exam table. "Liquor and pain meds are not compatible."

"Who's taking pain meds?" Jade swiveled her head from Doctor Sheppard to Maliki.

"You." The orthopedic surgeon was logging onto the computer that sat on a wheeled stand— the one she may have tried to log onto to surf the internet earlier, but she never made it past the lock screen. Where was Jewell when she needed her?

"No, I'm not. I don't take pain medications." Jade didn't need to say why, especially with Jason standing three feet from her.

"Excuse me?" Doctor Sheppard craned his neck and blinked back at her.

"Don't try to win this fight, Doc." Maliki sighed. "If I had a dollar for every time a King refused pain medications, I'd be rich."

"You are rich." Jade lifted an eyebrow and

defied Maliki to deny the truth. She knew his background.

He shrugged. "Rich-er."

"Jade, quit tormenting the good doctors. I'm going to go check on the operation at the compound." Jason turned his attention to the doctors. "I'll be in the hall if you need me. Don't hesitate to shout if she acts out."

"Hey, I'm not a child!" She yelled at his retreating back. When the door shut, Jade turned her mischievous gaze to the doctors. "I'm a fully grown woman. Want proof?"

Maliki groaned and shook his head, and the other doctor stared at her as if she was a science experiment. Jade winked at the man. That broke the spell. He snapped his head back to the computer, and Jade chuckled to herself. Damn it was good to be out of that hellhole.

CHAPTER 4

Nicolas DeMarco rubbed his eyes. He'd been awake for far too fucking long. Why in the hell had he decided that going on that rescue mission was, one, a good idea and, two, any of his goddamned business? Now, three days later, he was smack dab in the middle of paperwork hell. He fucking hated paperwork.

"Too bad you're so damn good at it."

Nic snapped his head up glaring at Jared King's comment. "Say what?"

"You're talking to yourself again, DeMarco."

Nic yawned and his forehead hit the conference room table with a resonating thunk. "Have we sent over the final transcripts on the chemist interviews we conducted after we brought them in? The DEA wanted to see if they could match anything we got to ongoing cases."

"Ahh…" Jared pushed at his tablet and shook his head. "No, but then again it is three in the morning… I think those guys are smarter than we are, and they are home asleep."

Nic lifted his head until his fisted hands cradled his chin. He closed one eye and squinted at his business partner. "You should go home. Go snuggle up with your man and get some sleep. At least one of us should get some." He wasn't just talking about rest.

"We've hit the end of the road for today." Jared started to roll down his shirtsleeves. "You should go home, too. Actually get some sleep instead of jumping into the sack with one of your women."

He responded with a derisive huff. If his friend only knew. He hadn't had a date in… hell… months. His womanizing ways had shut down when he'd attempted to get closer to Jewell. The woman was everything he'd always told himself he wanted. She was gorgeous, smart, dedicated, understood the crazy hours necessary, and as a side benefit, his mother would love her. Hell, Jewell worked harder than he did. He thought there had been a mutual attraction. Boy, had he called that one wrong. He'd gotten over it, but his pride took one hell of a punch when she chose Zane Reynolds over him. He'd acted like a total douche, and Jewell had called him on it. He should have blown the rejection off and got back on the horse, so to speak, but he wasn't sure if he wanted a life of nameless, faceless fucks any more.

He yawned again, cracking his jaw in the process. "I don't know. I'll probably catch a nap on the couch in my office. We need to confer with the program managers first thing in the morning. If they are hitting any speed bumps with the multitude of follow-up cases we've funneled their way because of this bust, we need to make sure we get them the resources to handle it."

Jared dropped his head into his hands and scrubbed his face before he gave Nic an exhausted and slightly glazed over stare. "Yeah, okay. I'll do the same."

"Nah, man, get out of here. Sleep for a solid eight and then come back and tag me out of this insanity. I'll handle anything that comes up until you get back."

Jared sighed and stood. He scanned the files and papers scattered across the conference room table. "It feels like I'm forgetting something."

"Dude, whatever it is, I'll handle it. Go home. Reintroduce yourself to your husband, and get some sleep." There was no sense in both of them imitating zombies. Although a zombie would probably have more energy than either of them currently possessed.

Jared gave him an owlish blink and nodded. "All right. If I remember what it is I'm forgetting, I'll message you."

Nic waved him off. "Don't worry about it, I got it." He watched Jared walk out the door and down the hall toward his office. Nic stood and gathered the fucking paperwork into semi-coherent stacks and cursed when his tablet lit up with the final interview transcripts. He tapped on the attached file and flung it up onto the ninety-two inch LED monitor hanging on the wall. There was no way his tired eyes were going to focus on the small tablet screen. He opened the document and cringed. One hundred and three, single-spaced, typed pages. "Fuck me. I'm going to need one hell of a lot more coffee." He cast a glowering look at the coffee station and grimaced. He'd consumed enough java over the last two days to sink the Titanic, but desperate times equaled desperate measures. He needed ten or twenty more cups of go-juice.

Four hours, seven interview transcripts, and twenty-three written statements later, he stood and stretched. It was official. He was brain dead.

"What in the hell are you still doing here?"

Nic jumped at Jason King's bellowed question.

He grabbed his chest and leaned forward, bracing himself on the table with his free arm. "Holy shit, man, what are you trying to do, give me a heart attack? I've consumed so much caffeine I'll explode if I move too fast."

"Yeah, let's not do the spontaneous detonation thing. I think the cleanup would suck. But seriously, did you work through the night, again?" Jason surveyed the carefully constructed chaos on the conference room table.

"Yeah. I sent Jared home about 3:00 a.m., but then the final transcripts of the interviews came in, so I dug in and finished them. The DEA should have all the information they need when they come into the office." Nic yawned so hard his body shook at the end of it.

"Did you forward them to Legal?" Jason studied his tablet as he spoke.

"Yeah, these were the last documents they

required to work up the cases we have open. I also put copies on the domestic server and courtesy copied all the department heads that need the information in order to pursue the suspects we're hunting."

"Excellent work. Why don't you head home and grab some sleep?"

"I will after Jared gets back. I'll pop back to my office, shower, change, and take care of the morning meetings and anything else that comes up. When Jared comes in, I'll crash, but one of us needs to be here. We have too many moving pieces right now with this meth manufacturing and distribution case on top of our normal workload." Nic folded his suit jacket over his arm and grabbed his tablet, making a move toward the door.

Jason snorted and followed Nic out of the conference room. "The scope on this is almost as large as the Morales Cartel takedown. We had a multi-organization task force working the fallout on that one for months."

Jason walked beside Nic as he headed toward his office. Nic tried to hide another yawn but wasn't successful. He chuckled before he spoke, because fuck, he was tired and he couldn't hide it, "I'm glad we've grown enough we don't have to beg a handout from the alphabet soup crew." Nic had zero love for the FBI, CIA, or any other XYZ organization. He'd run up against the bureaucracy when he was a cop and later. Of course, that was when he'd finally gotten smart, leveraged his Yale law degree, and taken this job with Guardian.

Nic shook his head as he considered the final interviews. "The Fathers had one hell of a network, I'll give them that, but they need to work on the loyalty of their employees. We had so many people rolling over that putting these guys behind bars won't even be a challenge." Nic paused outside his office with Jason and greeted several people heading into the office for the day.

Jason glanced at his tablet again and nodded to himself. He flashed the face of the pad toward Nic before smiling smugly. "Sonya has shuffled my meetings. It has been a couple years since I've held the helm in Domestic, but I'll take the morning meetings for you and hold down the fort until Jared comes back in. You've busted ass over the last couple days. Get some sleep. I don't want to see you for at least twenty-four hours, and since it is Friday, I'll alter that. Seventy-two hours. Nonnegotiable."

Nic would have argued the point, but the yawn

that currently stretched his jaw was an all-encompassing thing. Shit, he was done. He needed to sleep before he drove anywhere. When he finished his cell-restructuring yawn, he nodded his agreement. "We may need to send out more manpower to supplement the regional departments. The caseload we doled out has everyone stretched paper thin."

"Yeah, been there, done that. I got this. Go away." Jason cuffed him on the shoulder in a friendly gesture, only it sent him forward two steps. The mountain didn't know how fucking strong he was, or maybe Nic was that fucking tired. He watched Jason walk down the hall toward his office. Nic closed one eye and tried to keep him in focus. He was so tired he felt drunk. "Office, DeMarco!" Jason's voice snapped him back to the hallway.

He lifted his hand and waved off Jason's concerned look. At least he thought it was concern. The man had a resting bitch face that could make a person wonder. Nic opened the door to his offices and did a double take at the woman sitting at his personal assistant's desk. Since his administrative assistant had taken maternity leave, he'd been getting a rotation of temporary help.

This one peeked up at him through her fake lashes and smiled at him. He'd seen that type of smile before; hell, he held the patent on the prototype. This one was on the hunt.

"Mr. DeMarco, I'm Candi, with an 'i.' I've been assigned to you. I've printed out your calendar and put your messages on your desk. You have a stack from yesterday afternoon, one of which was from a Judge DeMarco. May I get you some coffee?"

Nic shook his head and literally shivered at the thought of consuming more coffee. He planted his tired body in front of the desk where Candi-with-an-i sat. Even in his comatose state, he could appreciate the fact that the woman was pretty. Big brown eyes, brown hair pinned up in a feminine style and a very tight dress that displayed an unnatural rack. Nature didn't hand out what he estimated to be 32 double Ds as a rule. "Candi, is it?"

The woman nodded.

"Yeah, my calendar has changed as of a couple minutes ago. Jason King will be taking my meetings today. I'm going in there…" Nic pointed to his door, "… and dropping dead on my couch. I do not want to be disturbed for any reason. At all. Period. What day is it, by the way?"

"Friday, sir."

"Right." Jason had said something about it being Friday, hadn't he? Nic stared at his tablet to confirm the date. "I think that's a record. No sleep in..." Shit, the last time he slept through the night was Tuesday, so it was... hell... it was too hard to figure out. "... a long time. Even if the zombie apocalypse happens, I don't want anyone to wake me up and tell me. Got it?" Which was really something, because being in the middle of that would be a major league thrill ride. But right now, the only thing he wanted was sleep.

The woman blinked at him and nodded before she lifted her hand, halting his turn. "Do you want me to wake you up before I go, and what if one of the Kings asks for you?"

Not the brightest bulb in the pack was she? Nic rubbed his eyes. It felt as if the entire Jersey shore lodged itself between his eyelids and eyeballs. He rubbed those poor tired bastards so he didn't have to look at Della the Double Ditz. Hell, that wasn't fair, but right now he didn't care. He wanted to go to sleep. Finally, he blinked his vision back to normal and shook his head. "Jason King told me to get lost. If he comes looking for me, the world has ended, and the zombies are storming the facility.

41

You have my permission to wake me if you actually see a zombie in person. There is no other reason on this earth that you should go near that door. Understand?"

"Yes, sir." The little brunette gave him a wan smile.

"Awesome. Good night." Nic turned on his heel and made it to his office five steps later. His jacket got tossed toward the coat rack. He had his shirt sleeves unbuttoned, his tie, belt, and shoes off in less than thirty seconds. He hit the remote dimming the lights in his office before he flopped face first into the Italian leather couch that occupied the far wall of his office. He'd slept many hours on the thing and knew it like a lover. He pushed into the cushions at the back of the sofa and unabashedly snuggled in. His messages could wait, especially the one from his mother. Nic took a deep breath and slowly exhaled, letting his body relax into oblivion.

Jade walked down the halls of Guardian noting the subtle changes in the building and the lack of familiar faces. Jared had told her not to show up today or he'd put her on admin duty tracking down some of the leads she uncovered while living at the meth complex. Bold threat, but having her on admin duty could bring Guardian to its knees. Hell, the last time Jewell left her unattended with her computer system she'd fried a server. No, a processor. And that event was just one of many she could list. No, admin anything wasn't her forte. She knew her limits, and so did her brother. She was bored. To tears. Well, not really tears because big girls don't cry and all that shit.

She'd hung out with the twins last night, enjoying a bottle of Gentleman Jack, and some honest communication with two men she respected and admired. The twins were funny, brilliant and fucking uber sexy. Could she jump in the sack with them? Hell, yeah, but that would ruin the connection she had with them. She honestly liked the twins. Having sex with them would fuck that up, and she'd be damned if her over-excited libido would take them away from her. Jade knew how she rolled. Fuck them hard and walk away. One and done with little to no chance of repeat hook-ups. She was allergic to commitment. That shit made her break out in hives and itch. Splotches were not in her future. Ever. Besides, she wasn't willing to walk away from Dixon and Drake, aka Double D, so she would never get physically involved with them.

Jade stopped in the hall and rubbed her thigh above her bad knee. The joint still ached like a mother, and it swelled when she was on it too long, so no clubbing for a while. Ha, as if. Dancing wasn't what was on her mind. Unless it was a tango between the sheets. Not that she'd been able to act on what was front and center in her thoughts because her mom had flown into town. Which was cool. Her mom filled her in on all the shit that had happened while she was undercover. They had a great visit, but Jade felt invigorated by being back at Guardian, by simply being in the building. Family was great, but she'd had an oversized portion of brothers, friends, and mothering in the last three days. Now she wanted to find something else that she hadn't had in over a year. She'd dropped her mom off at Jared's about two hours ago to find out Jared had rolled in after almost three days of around the clock work, and he was dead to the world. Her mom and Christian made plans to work at the youth center Christian had started. Not a good fit for her. It wasn't a secret that she didn't like kids, and man, could those little humans tell it. Kids could see shit adults couldn't. They freaked her out. How her mom raised eight kids was beyond her. Jade shivered as a chill ran up and down her spine. Take her nephews for example. Her nephews were cool as long as the parental units were around giving her no opportunity to fuck them up somehow. Because she would, it was a foregone conclusion. Jade plus little humans equaled a disaster waiting to happen. No, she'd work for Christian's cause in other ways. Like donating a healthy chunk of change to help the kids out.

With Jared down for the count, that meant Nic was in charge. Which was totes cool with her. She hadn't spent much time around him, but if Jared, Jason, and Gabriel liked him enough to hire him, she assumed the man was solid until he proved himself otherwise. At least he was really pretty to look at. The man was a jungle gym she'd wait in line to play on. She laughed to herself. If you believed the rumors, she probably would have to wait in line, because the man was popular with the women. Another reason the handsome hunk of man intrigued her.

She pushed open one of the glass doors to Nic's office. His assistant was on the phone with her back to the door, one foot on the ground and one foot tucked under her as she swiveled back and forth.

"I know! So I told her that there was no way. I mean can you imagine? As if that would happen."

Jade crossed her arms and leaned back against the doorframe, waiting for the woman to turn around and see her. Far be it from her to stymie someone's gossip time, even if it was in the middle of the workday.

"Seriously, he is to-die-for dreamy! He doesn't have much of a personality, though. I mean he showed up here looking like he'd lived in his suit and then had the audacity to tell me not to come into his office... Oh, you know I did! I snuck in a bit ago, and he was so sound asleep he was drooling. I thought all these guys were supposed to be like ninjas and stuff. What? No, didn't even stir."

Jade straightened and examined Nic's office door. Fuck, if the man worked the same hours that Jared had worked, he should be at home asleep, not trying to rest on an office couch.

"I would have taken a picture on my phone, but you know how it goes with all the security around here. They always catch me when I 'accidentally' forget and try to bring it in. So many good-looking guys. My Instagram and Snapchat followers would like double, you know? So, I grabbed his tablet, took a picture and emailed it to my account. What? Of course, I deleted it off his tablet. What do you think I am, stupid? Here, let me forward it to you." The assistant worked her keyboard and laughed.

Jade put her hands on her hips and glared at the little bitch. The woman pushed her chair around and froze. For a heartbeat before she tried to cover up her bullshit. "I'm sorry sir, I'll have to get back to you on that." She hung up the phone, crossed her hands on the desk, and assumed an air of superiority. "May I help you?"

Jade threw back her head and laughed because the little twerp had no idea what was about to drop on her. A pile of shit was falling fast. "Oh girlfriend, you're out of here. As of now. Get your shit and report to HR."

"I have no idea who you think you are…"

"Who I am, is the woman who overheard you telling whoever was on the other end of that phone call that you defied your boss' orders. You snuck into his office after he told you not to disturb him *aaand* dared to take a picture of the man while he was asleep."

"You can't prove any of that. Who are you?"

Jade stalked forward and picked up the phone. She pounded out her sister's extension and put the phone on speaker. "Hey, Jewell, hook me up will ya?"

"You got it sweets, whatcha need?"

"Two things. There was a photo sent from Nic's tablet to an undisclosed email address. Can you pull that photo, capture the email address and retract the message and attachment?"

"Amateur hour. Consider it done. Give me something challenging, would you?"

"Sorry, I have another easy one. The last phone call into or out of this office, where did it originate or go?" Jade watched the little bitch squirm, but she'd give the woman credit, it appeared as if she was going to follow the farce through to the end.

"Ummm... just a second..." The sound of fingers tapping on a keyboard filtered through. "HR department extension one, four... oh, well, hello my little friend. Paaalease tell me this is going to get someone in trouble," Jewell begged.

"Gonna get someone in hot water for sure." Jade crossed her arms and stared at the woman in front of her.

"What goes around comes around. The last phone call went to the desk of one Ms. Clarisse

Thompkins. The woman who doesn't follow security protocols and opens emails with viruses." Jewell's delighted little laugh danced over the speaker.

"Awesome. Would you get whoever is the head of HR now to pull Ms. Thompkins from whatever she's doing and bring her up to Nic's office? I have a little situation here that needs to be rectified." Jade watched the color drain out of the woman's face. Finally, she was starting to understand.

"Roger, can do. Do you need me to get ahold of Jason or... wait... hold on a second." The low indistinguishable rumble of a voice came through the speaker. "Zane read a memo that said Jason's covering for Nic and Jared today. He should be down the hall in the morning meeting. Hold on, let me access his calendar." Jade was taking more than a little delight in the way the woman's hands now shook noticeably, but she still held Jade's stare. Either she was braver than shit or too dumb to know better. Either way, she wasn't fit to be working in the executive wing.

"Yep, that meeting should be finishing up. Do you want me to message him to swing by?"

"Sure, I haven't seen him since yesterday. Get

the head honcho for HR and that other chick up here before Jason shows, would yah?"

"You got it sweets; I messaged him as soon as you asked. Hey, is Mom cooking dinner at yours again tonight? I just got done telling Zane about her red beans and rice." Jewell made a nummy sound over the line.

"Yeah, I don't know. She's with Christian right now working on a kiddie center issue, but if you call her, I know she will hook you up." Jade was sure her mom wouldn't mind cooking. They'd eaten take out the last two nights.

"Awesome. Should I call Tori and Jacob?" Jewell asked as the office door opened and Jason popped his head in. The frown he was wearing immediately turned into a smile.

"Give Mom a call first and make sure it's okay with her, if it is, we can gather the clan, again." Jade waved Jason in.

His attention tracked from her to the trembling woman in front of her.

"Will do."

"Cool. Jason's here, I'll call you later." Jade picked up the receiver and set it back down ending the call.

"Hey, how are you feeling today?" Two steps later, he enfolded her in a massive bear hug.

When he released her, and she could draw a breath, she replied, "I'm good. I was going to bother Jared today, just for the hell of it, but he was home sleeping when I dropped Mom off this morning. So, I came to see Nic."

"I sent Nic home. Is that why I'm here? You going to bother me now?" Jason shoved over the inbox on the desk and sat down with his back to the administrative assistant and gave his full attention to Jade.

"Yeah... no. Well, kinda. You see, I came in, and I find Miss Social Media here talking on the phone."

"Okay... and?"

Jason appeared like he was losing his patience so Jade dove in feet first. "First, she wasn't talking about company business."

"I wasn't doing anything that anyone else doesn't do."

Jade swung her head and nailed the woman with a stare. When she started to speak again, Jade threw her hand up. "Just keep your pie hole closed because you don't want to dig yourself deeper."

The woman glared at her but snapped her mouth shut.

"Okay, so on company time with her partner in crime down in HR, she was gossiping."

Jason groaned and rolled his eyes.

"Yeah, yeah, I know, not a big deal right? But it seems this one decided it was all right to go into Nic's office after he asked her not to and take a picture of him. Asleep on his couch. With his tablet. Then she forwarded it to another email account and deleted the photo." Jade let those little tidbits sink in.

Jason stood and rotated a full 180 degrees and leveled a stare at the temp. "How in the hell did you get his password to his tablet?"

The woman shrugged and looked away as a knock sounded on the office door.

Jason bellowed, "Come in." Everyone's attention swung to the door as it opened.

"Mr. King, we were told to report here?" Alexis Channing stopped halfway in the door.

"Oh, hey Jade, long time no see."

"Alexis." Jade's curt reply pulled Alexis up short.

She scanned the room and stopped when her eyes landed on Miss Gossip Bottom. "Ms. Foster, what are you doing here?" Alexis continued in the door and motioned for the person following her to come in. A small blonde timidly crossed the threshold while trying to make herself even smaller by curling in on herself.

"She was here acting as his admin. Why? Isn't she assigned here?" Jason shot a glance at Jade to confirm his assumption.

She nodded her affirmation.

Jason's query sent Alexis scurrying through her tablet. "No, she doesn't have the necessary experience or clearance for this position. I mean she has a clearance, but she hasn't been vetted for this area. I distinctly remember telling..." Alexis raised her head and glared at the young woman beside her. If it was possible, the woman shrank even further into herself. "Sir, I don't know what is going on, but I promise I will get to the bottom of this." Alexis turned to stare at the woman behind the desk.

Jason took off his glasses and pinched the bridge of his nose. Jade fought a smile. When the man made that move, shit was going to get real, and it was going to get there fast.

Jason directed his pissed off stare to the woman now standing behind the admin's desk. "Jade, call security. I want a complete report on what the f...

What happened here and how it happened. I want to know how she accessed Nic's tablet. Alexis, my office in ten minutes." He glared at the small woman cowering behind Alexis. "I don't know who you are, but if you are involved in this in any way, you better come clean." He glared back at Miss Foster. "I will bring the entire might of this company down on you if you don't cooperate. Consider that a promise, a threat, or an order, I don't care which."

Jade saw her opportunity and jumped in with both feet. "Are you sure you want me to call security? I mean, I don't have anything to do for the rest of the day, and someone needs to be here to answer phones, so let me conduct the interviews here, with Alexis present as a witness. I'll get to the bottom of it." Jade had the telephone receiver in her hand.

"Fine. Alexis, when you have answers, call Sonya and have her put you on my schedule." Jason waited for her to acknowledge his demand before he stalked out the door.

"Well, ladies, this is what we are going to do." She pointed at the little blonde. "You, go sit in the hall. Don't move and don't talk to anyone." Jade pointed at Ms. Foster. "You sit down." The woman started to sit behind the desk, and Jade stopped her. "Nope, over there."

The woman lifted and sauntered over to the small chair Jade had indicated.

"Now, I want answers, straight answers, or I'll stop this interview, read you your rights and charge you with fraud, industrial espionage, and violations of three Homeland Security articles concerning the violation of domestic security protocols." Jade called on every ounce of acting skill she had to keep a straight face. There was no such thing as a Homeland Security article and taking a picture of a sleeping man with a stolen password wasn't exactly espionage... unless the twit had done more than take a picture.

Jade held up her hand when Ms. Foster started to speak. The waterworks were falling in earnest now, but Jade wasn't going to leave any stones unturned. She punched Jewell's number up and asked her to make sure nothing else had been sent from Nic's laptop since seven this morning, which is when the majority of the administrative staff started coming to work.

Jade put the phone down and picked up a pen and paper. "Now, Ms. Foster, let's start at the beginning."

CHAPTER 5

Nic woke slowly. His arm was pinned underneath him, and his hand was numb. He peeled his face off the wet spot on the leather cushion and swiped at the drool on his mouth with the hand he could feel.

"Good morning, Sunshine."

Nic jumped at the low sexy voice. His head swiveled fast enough to cause him to wince. Who the fuck was that? No, it couldn't be? "Jade?" Nic cleared his throat to eliminate the gravel that he must have eaten while he was asleep, and spoke again. "What are you doing here?" Better, at least distinguishable as English. Nic rubbed his face and groaned. The couch was okay in a crunch, but he wasn't a spring chicken anymore, and his forty-year-old body complained bitterly over the mistreatment.

"I am here because Jared told me to come bother him at work today and then took the day off. So, I figured you'd be here."

Ah, so that was what Jared had forgotten. Or who. Maybe. At the moment, he didn't care. "What time is it?" Nic scanned his immediate vicinity for his tablet.

"Almost six. That's p.m. Are you looking for this?" Jade held up a tablet.

Nic wasn't a morning person, or afternoon person... or whatever-the-fuck-time-it-was, type person. Not without a shower and coffee. Coffee... uggg, maybe not. He drew a deep breath and stared at the woman sitting behind his desk. "Ummm... if it is mine, yeah, that's what I'm looking for. What are you doing with it?" Nic yawned and stretched.

"Well, that is a long story. Want to hear it?"

Jade's smile bordered on the evil side and that piqued his curiosity.

Nic nodded. Until he had hot water, soap and maybe some type of caffeine, he wasn't driving this crazy train. He'd settle in for the ride.

"Oh yeah, I love a good story, too! So, once upon a time, Ms. Foster, aka your recently acquired administrative assistant, decided to help herself to your tablet, take a picture of you while you slept, email it to herself, and then brag about it to her friend. She had her back to the door and was talking up a blue streak. Little did she know I had walked into your office. So, I kept quiet, and listened. You know Investigations 101 and all that. Let the bad guys incriminate themselves."

Nic sat for a moment and soaked up the information. He rubbed his face as he asked, "Well, fuck. First, how did she get my password?"

"From your full-time assistant, Adrienne. She left a 'help' file on the computer for the temp admins, the ones that really were cleared and vetted to be replacements. Oh! I heard she had a baby boy! Isn't this her second?" Jade's trajectory change on the subject made him pause and think for a minute.

"Third, two boys and a girl. Wait, Candi-with-an-i wasn't cleared to work here? How the fuck did she get into the X-wing?" Nic hated being behind the curve. He felt like his mind was moving through mud.

"Oh! That's a good part of the story. It seems her partner in crime was a young woman from HR who had access to this wing as a runner. Ms.

Foster got her friend in HR to change the temp assignments and place her with you. The runner from HR used her badge to escort Ms. Foster past security and into the X-wing. Obviously, your reputation precedes you. That woman *really* wanted to meet you." Jade threw back her head and laughed.

The sound was so full of light and fun that Nic couldn't help but smile. "You did the investigation on this?"

"Oh yeah! I wasn't going to miss it. Besides, I didn't have anything else to do today, so I answered your phones after Alexis took that twit back downstairs. Oh, I had a long talk with your mom. So, she's a judge, huh?"

Nic groaned and fell to his side, face planting onto the cushion of the couch. His ma was the living personification of an Italian mother. She was a loud busybody that was way too deep in her kids' lives. She loved to feed her boys her old-world, Italian family recipes learned from generations of women before her. Yet, Judge Bettina DeMarco was also a no bullshit, career-minded woman. She'd earned her law degree at night and worked her ass off to raise three boys as a single mom after Nic's dad died in a freak accident.

Nic turned his head toward Jade and held up his finger. "Can we never mention my mother again? Let's get back to my stalker admin. Did she do anything else with my tablet, as in access any files, or send anything other than the photo?"

Jade scrunched up her face but shook her head, causing a miniscule ripple in the lush black pony-tail that fell over her shoulder. Its sensual, luxurious slither drew his eye. He'd always thought she was stunning—a supernova that burned too bright for the human eye to understand. If he'd seen her in a club, he'd have put his best moves on her. He'd heard stories about the woman's antics, but at the time, he'd believed the outrageous recounts had grown as they passed from person to person. Not anymore.

She lifted her hand and waved his question away with a light laugh. "Nah, Jewell did a forensic something or another and said Smurfette entered your password, took the picture, emailed it to herself, get this, a Guardian email account, and then deleted the picture off your tablet. Basically, they were airheaded Barbie-types that wanted an M.R.S. degree, and one of them targeted you."

Nic pushed himself up on his elbow and shook his head. "A what?"

Jade's brilliant green eyes popped wide. "Dude, an M-R-S degree. It was what oh... twenty percent of the college co-eds majored in when I was in school. Marrying a good-looking man with the means to take care of her for the rest of her life. A Mrs. degree."

Nic threw back his head and laughed so hard his gut hurt and his eyes watered. When he could control himself, he declared, "Holy shit! I am so not a candidate for anything permanent."

Jade's laughter lilted lightly over his admission. "You and me both! What do you say we go get something to eat and maybe a drink? I was under-cover for over a year and had zero alcohol, zero sex, and zero fun. I need to rectify that, and by the look of that suit, you need to get the hell out of Dodge for an evening of fun. You can be my wingman."

"Your wingman?" His voice cracked a little. Damn, his sex appeal had spiraled into the toilet if a gorgeous woman expected him to scope out other guys for her. Perfect. Welcome to life at the bottom of the drain. He really needed to get out and get laid.

"Sure, I need a big strong guy like you to keep the assholes at bay. Tonight I want to get drunk, falling down, shitfaced drunk, while I listen to music and eat bar food. I need to blow off steam, but you need to change, because..." her gaze evaluated him from head to foot. "... no, just no."

Nic peered down at the wrinkled, rumpled mess he wore. "I doubt you need anyone to keep assholes at bay, and hey... pretty damn judgmental for someone who is the reason I look like shit."

"Say what, now?"

"We've been busting ass working the leads and cases that your investigation spawned. The people in that cult have been rolling over faster than we can transcribe the interviews." Nic yawned and rotated his neck, cracking it. *God that felt good.*

Jade stood up and came around the desk, leaning on the front before she crossed her arms. She wore faded jeans that fit snug in all the right places, and her long legs accentuated where they'd thinned until almost white in color. Her black silk blouse fell in a deep, plunging vee from her shoulders, and clearly showed the full mounds of her generous breasts supported by a bright-yellow lace bra. She wore bright-yellow, peep-toe stilettos that matched her bra and showed off her blood red toenails. Hell yeah, that combo was sexy as fuck. He was a foot guy. And a leg guy. And an ass guy.

Whatever. Too many men had no fucking clue how erogenous a woman's foot could be. He'd learned to never overlook an opportunity to make a woman writhe under him. Or rather, he hadn't until a couple months ago.

"Well... as glad as I am that my work is paying dividends, for your information, the only way I would ever admit responsibility for a suit looking like that was if I had just spent twenty-four hours fucking the brains out of the man in it."

It literally took several seconds to, number one, believe the woman actually said the words he'd heard—and number two... that the woman actually had said the words he'd just heard.

"Dude, did I break you? You ought to see your face." She chuckled and pointed at him as she spoke.

Nic opened his mouth to reply and shut it again. He started again and stopped.

Jade threw back her head, and her laughter filled the room.

Nic chuckled and rubbed the back of his neck. "In my defense, I guess I've never heard a woman say something like that?" Nic offered the question as an explanation, still stunned by Jade's statement. Shit, the stories had to be true.

"Well, you and most men on the planet are woefully unaware of what women talk about when men aren't around. Sex is a popular topic, and believe it or not, some of us really, really like it. Just FYI, my default is the kind of sex that happens without strings, relationships, and expectations of more than one hell of a good orgasm. Don't you think women should be honest about what they want from a hook-up?"

Nic stood and stretched. He had no idea how he landed in a conversation about sex with the sister of his best friend, but he sure as hell was there now. "I guess I never gave it much thought. I'm ahh…" He motioned toward his office's ensuite bathroom. "… going to grab a shower and change. Shouldn't you be having dinner with your family?" The Kings had been doing the family group hug thing since Jade had been back. Except for Jared, who had been with him most of the time since they returned from the compound. They'd put in some long hours. He debated the wisdom of going out with Jade for about a half second. Why the fuck not? He deserved a night out and a new bed partner. It had been too damn long.

"Nah, Jewell and the boys are at Jared's tonight. Mom's cooking, but I talked with her earlier. She understands that I need to go out and try to find my normal again. You game or what?"

Normal? From what he'd heard about her from her family, the imagination could not be stretched enough to define Jade as normal. He couldn't believe he was going out with Jade King, being her wingman. *The Matrix*. Yep, he'd woke up in the middle of The Matrix or at a minimum an alternate reality. He'd let his little infatuation with her sister knock him on his ear. Perhaps it was time to change that.

"You didn't answer my question."

Jade's word's startled him out of his thoughts. He nodded. "Yeah. I could use a drink."

Jade watched Nic head into the bathroom and shut the door. She'd always liked the way the man looked. She'd been a perv and watched him sleep for about a half hour. He was a beautiful man. Classic Italian with dark hair, strong chiseled features, and his body made clothes look damn good. Even if they were wrinkled beyond repair. He was sexy as hell and just her type, a man whore. Nic was easy on the eyes, had a body that made her drool, and understood what no strings meant. She wasn't going to lie. The semi he sported as he woke up was drool worthy—a promise of great things to come. Yup, he had the equipment to make her very happy. Then he woke up, and yeah, a sleepy, rumpled Nic was sexy as fuck, too.

She waited until she heard the water running before she picked up the receiver to the phone on his desk and punched in the number. She hadn't really told her family she wasn't coming to dinner tonight. Time to rectify that situation.

"Hey, Momma."

"Hi, sweetheart. Where are you? Everyone except Jason, Faith, and Reece is here, and Jason called to say they were on their way."

Jade could hear laughter and the sounds of pots and pans banging in the background. "Yeah, about that. I'm going to ditch tonight."

Her mom didn't speak for a short time, and the sound in the background grew distant. "Why? Is everything okay?"

"Honestly, I want to go out, get drunk and find a man to make me feel good. It has been over a year since I've had any relief except what I could provide for myself if you get my drift. I've been good and stayed off my knee like the doctors told me, but I'm ready to get back to being me." Jade had always been unerringly honest with her mom.

"Well, I guess I asked." Amanda King chuckled into the phone.

"Yes, you did." Jade smiled at her mom's obvious embarrassment.

"All right, I'll let the others know you've got other plans, but tomorrow night we are having a girls night, so no bailing on us. I have to get back to the ranch soon, and I want an evening for us ladies."

"You're wanting to get back because you're missing your man, aren't you?" Jade teased her mom. She loved Frank. The cowboy was perfect for her mom. Strong and silent, and he loved her mom something fierce. It was obvious to anyone who had eyes.

"Yeah, I am." Her mom's voice held a wistful edge.

"See, I knew you'd get what I meant, Mom." Jade leaned back in Nic's chair and put her high-heeled shoes up on the desk. She might as well elevate her knee.

"Slight difference, I'm married to him."

"Lucky me, I still have so many options. Settling down with one is not on my agenda." Jade snorted to herself. As if she was ever going to settle down. "And you're telling me you never had sex with him before you got married?" Jade taunted.

"I'm not telling you anything, young lady." Amanda's weak admonishment held no anger, and they both laughed at her attempt.

The shower turned off, and Jade's attention once again drifted toward the naked man behind door number one. "Hey, I'm going to get going. Y'all have fun. Love you."

"Love you too, and for the salvation of all things holy, do not get thrown in jail."

Her mom had adopted that very specific caution after the second time bail money was required. Honestly, Jade was still pissed about the cops throwing her in jail for that one. She'd only finished the fight those bastards started. "But where is the fun in that, Mom? Besides, now I have a savings account set up just for my bail issues."

"Somehow, I don't doubt it. Good night and have fun."

"Night, Mom."

Jade replaced the phone and leaned her head against the headrest of the massive executive chair. The sounds of Nic moving around next door kept her attention on the man. She needed an escape, a good time with no strings attached, and she wanted that good time to be with Nic. She'd thought of the man fucking her to oblivion five or twenty times since she'd met him a couple years ago. It never seemed there was an opportunity to jump onto that particular ride. Until now. He was perfect. She didn't work directly for him. They rarely saw each other, and he was smoldering hot. Jade smiled to herself. Now she needed to convince Nic sex with her would be the best idea he'd ever had.

The door to the ensuite opened, and Jade was pleasantly surprised at the man who reappeared. He wore dark wash jeans, designer boots, a dark blue button down and a chunky silver watch. To say the man was sexy was like saying the Great Wall of China was long. While technically correct, the description vastly misrepresented reality. Nic DeMarco was sex personified.

He flashed her a brilliant white smile. "Ready?" He rounded his desk, nudged her feet off where she'd propped them and pulled the top drawer out, grabbing his keys.

"Oh baby, I'm always ready. For anything that happens." Jade purred the response as she lifted out of the chair and pushed by him, making sure to graze his body with hers. She sauntered toward the door and glanced back over her shoulder at him. "Come on; time to go find us someone to take home tonight."

She laughed softly as she walked out the door, because she was happy, and because she swore she heard him groan before the door closed. 'Operation Get Jade Laid' was underway.

CHAPTER 6

"God no, she's a creeper." Jade poured another finger of very expensive whiskey into her glass and refilled Nic's.

"I've got something she could creep." Nic wagged his eyebrows at Jade. They'd had dinner at a bistro down the street from the exclusive club where they now drank top shelf whiskey. The conversation had been brisk and engaging. They had similar likes and dislikes in movies and in music and had common work experiences, so there had been no awkward pauses or silences since they'd left Guardian Headquarters.

Jade shook her head at Nic's crude remark. She'd known he was going to say it before the words came out of his mouth. "Nic, you do not need a vine, someone who just clings to you and doesn't participate. You need a woman who knows what she wants from a man and takes it."

He tossed back his drink with a shrug. "Yeah, well, your interpretation of what I need may be better than mine. Hell, I thought I found a woman who'd fit pretty damn good with me, but that shit sure as hell didn't work out."

Whoa! Bombs lobbed over the deck! "Seriously? Fuck man, I'm sorry. Had no idea you'd been dating someone steady."

He filled his glass again and set the bottle down. "See that's just it. I wasn't. I wanted to be, or at least I had convinced myself I wanted to be. You said you had a conversation with my mother today, right?"

"Oh yeah. Thirty minutes if it was a second."

He flinched at her words. "Yeah, well imagine having that voice in your head every day for as long as you've been an adult. 'When are you going to settle down, Nico? Why haven't you introduced me to your girlfriend, Nico? When are you going to give me grand babies, Nico?'"

Nic's imitation of his mother's voice was spot on. Jade sputtered and choked down the sip of whiskey she'd swallowed. Coughing to clear her throat she croaked, "She calls you daily?"

"Every. Single. Day. She's an amazing woman, but really, I'm forty, and she's still nagging me about settling down."

"Oh, my God! You're a momma's boy! That is so fucking cute!"

A blush crept up his neck, and he looked away. He shrugged and spoke while looking across the room. "That woman has dedicated her life to my brothers and me. We're tight, and yeah, I'll own that title. She deserves my respect."

Jade reached over, tapped his arm, and got him to look at her. "Listen, I may give you shit for it, but that right there is a hallmark of a good man. I heard somewhere that the way a man treats his mother tells a lot about him. Hell, every one of my brothers is one hundred percent a momma's boy."

Nic glanced up at her and nodded.

"So you tried to settle down?" Jade prompted him before she took a long sip of her whiskey and thanked the stars she'd eaten before they started drinking. The year without alcohol had seriously fucked with her tolerance level.

Nic smirked. "Get this, I asked Jewell out about

the same time as Zane did. I didn't stand a chance but wasn't smart enough to know it."

"Jewell, as in my sister, Jewell?"

Nic nodded and refused to meet her eye.

Jade took another sip trying to understand, but yeah, that wasn't happening. Two plus two equaled about five million in this case, so there was no way to make sense of what he said. "Why?" She really was at a loss. Jewell wasn't Nic's type. Like at all. Nic was free and loose. He was a "no strings attached" kind of guy. If you went by the rumors and threw a shit-ton of salt over your shoulder to balance out the bullshit factor, the man was a sexual legend. Jewell, well that girl was a hot mess, but she was also a permanent relationship waiting to happen. Jade had always known Jewell just needed to find the right man—one strong enough to make her realize a relationship was exactly what she needed. Obviously, Zane was that man. Jade had never seen Jewell as happy or as animated as she was when she was with Zane.

Nic frowned at her. Jade wanted to push her finger between his furrowed eyebrows and smooth out the tension that had settled there.

"Suffice to say, I thought it was a good idea at the time. Hindsight being twenty-twenty, I know I was looking for something that wasn't going to happen, for her or me." Nic's eyes stopped searching the crowd and froze on a target. Jade took a gander in the same direction. There were three women, two blondes, and a redhead in the general vicinity. Oh, not tonight, ladies. Jade had absolutely no plans on letting anyone take off with Nic.

"I have a better idea for you." Jade turned so she was facing him and drew his attention from the women across the room.

"Yeah? What's that?"

Jade lifted her drink to her lips and licked the rim. Nic's eyes followed the motion. She took a small sip before she whispered, "Fuck me instead." Jade watched surprise, then confusion, and then disbelief cross Nic's face.

"Ahhh… that would be a no."

She saw the second Nic realized exactly how close they were sitting. He pulled away and cleared his throat before he focused his attention across the room again.

"Why not? Sex with you sounds like a great idea to me."

"You are my best friend's sister." Nic shot the retort back at her without a second's delay.

"Wait, what? So was Jewell!" Wow, why were the sexy ones so damn slow?

"I wasn't going to take her to bed. I was going to date her and build a relationship with her. I would never disrespect Jared or Jason by just screwing you or your sister." Nic tipped the empty glass back and growled in frustration as he slammed it down on the bar and poured a double fingers worth into his glass.

"Wow. I had no idea you were such a conceited, self-righteous, pompous, misogynistic asshole. Good to know."

"Excuse me?" Nic's eyes pinned her, and he wasn't a happy camper, but Jade had a point to make.

"No, I will not excuse you." Jade jabbed a finger at him and mimicked, "I wouldn't disrespect your brothers by sleeping with you." She put her glass down and carefully clasped her hands in front of her, keeping her soapbox of emotions in check.

"Right." He nodded, affirming what she'd said.

"Wrong. My brothers have nothing to do with what goes on in my sex life. Ever. You won't disrespect them, yet you'll disrespect me by insinuating that a man, any man, including my brothers, has the right to approve or disapprove who I fuck?

And believe me, that's what I do. Talk about an antiquated and chauvinistic heap of steaming bull-shit. If I ever want to give a man that much control, I will sign a contract beforehand and there will be safe words involved. I want sex. Fucking. If not from you, then from…" Jade scouted around and found a likely prospect. She pointed at a guy that was tall, hard with muscles, and smoking hot. "… him." Jade downed her drink and stood up. "Thanks for dinner and the drinks. I hope you find a woman to live up to both you and your mom's expectations."

"Jade, wait," Nic called after her.

Fuck that and fuck him. Or not, as the case would be. She tossed her ponytail off her shoulder, held up a middle finger in response to Nic, and put the handsome hunk of man meat she'd identified in her sights. She was having an orgasm tonight. One that wasn't given to her by her own hand, and she was having it within the next hour.

The guy must have felt her eyes on him because he turned and watched her as she sauntered toward him. Jade licked her lips and smiled. Target acquired, now it was time to launch the attack.

"Jade, wait a minute." Nic grabbed her arm and spun her around.

Oh, hell no, he did not just do that. With a practiced calm, she slowly moved her stare from the hand holding her forearm to the man who had crossed one hell of a line. "Unless you want to be laid out on your ass in less than three seconds, take your hand off me."

Nic released her arm and raised his hand, palm out, toward her. "I can see that I may have screwed up back there."

"May have screwed up? May have? Whatever. Good night, Nic." Sometimes sexy men were too stupid to fuck. It wasn't often she found an example of that rare and elusive creature, but it seemed Nic DeMarco was that special unicorn tonight. Lucky her. She spun on her heel and found her mark again. The man's glance bounced between her and Nic. Tall and sexy raised a questioning eyebrow. Great, now Nic was cock blocking her orgasm.

"Whoa!" Jade gasped the word when a strong hand spun her around. She tensed and pulled back her fist. Oh, hell no, and she'd even warned the asshole. "You son of a…"

Nic's hand caught her fist, stopping her forward momentum. His lips landed on hers in a punishing kiss. Teeth pushed against her with demanding force, crushing her lips. The initial shock lasted a split second. Jade reached up and grabbed his neck, pulling him closer. The feel of Nic's strong arms pinning her to his hard chest swamped her senses. *Fuck yes. This.* She wanted this. She needed the contact and the feel of a man against her. God... Nic could kiss. She opened for him when his tongue swiped at her lips. He wasn't gentle and thank fuck for that because she didn't want gentle. She wanted raw, sweaty, mind-blowing sex and she wanted it now. Nic pulled away, and she chased his lips catching his bottom one with her teeth. She pulled on it not so gently before she released it. He waited until she looked up at him and met her heated stare. The lust in his eyes had to match what he must see in hers.

She ran her thumb over his swollen bottom lip. "That's just a sample, big boy. Put your issues in your back pocket and keep them there. Take me home and let me get my freak on. I guarantee it will be a night you'll never forget." Jade leaned forward and bit his lip again, pulling it out with a tug.

Nic pushed into the kiss forcing her to release him. He lifted away and grabbed a handful of her hair as he spoke. "I don't take anyone to my house."

Nic ran his free hand down her arm and up her back.

"I don't live alone right now, but hey, if you want to fuck me with my mom down the hall..."

Nic groaned, grabbed her hand, and pulled her toward the exit. Jade felt a bubble of laughter well up and escape. Go, HeMan! Thank God. She was so getting laid tonight!

CHAPTER 7

Nic hailed a cab the second they broke through the nightclub's door. He'd had too much whiskey to drive. Besides, his mind wasn't on the rules of the road. No, his mind was on a tall, leggy, bossy, sexy... *fuck*... Nic pulled Jade into him and found her mouth again. She met his tongue stroke for stroke and grabbed his shirt in a grip that wouldn't let him leave even if he wanted to break free. But that was the last thing he wanted. He wanted her. Fuck, the aftermath was going to be messy, and he'd probably lose his best friend when Jared found out what he'd done, but God help him, he was going to take the demanding woman to his house, and he was going to fuck her like she'd never been fucked before.

A horn blasting at his hip separated them. He gathered what remained of his brain and opened the back door of the cab, practically throwing Jade into the taxi. Once he ducked in, she bounced closer to him and threw her head back laughing as she grabbed at his shirt pulling him even closer. The melodic sound was lighthearted, free and unbridled. He somehow managed to give the cabbie his address and leaned into a kiss that sent his rock hard cock into titanium-coated-tire-iron category.

He vaguely remembered throwing a wad of bills at the driver when the man announced they'd arrived. Their shuffle to the front door entwined in a dance of grasping hands and searching lips was a mere wisp of a memory. When he slammed the door shut and Jade grabbed the front of his shirt and ripped the fucking buttons off it before she pushed him into the wall... *that* he fucking remembered.

He grabbed her wrists and captured her, pushing his leg between her thighs. He damn near came in his pants when she moaned and ground herself against his leg while rubbing his cock through his jeans. Fucking hell, he'd never had a woman act so aggressive, and he loved it. He grabbed her ass and picked her up.

"Fuck yeah!" Jade wrapped herself around him. Her teeth, tongue, lips, and hands never stopped their chaotic exploration of his body. He kicked his bedroom door open and fell onto the bed, pinning her underneath him.

Clothes disappeared between lust-filled kisses and desire-fueled groping. It took twenty seconds for them to perch their concealed weapons and identification on the bedside tables. They lunged at each other, collapsing the space between them. Jade pulled his jeans down and grabbed his cock as she shimmied out of hers. He shuddered at the feel of her hand. She pushed him off her as if he was a one hundred pound weakling. The wildcat pounced on top of him and pinned his arms to the bed with her knees. She reached behind her and flicked the clasp on her bra, and shrugged out of it. Nic watched as she pulled her hair out of the ponytail. Long black tresses floated down past her fucking gorgeous full breasts. In one fluid motion, she stood over him, turned around, so she was standing next to his hip on the bed and bent over, sliding her panties down at the same time. Holy fucking hell, those long sexy legs and phenomenal ass were a work of art. Nic swallowed hard. She peeked around her legs and smiled before she dropped to her knees and spun around landing on top of him. He lost all the air in his lungs, but who needed to breathe?

"Where are your condoms?" He pointed, and she reached across him to the nightstand and opened the drawer. "Score!" Jade lifted her arm and a line of condoms trailed after her. Nic rolled her over and fell between her thighs. She put a foil packet between her teeth and ripped it open. Fuck, she was the epitome of a wet dream. He took the damn thing from her and suited up.

Nic stopped and made her look at him. "Are you sure?"

"Don't you fucking dare stop now. If you do, I'll kill you, and it would be a justifiable homicide." Jade grabbed him by the shoulders and pulled him down into a teeth-clacking kiss.

He lined up and thrust into her slick, wet heat. His moan married hers as they continued to kiss. Damn, she felt amazing. Nic broke the kiss and bucked forward seating himself deep inside her. She wrapped her legs around his thighs and grabbed his ass with her hands keeping him there. He lifted and gazed down at her. Intense green eyes stared back hooded with lust, and her face flushed red from the exertion of their extreme foreplay.

She grabbed a handful of his hair with one hand. "Fuck me, Nic. Pound me with that big cock. I need it hard and fast. Don't stop unless you're coming or dying."

"Holy fuck, your mouth, woman." As he lifted to his knees, he grabbed her thighs and pushed them back toward her shoulders in a wide vee.

"No, you don't get my mouth this time. Next time, I'll let you fuck it." Jade put two of her fingers in her mouth and circled them with her tongue. He had to close his eyes, or he'd fucking bust his nut. Her laughter popped his eyes back open. He smiled and then winked at her.

Her fingers still in her mouth, she smiled and used her other hand to pinch his nipple. He sucked in a breath as she demanded, "Fuck. Me. Harder."

Nic rocked back and slammed into her.

"Yes! Just like that!" Jade's shout echoed around the room. Her breasts swayed up and back with the force of his cock's rhythm. Her hand traveled from her mouth to her nipple, and she played with it as she watched him watching her. The only thing that eclipsed her hot, dirty talk was her brazen actions.

He would love testing her limits—if she had any. Grasping her thighs, Nic jerked her to him and abandoned any physical restraint. He was a substantial male in supreme condition, and his cock powered into her in a savage rhythm as her growled demands drove the ever present worry he could hurt the woman beneath him out of his brain. Nic was losing the war against the demands of his body. The orgasm building became an all-consuming demand he couldn't resist. He released one of her legs and reached between them to find her clit. There was no way he'd come before he made her scream his name. His fingers found her hard nub and massaged it with a skilled touch perfected from years of experience.

Jade's body arched. "Yes! God... Yes! Yes! Yes! Nic!" Her body tightened and her pussy constricted in waves around his cock.

Nic slammed home at the sound of his name echoing around his bedroom. White spots split the darkness behind his eyelids when his orgasm tore through him. He pounded her through his release, because he'd fucking die if he didn't. Nic shuddered and stayed frozen for several seconds before he dropped down on top of her gasping for air.

"Holy fuck. That is so going to happen again, but you need to get off me so I can breathe." Jade's voice came in breathless pants.

He grunted an assent and slid off her. Nic took care of the condom, dropping it somewhere near the trash can beside the bed. His hand flopped back to his chest as he tried to regulate his breathing. They lay like that for several minutes. Just pulling air in and pushing it out.

That orgasm was one of the best he'd ever had. He put Jade in the top five encounters of his life. Okay, top two. His first teenage orgasm in a girl, not his hand, would stay at number one. Jade rolled toward him, and he turned onto his side facing her. A tumble of dark hair fell across her brow. Nic pushed her hair away so he could see her eyes.

"Anyone ever tell you that you're pretty okay at this sex thing?" A mischievous smile spread across her face.

"Maybe once or twice, but I'm considering 'pretty okay' as a compliment coming from a wildcat like you."

"Wildcat? Maybe tonight. I mean, dude, I

haven't had contact with anything but my vibrator or my fingers in over a year. I deserve to cut loose tonight."

Nic rolled his hips toward her. "So how about you reward me for a job well done?"

Jade reached down and cupped his cock. "Seriously, you are ready to go again."

"Let's just say you lying here on my bed is quite the incentive."

A smile spread across her face as she stroked his hardening shaft. "Color me impressed."

"It's been a couple months for me. I don't know how you went a year without sex. You and your DEA partner never...?" Nic wasn't expecting the undignified snort of laughter that blasted out of the sexy woman next to him. She slapped her hand over her mouth and rolled onto her back, laughing harder. There was nothing he could do to stop his own laughter. Jade was the antithesis of every woman he'd ever dated. She was boisterous, not demure, callous and crude, not poised and pretentious. Her love of life and self-confidence shone like a beacon for the world to see.

"Dude, I so wish. Unfortunately, I'm told sex with your undercover partner is a big no-no. Also, Garret is gay." Jade gasped between bouts of uncontrollable laughter. "We were both miserable!"

Nic pulled up short. "Wait, you wouldn't cross that line while you were on a case, because, and I quote, that 'is a big no-no'. But this one, the one between us, you blasted through? What the fuck is the difference?"

"Well as I see it, I'm not on a case right now; I'm on mandatory time off. You know Jared handles all my assignments, so there is no boss/employee bullshit we need to worry about and..." Jade launched him onto his back and straddled him in the process, "... according to all accounts, you are a love 'em and leave 'em type guy. Just the flavor of M-A-N I prefer." Jade bent down and licked a stripe up his neck. "Delicious and disposable."

Nic couldn't deny the fact he had a reputation, and right up until the time he observed the Kings settling down, he honestly thought life as a confirmed bachelor was the way he wanted to live. As much as he wished he could deny it, witnessing his friends falling in love had an effect on him. Now he wasn't so sure being the disposable bachelor was the way he wanted to continue, but that little revelation was going to stay hidden, especially from her.

Jade rocked her hips, grinding down on top of his cock. "I deserve a second helping, big boy. I've been a very good girl. Give me another taste?"

Nic grabbed a handful of hair and tugged gently, bringing her down closer to him. "You deserve more than a taste." He pulled her in for a kiss and then rolled on top of her. He trailed kisses down the slender column of her neck to her collarbone where he nipped and licked the tender skin. Her happy giggles turned into a long, low moan as she arched under him.

Nic continued his sensual exploration as her hands snaked through his hair. The last time, sex between them had been hard and fast, but now Nic wanted to give her what she'd been missing for the last three hundred and sixty five days. He knew how to make a woman writhe with pleasure, and he wanted this woman's definition of great sex and his name to be synonymous.

He lost focus on anything except the woman under him. His mouth and fingers worked their way down her body, finding the sensitive areas that made her moan, gasp and beg. She grasped his shoulders when he centered over her hot sex. Her fingers dug into his flesh, punctuating her lust-filled symphony of sensual sounds. A soft swirl of his tongue over her hipbone won him a low, needy moan. He copied the move on the other side, and she started to beg. Her hands once again found purchase in his hair. Nic opened her up. Beautiful, red and swollen, her body told him how urgently she needed his touch. He blew a gentle breath across her heated sex and her torso bowed off the bed. Nic pinned her hips down with his forearm and feasted on her flesh. Jade writhed under him. His name became a chanted plea. The pleas turned into begging, interspersed with a helpless mewling sound that singed a pathway straight to his balls. Making this strong, independent woman beg and plead hit him like a nose full of cocaine. Powerful, electrifying, and addictive, her desperation lit him up from the inside and exploded with the vibrancy of a million lights. Nic lifted off her, suited up and slid home. His mouth consumed hers, because unlike last time, Jade wasn't fighting him for control. Absorbing her submission, he let the demure side of her fuel the endless slide of his cock in, the slow withdrawal to the tip, out. He broke the kiss but held his lips over hers. Their breath mingled with soft pants and quiet sounds of pleasure. His fingers traced her thigh before he lifted one of her legs and held it at his hip, balancing his weight on one elbow. Jade opened her eyes and stared at him. What he saw mystified and beguiled him. The demanding, bossy woman who'd taunted him into bed tonight had a soft side, and she'd allowed him to see it. But it was only for a moment. She closed her eyes and shut him out. Nic lowered the scant inch to her lips and pressed a soft kiss against them.

"Nic..." Jade's plea fell from her lips as soon as he lifted away.

"I've got you." Nic lowered again, taking another sip of her lips. "Let go and feel how good we are." Her hands kneaded his back in a fruitless effort to bring him closer. Nic fought the desire to give in and seek his own release. He nuzzled her ear and whispered, "Let go. You can drop the act. You're safe with me." He had no idea where the words came from, but they spilled from his lips before he could stop them. He felt her stiffen in his arms and regretted the words immediately. God, he clenched his jaw to shut up his fucking mouth. He changed his angle and ground into her.

Jade arched under him and moaned, her hips pressing into him as he hilted against her. His thrusts built in speed, driven by the undeniable wave that strove for release at the base of his spine.

Jade's fingernails scored the skin of his back and shoulders as she damn near pushed off the bed. Her body tightened around his cock as she gasped and shuddered under him. Nic released a groan of pure pleasure and chased his own release. Five hard, deep strokes later, he exploded into the condom. He bucked through his orgasm and draped over her, exhausted.

Their sweat soaked bodies squelched when he shifted. Damn, he hadn't ever worked up such a sweat while making love. No. Fucking. That's what they were doing. Fucking. Sexual release, no emotions, and no attachment. With that thought in mind, he lifted off her and rolled onto his back.

Jade didn't waste a second. She rolled the opposite direction off the bed and headed toward the bathroom. He watched her bend down to pick something up off the floor before she entered the bathroom and shut the door. The sound of water running escaped the confines of the ensuite seconds later.

Nic pulled the condom off, tied it in a knot, and tossed it the same direction as the last one. Sitting up in the bed, he scrubbed his face and glanced around the room. Their clothes were scattered across the hardwood in a jumbled mess. He got up, opened his dresser and pulled on a pair of basket-ball shorts as Jade exited the bathroom. She'd put her hair up into some kind of floppy bun thing. The woman didn't even glance at him before she started picking up her clothes and dressing. The quiet between them was a physical thing, kind of a like herd of fucking elephants. Impossible to miss and too damn big to ignore.

"You don't have to go." Nic cringed. Hell, his words sounded disingenuous even to his own ears. In actuality, he needed her to go, and go now. There was so much wrong with what had just happened between them that he needed time and space to process it. A lot of time and a lot of space. It was a damn good thing they rarely saw each other.

"Yeah, I do. I'm not much for the post-hook-up snuggling thing. Not a fan." She grabbed her blouse and attempted to slide the material over her head. He stared at her pale skin as she struggled with the tangle of sleeves. She was a strikingly beautiful woman, even when she was in full evasion mode.

"I'll call you an Uber or a taxi." Hell, it was the courteous thing to do, right?

She finally pulled the black silk over her head and tugged it down. "No need, I ordered one when

I was in the bathroom." She lifted her cell phone and moved it in a small waving motion as if in evidence of her call before she slipped her feet into her shoes and stuffed her bra and panties into her pants pocket. "Right. So, later then?" Nic felt like a high school boy trying to talk to the popular girl. He'd never been in this position before. He'd always been the one to get up and leave. He was the one who left them wanting more. That thought made him pull up short. He didn't want more. This was a hook-up to scratch an itch, right? This uncertainty as to what to do afterward was why he never brought anyone home. Never.

"Nah, I'm authorized more vacation time. I'm heading to the ranch for a couple weeks. I'm sure Jared will have an assignment for me soon, so..." A vibration caught their attention. Jade patted the pockets of her jeans and then spotted her phone on the bed where she'd been sitting. She picked it up. "My Uber is almost here." She slipped the phone into her back pocket.

"All right, well then I guess this is goodbye." Nic walked with her toward the front door.

"Yep. Thanks for the good time." Jade's voice was cool, polite and distant.

"You bet." Nic opened the door for her.

"See yah," Jade said as she passed by.

Nic shut the door and leaned against it. "Yep." He pulled his head back and dropped it against the door. Hard. *Fuck, DeMarco, only you could screw up a no strings attached hook-up with the hottest thing this side of the Mississippi.* The problem was, he had no idea what he'd done to ruin the good time they were having. What had he said? That was benign pillow talk. Right? Of course, it was. Granted, he'd never said those words before... He thrust his hands through his hair. Women. Fucking complicated and crazy.

CHAPTER 8

S *tupid. Stupid. Stupid! You couldn't limit it to fun and games, could you? Damn it Nic, you weren't supposed to be observant, or caring, or... anything other than a one-night stand. No, no, no!* Jade wanted to slam her fist into the wall. She wanted to scream to release the stress that tonight's activities were supposed to have already released! "Fucking men."

"All men or just one?" Her mom asked from behind her.

Jade dropped her head and groaned. "All men in general, but one specifically."

"Sounds like we need cocoa."

Jade snorted. That was her mom's fix all. Well that or a glass of wine, but it was a little late, or rather early, to be consuming alcohol. Well... at least for her mom it was. Jade was willing to chug a fifth and find oblivion with her friend Jack Daniels.

"What happened?" Amanda King-Marshall walked past and headed into the kitchen. Jade followed. Her mom grabbed a saucepan and pulled out the milk. Jade pulled out a chair and plopped down into it. She pulled her hair out of the haphazard bun she'd shoved it into before she left Nic's and rested her head in her hands.

"I went out with a guy. We had a good time and then he had to go ruin it." Jade lifted her head and started rubbing her temples. Why the fuck had Nic said that? Better yet, what the fuck had he seen to make him say those things? She didn't need anyone to make her feel safe. She'd dedicated her entire life to being the one person who didn't need anyone. She was the one they called when shit got real. She was the one who kicked ass and took names. God knew she didn't need anyone to make her feel safe. *"Let go and drop the act." Fuck you, Nic.* She didn't need to let go of a damn thing. Act? There was no fucking act. This was who she was. Unapologetically this. Fuck Nic-fucking-DeMarco for assuming she was anything like one of the Barbie dolls listed in his series of little black books.

"What did he do?"

Her mom's question startled her. Jade blinked back the fog of her mental tirade. "Sorry, what?"

"What did your date do to make you so upset? He didn't try something inappropriate did he?" Her mom's eyes widened, and her hand snaked out to grab Jade's forearm.

"What? No, shit, Mom, you know me better than that. If he'd done that I'd have kicked his ass."

"Well, then what happened?" Amanda released her arm with a gentle pat and turned to stir the milk and cocoa powder while she added the sugar.

"He ahh..." Jade closed her eyes and clenched her fists. "He insinuated I needed a safe place to... Let me see if I can get this right." Jade released her hands and threw a pair of air quotes up. "He said I could let go and drop the act. That he had me and that I was safe. As if I'd ever need a man to be safe." Jade bit out each word. She was so fucking pissed that Nic insinuated she wasn't capable of taking care of herself.

"Oh, okay. I'm sorry." Her mom pulled two mugs down from the cupboard and carefully filled them with the cocoa.

"You're sorry? For what? What does that

mean?" Jade accepted the hot drink. "Thank you for the cocoa, Mom."

"You're welcome, and the I'm sorry is because I think you probably went out with a remarkably perceptive man tonight, and I know for a fact that you do need to let your guard down and you do need a safe place to relax."

Jade tensed at her mom's words. She really didn't think her mother of all people would agree with Nicolas Fucking DeMarco. "How can you say that? Have I ever given you the impression that I need a man to protect me?"

"Nope." Her mom popped the 'p' in the word. She'd always done it when she was making a point. Hell, every woman in the family did that when they were making a point.

Jade blew on the hot liquid in her cup and tried to resist the pull to ask her mom what she meant. She made it a full thirty seconds before she caved. "Fine. Go ahead, tell me."

"You don't want to know what I think." Her mom smiled and drew her finger around the rim of her cup. "But I'll tell you a secret. Over forty years ago, your dad held me, and he told me that I would always have a safe place in his arms. I believed him, and I will never regret the time that I spent feeling safe, protected, cherished... loved."

But he died. He wasn't there to take care of you or us. We weren't safe or protected. Of course, Jade didn't say any of that. She wouldn't do that to her mom. She couldn't tell her mother that as a young child she felt angry and abandoned. Her dad had died. He wasn't supposed to leave her. How could she feel safe? Even now, when she thought about losing him, the immense void left after her dad's death threatened to swallow her up. She wished she could remember the good times, but the fact was she was still mad at her father. She'd loved him desperately growing up. He was her idol, her hero, and she did everything to make him proud of her. Everything. Every night when he tucked her in, he promised he'd protect her and take care of her, forever. And then he was murdered by a waste of sperm who didn't deserve to live. She'd believed her daddy. She'd never doubted that he would be there forever... until he wasn't.

Loving people made you vulnerable to unimaginable pain, and as she watched them lower her dad's casket into the ground, she swore she would never depend on anyone else to make her feel safe. She would never trust in promises that couldn't be kept. The world knew an irreverent, impulsive Jade, a woman in search of a good time, and that was the image the world would continue to see. Her "acting out" had those closest to her wondering which screw was loose, but her uncensored behavior kept those who sought to be close to her at arm's length. *He wasn't there to take care of you or us. We weren't safe or protected.* No, she couldn't speak those words and admit the pain she held inside her. Instead, she took a moment to swallow the bitter feelings and a sip of cocoa.

Finally, she managed a shrug. "Yeah, and that was after you dated all through high school. It was after you graduated he asked you to marry him, right?" Jade couldn't find a parallel between her mom and dad's long, loving relationship and a single night of great sex with Nic. Hell, it wasn't even an entire night, it was two hours in the sack. Tops.

"True, but the idea is the same. We all need a safe place, a place where we can be vulnerable." Her mom lifted her eyes and cocked her head giving Jade an assessing look. "When was the last time you let yourself be vulnerable with a man?"

Jade snorted. Yeah, about an hour ago. She'd let her guard down and fucked it all up by letting the man she was with see it. "I don't know." It was a bald-faced lie, but she was damn good at telling people what they wanted to hear.

"Maybe you should try it sometime? I promise it won't hurt nearly as bad as you're imagining." Her mom stood and took her cup over to the sink, pouring the majority of the beverage out. She turned around and stopped to kiss the top of Jade's head. "You'd be surprised what a difference letting someone in your life will make. Stop pushing so hard, sweetheart. You may push away the one who could make you happy."

Jade leaned back in her chair and listened to her mom go back to the guest room. Oh, it would hurt. Of that, she had no doubt. Letting people see you vulnerable was nothing but an invitation for the assholes in the world to kick you in the teeth. No, there was no way she'd ever let anyone get that close. Especially not when there were so many men willing to keep it casual. When it came to relationships, Jade was all about casual, and fun, and absolutely no commitments. Life was one huge smorgasbord of delectable men, and Jade wanted to sample each offering.

She sighed at the unwanted feelings of discord Nic DeMarco had stirred. All she'd wanted tonight was a little fun and an orgasm. She had the orgasm. Jade smiled despite herself. She'd had two stupendously satisfying orgasms. Hell, she could validate the reputation Nic had earned. Punch his ticket girls; the man had sexual skills. He was remarkably talented in bed, and his body was a fucking playground that consisted of hard muscles, strong arms, and a sex-fueled libido that very few of her previous partners had ever surpassed.

Pushing those thoughts from her head, Jade moved her attention from her cocoa cup to her phone. There was only one thing to do. She picked up her phone and tapped out texts to her friends in Manhattan, and one to her brother, Justin. She needed a place to crash in the city. Justin had a sick apartment overlooking Central Park. Maybe she'd even luck out, and he'd be in town. She hadn't seen him in... hell, well it was too fucking long if she needed to think about it. Tomorrow night was girl's night out and then Monday she'd hop up to NYC and blow off some steam. Who the fuck needed Nicolas DeMarco? Not. Her.

She jumped when her phone suddenly vibrated. It was almost two in the morning. She hadn't really expected an answer from anyone. She picked it up and smiled. It was a text from Justin.

Justin:> I'll be in town, guest room is yours.

> :>) B there Monday. YU awake?

Justin:> 7 a.m. in London.

> YRU in London?

Justin:> New restaurant.

> No shit? How many now? 12?

Justin:> Something like that. CU Monday.

> Can't wait.

Jade grabbed the phone and stood up. What she needed right now was a shower and some sleep. She took a deep breath, rolled her shoulders, and made a resolute decision. Life was way too much fun to let the careless words of one man disrupt her Zen.

The phone skittering across his nightstand pulled him from a dead sleep. Nic slapped at the offending object and pulled it toward him. He swiped the face without looking at who was calling.

"What?" He croaked the demand not giving a shit who was calling. It had taken far too long to fall asleep after Jade left. He was tired. Capital T and it was Saturday for fuck's sake. Unless the cases they'd been working on were falling apart, nobody should be calling, especially at the fucking ass crack of dawn.

"Nicolas Giovanni Constantino DeMarco is that anyway to answer a phone? I think I taught you better manners." His mother's voice lanced through his hostile attitude.

"Ma, it's early. Zombies are probably still patrolling the streets." Nic rolled onto his back and inhaled a soft whiff of Jade's perfume that lingered on the sheets. He groaned, not wanting to rehash the evening's events again. He'd spent more than enough time last night wondering about the fallout.

"No, all the undead have retreated for the day. It's almost ten in the morning. Why haven't you been taking my calls? It isn't like I call just to bother you."

"Ha! Yes, yes, you do, Ma." Nic belted out the comment and chuckled at his mom's laughter.

"Well, maybe I do, but it's only because I don't get to see you enough. Mario and Carmine are going to be available next week. Take a couple days off and come up here. I want to have dinner with my sons and my docket after next week is insane."

"Yeah? You telling me the criminals in your

district aren't behaving?" Nic sat up in bed, threw two pillows against the headboard, leaned back, and got comfortable. His mom could talk the bark off trees, and it was Saturday, so he wasn't going to get her off the phone with an excuse about work.

The evil laugh she gave him put a smile on his face. The Honorable Bettina Giada Isadora DeMarco, Federal Judge of the Southern District of New York, wasn't someone you wanted to face in a courtroom if you were a criminal or a defense attorney that didn't know what the fuck you were doing. The woman's mind was sharper than a rapier. She didn't put up with any bullshit in her courtroom. She'd earned her reputation as a judge you shouldn't fuck with.

"It wouldn't be so bad if it was just my caseload, but Judge Salisbury recused himself from a case the Appellate Court remanded back to District, and now I'm stuck with it. Silas and I had to juggle all my other cases so I could hear a case that has already been tried, all because Salisbury won't be able to hear the case."

"What is it about?"

"Oh you know, the usual: greed, crime, corruption, murder, and something else, but I can't remember what." That answer waved a red flag under his nose so hard he sat up in bed.

"Hold on a second. There has never been a case in which you couldn't recall the particulars. What's the case, Ma?" Nic got that hot pinched feeling in his gut, the one that told him shit wasn't adding up.

"Well, you've heard about the RICO case involving the Triad that happened about four months ago?"

"Yeah, it involved the Shāshǒu de Yīnyǐng Clan right?" Hell, Nic followed the case because Guardian had been involved with another branch of the Triad in California, but they weren't able to pull a RICO on the members, and most of them walked. RICO cases, or Racketeer Influenced Corrupt Organization cases, allowed the federal government to prosecute the leader of the organization for crimes he ordered but did not personally commit. From what he recalled, the leader of the Shāshǒu de Yīnyǐng didn't have a chance in hell because the FBI had done one hell of a job. He heard about it from Cole Davis, Guardian's pseudo-liaison to the FBI. He was actually one hell of a decent guy and on a trajectory to make it to the top of that agency.

"Yep. Well, that's mine now."

Nic winced at his mom's words. Making key people, like judges, disappear was a hallmark identifier of the Triad.

"Has it been announced yet?" Nic threw the sheets off and strode naked through his bedroom into his office. Flipping the light switch, he padded to the computer. He turned it on and started the log on process to the Guardian Server.

"Not officially. But the clerks know, and you know how juicy stuff like this spreads."

"Like wildfire." Nic knew it only too well. He and his brothers had lived his mother's career with her. All three of her sons had gone to law school. Carmine and Mario were in practice together in Manhattan. Their firm was immensely successful. Nic had taken an alternate route after he passed the New York Bar. He took a job on the Washington DC police force. He wanted to see the criminal world from the bottom up. At the time, he wanted to be a criminal defense attorney, and he wanted to know the process better than any other lawyer did. He needed to understand how and why the cops bent the rules and regulations to suit themselves. Boy did he get his pious, preconceived notions—along with his ass—handed to him on a silver platter. Over and over and over again. His Ivy League education had fed him a crock of shit, and he'd believed it until he'd seen the war going on between the criminals and law enforcement. Moreover, it was a war. Classifying it as anything less was a gross misperception.

"Yeah, so I'm sure the people who are listening to the gossip know. But that case doesn't come home to roost for another week, so in the meantime, I want to get my sons together and go to dinner."

Nic watched the screen of his computer as it went through its log on process. "What? You're not going to make me my favorite manicotti?" Nic laid that unapologetic whine out there, as he always did.

"Of course I will, but one night you and your brothers will take me out to a nice place. I want atmosphere and someone else doing the cooking and dishes."

"Ma, you just want to grill us on our love lives," Nic chided her. If she had them at a restaurant, they couldn't get up from the table and leave. Well, they could, but Bettina DeMarco didn't raise stupid boys.

"And what's wrong with that, Nico?"

He smiled at his mom's use of his nickname. His father had named him after his childhood friend, so he was Nicolas instead of Nico, but his family had always called him Nico.

"Ma, I'm forty. I think you'd know by now I'm a confirmed bachelor." He typed in his password and pulled up his schedule for the next week. God, it was a fucking zoo.

"You are only as old as you feel, Nico, and you still have time to get married and give me a grand-baby or twenty."

"Twenty, Ma? Not asking much, are you?"

"Nah, knowing what I know about you and your brothers, you enjoy the practicing part of making a baby all too well. Now you need to get busy with the actual baby production."

"Jesus, Ma." Nic felt his face flush with heat. She didn't pull any punches.

"Do not take the Lord's name in vain, Nico. It wasn't like you boys were inventive when you hid your condoms or dirty books."

"Ma, seriously, you need to change the subject!" Nic closed his eyes and groaned the words. How did she always make him feel like he was thirteen years old?

"Point in fact, I wasn't the one who brought the

subject up; it was you. Not my fault I followed the trail of evidence." The mirth in her voice was the only thing that stopped him from ramming a pen through his eye. Sometimes talking to his mother was an act of insanity. He loved her to death, but she was a force of nature when she latched onto a subject.

"Why don't you date that nice girl I talked to yesterday? She sounded pretty, and she had a sense of humor. None of your other assistants sounded like they had a brain in their head."

"What are you talking about, Ma? How can anyone sound pretty?" His gut pinched again. Until this second, he'd forgotten his mom had talked to Jade yesterday.

"She was like a breath of fresh air. Nico, that woman laughed, I mean actually laughed, not the pretend tittering of all your other temps. When is your regular assistant coming back to work? She's very nice, too."

"And very married. She's on maternity leave, Ma. I don't know when she'll be back. I assume she'll show up when she's ready. What days are Carmine and Mario free?" He needed to divert her attention and quick.

"Carmine is back in town on Tuesday so any

day after that. Does this mean you're going to try to come up?" The hopeful sound of his mom's voice made him feel like shit for not going home more often, but life has a way of making best intentions look like bullshit excuses.

"Yeah, I need to call my partner, and his secretary will need to take a look at both of our schedules, but I'll be home this coming week. I'll even make the reservations for Friday night. I know a guy." He hit his contact list on the screen in front of him and scrolled down to Justin King's personal cell phone number. One of the perks of knowing the King family was having access to the friends and family seating at Justin's Michelin three star restaurants.

"As long as it isn't owned by organized crime, I'm game." His mom's reply should have been funny, but there were at least twenty restaurants that she couldn't go to due to known or suspected ties to organized crime."

"Guaranteed no affiliation, and I know the owner." Nic typed out a text to Justin and hit send.

"Thanks, and Nico?"

"Yeah?"

"I don't mean to be a nag. I love you. I want to see you happy, to have what your dad and I had."

Her soft voice echoed with loneliness. She'd dated occasionally but never found anyone after his dad had passed. She'd told him once she'd lost half her soul when his dad died. He couldn't imagine loving a person that much, but it was obvious that his mom and dad had been each other's world.

"I know, Ma. I know." Nic cleared his throat and his gaze bounced around the room as if the act would clear the emotion that dangled between them. He didn't do emotion well, which is why the angsty bullshit from last night had driven him insane until the early hours of the morning. "I'll see you soon, yeah?"

"Good. Love you, Nico."

"Love you too, Ma." He ended the call and glanced at his schedule again. Fuck, it wasn't going to be easy to extract himself with all the cases that had dropped out of the sky and stacked like pancakes on top of their normal workload, but he needed to make it work. Hell, he hadn't requested a vacation day in years. Maybe it was about time.

CHAPTER 9

J ade stood outside on Justin's balcony. The summer heat had dipped because of a massive thunderstorm earlier in the evening. The noise and bustle of New York faded beneath her. The apartment she remembered had doubled in size. Her brother had bought the unit next to his and knocked down walls. The interior was a marvel of masculine design—dark woods, leather, chrome and smoked glass. Things that shouldn't go together seemed to merge seamlessly. The paintings on the walls were obviously originals, but Jade had no idea who painted the canvases, and if Justin had told her the names, she still wouldn't have a clue if she should be impressed or not. The art was nice to look at, and they made the apartment feel like a home. She took a drink of the very old scotch that she'd found sitting on one of the shelves of his grandiose bar. The subtle lighting on the marble and ornately carved wood held more bottles than most downtown bars. She slid open a pair of beautiful double doors and marveled at the wine collection. A glass face to the chamber hidden behind the doors was something she wouldn't touch because, although she didn't know much about wine, she did know these bottles were priceless. Her brother Justin was pure class, through and through. Of course, that meant their personalities were polar opposites, and maybe that was why they got along so well. Justin had always been a loner, quiet and studious. He observed more than participated. His interests lay in things she couldn't or didn't want to understand—things like ballet, opera, art, and of course, food. He could talk for hours about priceless sculptures, the exhibits at the Louvre, or the latest scandal in the highest social circles. He'd obtained the rank of Master Sommelier, a three year endeavor she'd never dream of trying to achieve. Justin could tell you where wine was grown by tasting it. He was never wrong, and her family had tried countless times to stump him. She never imagined him as a millionaire executive while they were growing up, but he wore the mantle the same way he wore his bespoke suits. Perfectly.

The sunset cast an eerie yellow hue to the sky. It was nothing like the sweeping vistas in South Dakota, but it was... urban beautiful, if that was a thing. She could appreciate the architecture and city skyline. The abrupt rise and fall of hard structures held a beauty all their own. Her lungs filled with the unique scent of the city. Yeah, this was her vibe, more so than the ranch where her mom lived, or the home she owned in Virginia. She felt the pulsing energy of the city beneath her and longed for the distractions the metropolis provided. Her knee was healing well; it still hurt when she pushed it hard, but life hurt so what else was new? She took a long sip of the amber liquid in her hand. A distinct oak flavor followed the warm slide of the top-shelf hooch. God, life was so good. She had no idea how it could get better. She was on top of the world and flying.

"It didn't take you long to break into my best scotch."

Jade twirled toward the open French doors. It took two seconds to hop across the space that separated her from her brother. She threw her arms around his neck and pulled him down and in for a hug. "Damn, it is so good to see you!" Jade pulled back and gave him a once over. Even after a transatlantic flight, the man looked immaculate. Except for the dark circles under his eyes.

"Good to see you, too." Justin released her and tipped his head toward the bar. She followed as he rounded a marble-topped counter and pulled down a crystal tumbler. He dropped two ice cubes into his glass and poured a healthy dose of a vodka with a label she couldn't pronounce. He lifted it in a silent toast to her and took a sip. "Heard you got yourself into a sticky situation." Justin motioned toward the leather seats, and Jade headed that way.

"What? Who said that? No, I didn't." What the hell was he talking about?

"Oh, so Jacob and Jared didn't have to come rescue you from your last assignment?" The corners of his mouth twitched at his taunt.

Jade stuck out her tongue at him. "Brat, you know I don't need them to take care of me. No, they had intel that my cover was compromised, but as far as I can tell, that was never validated. I was doing fine, thank you very much." Jade wasn't about to tell him or anyone else that she was more than happy they'd shown up when they did. That was information nobody needed to have in his or her back pocket.

"Glad to hear it." His smile contradicted the obvious disbelief in his deep voice. "What brings you to New York?"

Jade dropped her head back on the couch, scrunched her eyes shut and blew out a lungful of air. She tapped her glass and rolled her head to look at him. "I'm here to blow off some steam, destress and let my hair down. I was on that last assignment for over a year. I deserve some me time." All of that was true. She was also trying to forget the man who was responsible for her trip up from DC.

"Sounds like a plan. I'm starving. You?" Justin took a long pull on his drink.

"I could eat." Hell, she was ravenous.

"I'll call the restaurant from my bedroom phone and have them send up two specials." Justin palmed his cell phone and stood.

"I guess it is good to have one of your restaurants in the same building, huh?" Jade teased her brother after he finished his call.

"It's even better to own the building. I'm going to go take a shower and wash off the travel dust. They'll call my cell when the wait staff is on the way up. Answer it, will you?" Justin threw his phone onto the ottoman and headed toward the master suite.

"Sure, that's why I came all the way to New York, to answer your phone for you," Jade called after his retreating back. His hand came up, his middle finger waving back at her. She laughed and grabbed the remote off the huge ottoman. Twenty minutes later she'd landed on BBC America because watching any of the American news channels led to a headache of biblical proportions. Jade was transfixed watching a news report on a corporate espionage-slash-theft that had happened sometime over the last two days in London. Closed for the weekend, when employees went back to work they found the contents of their server and hard copy backups in a hardened vault were gone. According to Scotland Yard, the company's high dollar alarms never activated, but it was not releasing any further information. God, she'd love to be part of the team working that case. It was rare for Guardian to get gigs like that, especially overseas, but if the client was big enough, they could afford to bring in Guardian. Unfortunately, that kind of case wasn't her forte. She didn't doubt she'd fall back into the rotation on the personal security side of the house as soon as she was cleared and done blowing off steam. It wasn't an easy job, and Jade loved meeting new people and experiencing their lives for a short period of time. But what she loved the most about PSO duties was the unknown. She was on a knife's edge every minute she was with a primary, and the thrill of that adrenaline rush was sexy, alluring and addictive. She fucking loved getting new assignments.

"Have they called yet?"

Jade jumped at Justin's voice behind her. "Huh? Ahhh... she peeked at the phone and shook her head. "Nope." Her eyes flitted back to the talking head on the television.

"What's so interesting?" Justin, now clad in designer blue jeans and a silky looking t-shirt, walked back to the bar.

"Corporate espionage thingy over in England."

Justin contemplated the television and shrugged. "As long as they didn't steal the building I acquired for my restaurant, I'm good." His phone vibrated beside her.

Jade picked it up and swiped the face. "Hello, this is Jade, Justin's indentured phone servant. He's too damn important to answer his own line, but I'll be glad to speak with you. How may I direct your call?" Justin snorted in laughter behind her while she waited for whoever was on the line to answer. When no one spoke, she pulled the phone away from her face and looked at the display. Nope, still connected to a number in Virginia. ND displayed above the number. "Hello? Is anyone there?" She wanted to bust out with the chorus of Adele's song, but with her tone-deaf music sense, that stunt could break someone's eardrum. She wasn't that cruel.

A man cleared his throat. "Hey, Jade, is Justin available?"

Oh, holy fuck. Of all the people in the world. Did she have to fly to New Delhi to get some space from the man? "Hey, Nic, just a minute." She pulled the phone from her ear and held it up in the air pretending to focus on the London news coverage. "Nic DeMarco for you."

Justin grabbed the phone from her. "Hey, Nic. What? I'm pretty sure I did, but I'll admit I'm jet lagged and can't be one hundred percent positive. Let me double check and make sure that it was done." Justin headed off toward his home office. Jade heard her brother laugh as he walked down the hall. His low rumble disappeared when he went into the office and shut the door. Jade reached for her scotch and downed the remainder. She drew a breath, battling the burn of her throat. She would not let one man get to her, not when there were so many fish in the sea. Wait, bad choice. She hated fish. Okay, so many steaks to eat. Yeah, that was better.

"Yeah, I have you set up. A table for four at seven thirty for this Friday."

Nic listened to Justin's response with half his mind. The other half was trying to decide if he was pissed about Jade lying to him about going to the ranch.

"Thanks. My family doesn't get together very often. I appreciate you squeezing us in." His mom's voice floated toward him. She was talking on the phone in her den. The sound sent a warm feeling of comfort around him.

Justin casually pushed off his gratitude with a laugh. "Not a problem. I always have two or three tables I hold for family and friends or the occasional senator, Supreme Court Justice, or Hollywood A-lister."

"Yeah, well the DeMarcos don't qualify as any of those, so I appreciate it. You and Jade hitting the town?" Nic squeezed his eyes shut and tried to figure out where the fuck that question came from.

"Nah, I just flew in. I think she's hitting the clubs with some of her friends. Said she wants to blow off some steam and destress. I guess her last assignment was epic, but you'd know more about that than I would."

"Yeah, she did a great job and deserves to have some fun." Nic acknowledged Jade's work.

"Hey, if you're in town all week, maybe we can get together and have a drink. I know Jade would be down with that."

"Yeah, unfortunately, the family and other obligations will prevent that. But the next time you get down to your place in DC, I'm taking you out for a night on the town."

"Dude, I might take you up on that. Seems the only thing I do now is work."

"Hell, I feel your pain, man. We need to learn how to relax." Nic couldn't remember the last time he took a week off. He felt guilty for sticking Jared with the administration of the caseloads they had now, but his partner had swatted away his objections, reminding him that Nic had held down the fort while he and Christian had taken several trips and short vacations.

"Isn't that the truth? Speaking of which, I'm going to eat and then fall into bed. Flying back from Europe always messes up my body clock. You'd think it would get easier."

"Never does. Thanks again."

"No problem. Take care"

"You too." Nic pushed end on the call and stood staring out the window into his family's neighborhood. The long row of brownstones had gone through a revitalization, and instead of bicycles and scooters lining aging wrought iron fences, perfectly manicured stoops now welcomed home professionals and people with seven figure incomes. The families who used to live in these houses had sold out, taking the money and moving to less desirable areas. His mother and old Mr. Conti, who owned Pappi Conti's Pizza, were the only two from the original families, or at least the families that Nic remembered growing up. Old man Conti had franchised his restaurants, and it was now a national chain. His daughter, Carla Conti, had been Nic's high school sweetheart. God, he hadn't thought of her in years.

"What's holding your interest out there?" His

mom came up beside him and put her small hand on his back, rubbing it as if her touch could soothe away the tensions of the world. Once upon a time, it had done just that. Those were good memories that Nic held onto.

"Whatever happened to Carla Conti?" Nic stared across the street toward the Conti house.

"She got married, had a baby. A tragic accident took both her husband and son from her. She comes around sometimes. Gio talks about her whenever we see each other. Why?"

Nic shook his head. Life really had a way of wearing a person down. "Just thinking about years gone by. The neighborhood is so different now."

"Ahhh… that is true. I'm not complaining. When your dad and I bought this house, it was the best we could do. If I sold it now, it could fund a third world country for a week."

"Only a week?" Nic turned his smile toward his mom.

She swatted at his arm. "Two if they're frugal."

A comfortable silence settled over them. Nic continued his wander down memory lane.

"Do you want Carla's number? I have it. She is still as beautiful as ever, and I think she'd enjoy a cup of coffee to catch up. I gather from Gio, she doesn't have many close friends. She works all the time. He worries."

Nic blinked back to the present from his mental road trip. He focused across the street again. Why the hell not? It wasn't as if he had any better prospects, other than a countless string of one-night stands, and even that had run its course. He wasn't interested in the chase anymore. "Yeah. Okay."

"Okay? Really?" His mother's shock drew a chuckle from him.

"Yeah. I'd like to see how she's doing." She was a friend from back in the day. He was here for the week and contrary to what he'd told Justin, he didn't have any solid plans except for Friday night. Dinner with the entire family. Meeting up with Jade for a drink was the last thing he wanted to do. His brain floated a vision of her long legs through his mind. Okay, so maybe it wasn't the last thing, but meeting with her outside the office would be a mistake.

CHAPTER 10

J ade cracked her eye open then shut it immediately. She said a simple silent prayer to the porcelain god that whoever was pounding her fucking skull with a sledgehammer would die. Die a brutal fucking death, the bastards.

Her mouth felt like the floor of a New York City subway platform. Disgusting, smelly and sticky. It would take a jackhammer to peel her tongue off the roof of her mouth.

One heavy eyelid opened at a soft tap on her door. "What?" The morning after taste of tequila pushed a bile-inducing, double-flip action through her gut.

"Hey, sorry to bother you, but Jared said he called you three times. He told me to tell you, and I quote here, 'Unless her cell is dead, or she is, her ass needs to call in for a briefing.'" Justin kept his voice low.

"Fuck me. When?" Jade lifted her head and immediately dropped it back down.

"Forty-five minutes. I brought you something for the hangover." Shit. His voice right next to her shocked her. She hadn't heard him cross the room. But then again, the sledgehammer concerto tapping out a techno-dance thrum in her brain was fucking loud.

Jade pried open her eyes and grimaced at the vile, greenish-brown, gelatinous liquid he was holding out toward her. "What's in it?" Jade slowly rolled to her side and pushed up on an elbow. *Shit. Never again.* Emory, Danni and she had gotten stupid drunk last night. Thank God, they had sense enough to take a limo, otherwise who knows where they would have ended up. Jade didn't cut loose often, but she'd drank way too much, and they had closed down the dance club. She bent her legs and groaned. Her knee was a little stiff, but that was to be expected.

She reached out for the glass and closed the slits she was looking through. She took a deep breath and chugged the drink. Her eyes popped open, and she bolted to the bathroom. Fucking son of a bitch!

Twenty minutes later, minus what remained in her stomach, showered and shampooed, because long hair and paying homage to the porcelain toilet gods never worked out well, Jade walked into Justin's kitchen.

"Feel better?" Justin leaned over a saucepan stirring whatever was in the small ceramic pot.

Ewww... food. No. Just no. "What the fuck was that shit?" Jade made a beeline toward the coffee maker.

"A little of this, a little of that." The laughter in his voice irked her. "But you've got to admit it. You feel better, don't you?"

Jade lifted the small silver pitcher and frothed the milk for her coffee. She did feel better, but admitting that to him wasn't going to happen. "Shut up." Not the most eloquent comeback, but hey, it worked.

Justin laughed as he crossed the kitchen to the oven. "Biscuits with honey?"

Jade wanted to hate him for being so chipper, but he'd made her biscuits and Justin made the best biscuits. Better than their mom could make, but that was a secret the siblings would take to their graves.

"Thank you." Jade walked over and stood behind him, dropping her head on his back.

"I've never known you to get that wasted." Justin plated a biscuit and ladled a small amount of warm honey and butter mixture into a ramekin. "Anything you want to talk about?"

Jade pulled a piece of biscuit off and dipped it in the honey. She let the excess drip off while she considered his question. Finally, she shrugged. "Long assignment with zero alcohol. My tolerance level is in the basement. Admittedly, I drank too much last night, but we had a limo. Before you ask, I was with it enough to make sure Emory and Danni got home okay. Do I regret the last three rounds of tequila shots? Hell yeah, but it wasn't like I was out drowning my sorrows at the bottom of a five dollar bottle of rotgut."

"So you admit you have sorrows?" Justin popped a bite into his mouth.

"Ahhh... no, I didn't say that."

"Sure you did."

"No, I didn't. I have no sorrows, no regrets, and no problems." Jade pointed her piece of honey-dipped biscuit at him.

Justin looked up at her and let a wide smile

slowly spread across his face. "Methinks the lady doth protest too much."

Jade tore another piece of biscuit and busied herself dipping the fragment to avoid her brother's gaze. She wasn't protesting. Was she? And what if she was? It wasn't as if she was the touchy feely one in the family, that was Mom's forte, but hell, she was authorized a me moment, wasn't she? "I am not protesting, but even if I was, I've decided I'd be authorized. And, dear brother, I don't think that was the line we learned in high school. Why the sudden interest in my sorrows? Not that I'm admitting to having any."

"Just trying to catch up. I've been running at full speed for the last five years, and regrettably, that means I don't get to spend much time with the family." He walked over to the stove and placed a small sauté pan on the massive cooktop. "You ready for some eggs?"

"Scrambled with the yummy cheese?" She had no idea what type of cheese he put into her scrambled eggs, but she could never recreate the flavor of Justin's cooking.

"You got it." He reached for a bowl and whisk.

"Can I ask a question?" Jade dragged the last of

her biscuit through the bottom of the honey pot on her plate.

"Sure, but I reserve the right not to answer." He didn't look up from his work as he spoke.

"Why are you working so hard? I mean, you never stop." She couldn't understand his drive to keep adding more and more responsibilities to his plate.

Justin paused grating the cheese block in his hand. He regarded her for a moment and shrugged. "If you listen to my shrink, I'm compensating for not being able to control my past."

"You have a shrink?" Jade blinked back her surprise. One of the prerequisites for employment with Guardian mandated she go through several sessions with a psychiatrist, but she was very careful to answer the questions so there would never be a doubt as to her mental stability... or lack thereof. She smirked at that thought. She'd admit she was a bit crazy. She embraced the wild streak in herself and loved to shock people. A shrink would have a field day with her, of that she had zero doubt.

"Hmmm... yeah. I had some issues in my past, and I needed to get my head on straight. Now my sessions are more of a security blanket than anything else, but yeah, I see a therapist in DC about once a month or so. Sometimes more if the stresses of the world get to me. She does video chats with me when I can't physically get there." Justin dumped the egg concoction into the sauté pan and stirred the mixture.

Jade cocked her head and really examined her brother. "What issues?"

"I thought we were talking about your sorrows."

"Did it have to do with Dad's death?" Jade knew many of her own issues centered on that event. The murder had fractured a close family and left deep fissures in each of them. Fissures that they didn't discuss. The damage had affected each of her siblings in different ways. The events mani-fested by the loss of their father irrevocably changed each one of them. She was smart enough to recognize that fact.

"Yes and no. I lost my way and started getting involved in some situations that would have inevitably led to jail time. I had started doing some extreme things to hit an adrenaline high. A person I barely knew called me on it. He put me in touch with this therapist and helped me to find an appropriate outlet for my... adrenaline addiction."

"What was the outlet?"

"Hmmm? Oh, typical adrenaline junkie things, like skydiving. I'm also a part owner of an Indy race car team, and I take hot laps in the car every now and then. It is all controlled and safe, but it still gives me the thrill I need to feel... alive."

Jade stared at her brother and blinked, hoping to reboot her brain. Her image of her overworked brother just shattered into about a gazillion pieces. "That's... really?"

Justin laughed and slid a plate of scrambled eggs and sliced tomatoes, decorated with some green curly leaf thingy, plus another biscuit, in front of her. "Really."

"Damn, Justin, and here I thought you were a fuddy-duddy ole businessman."

He shrugged and cracked an egg into the pan for his breakfast. "I think we all have sides of our personality that we hide from each other. I enjoy building my businesses because they allow me to seek out the type of thrills that are beyond the means of others."

Jade nodded. She got that. She worked the job at Guardian because she was addicted to the adrenaline that pulsed through her every time one of her primaries was in danger. She trained relentlessly to hone her skills, walked a razor's edge and put herself in harm's way to protect those that Guardian assigned her to watch. She loved every single second of the unknown. It was her adrenaline addiction, and she owned it. Well, that and sex. Jade poked at the scrambled eggs while she watched her brother move around his high-tech, monster-sized kitchen.

Nah, sex wasn't an addiction for her. She'd gone a year without it. Jade pushed her eggs around her plate and thought of that night with Nic. Holy fuck, the sex had been amazing. Sure, any sex after a year would have been amazing, but Nic had made her feel... valued? She stabbed at her eggs at that thought. No, he was a player, just like her. He had the moves and knew the words to make a woman feel like she was the only one. She stopped moving her food around when she remembered her drunken epiphany last night. Yes! That! That was what had happened. Jade was a fool for thinking that his words had meant anything else. She'd figured it out last night... after the fourth or fifth shot of tequila. The technique she used to reach that conclusion wasn't necessarily recommended, but her logic was sound. She was such a putz for letting his words get into her head.

She could have stayed that night and had two or three more orgasms, but no… she'd actually let his words mean something when there was absolutely no way they meant a damn thing.

"Are you going to murder the eggs or eat them?" Justin sat down across from her as he spoke.

"Huh?" Jade peered down at the once fluffy plate of whipped eggs and released a small laugh. She'd obliterated the damn things with her fork while she'd been lost in thought. Jade broke open the biscuit, forked it full of egg and covered it with the top.

"Remember, Jared wants you to call in…" Justin read the digital clock on the double oven. "… five minutes."

Jade bit down on her makeshift sandwich and nodded. She had no idea what Jared wanted. She was on vacation, and unless the earth, moon, and stars were in jeopardy of falling out of orbit, she was going to use every freaking day owed to her.

CHAPTER 11

J ade left the treadmill after a short, low-speed jog. She'd worn a brace on her knee, but there hadn't been so much as a twinge during her cardio warm up. Well, not from the knee. She'd swear her sweat turned to pure tequila around the half mile mark, but she was feeling much better tonight; hence the workout at Guardian's New York facilities. Jared had given her an update on the fallout from her undercover work. It seemed she'd found the loose thread and the organization was unraveling almost faster than Guardian, and the associated agencies working with them, could pull the string. Jade listened to the multitude of investigations that her undercover operation had spawned. She'd be lying if she said she wasn't impressed with herself. The explosion she and her DEA partner had detonated across the sphere of the Fathers' influence made the yearlong effort well worth the sacrifices.

Jade headed for the locker room to tape her hands. She had an appointment with the heavy bag and then hopefully she could get someone to spar with her. Working undercover didn't give her any time to work out or even perform her kata to keep her mind and skills sharp. Muscle memory, pride and a stupid amount of luck had gotten her through the fights the night Guardian infiltrated the compound. She wasn't a fool. She needed to get back into fighting shape, and that meant cardio, weights and sparring against opponents who were bigger, faster, meaner and better at the skills she was trying to hone. The process wasn't fun, but Jade fucking loved the challenge and competition.

She pulled the last wrap tight and taped it into place. The heavy bag was calling her name. She skirted around the weight room and rolled her eyes at a couple of guys who tried to catch her attention. The gym was the only place where she wouldn't troll for a piece of man meat. Here she was working and, as much shit as she talked, she'd never jeopardize her training with a distraction.

Jade threw a couple light punches at the bag and rolled into a routine she'd been doing for years. She upped the torque and speed of her attack. Her knee held up when she moved into rapid succession punches. She ducked and bobbed while thinking about her last opponent, the one who'd taken out her knee. The bastard shouldn't have had the upper hand during any of that exchange. Jade attacked the leather with a flurry of uppercuts. Someone grabbed the swaying bag and held it firm against her assault. Jade shifted her attention from her assault of the bag. Fuck. She stopped her workout. Her lungs burned from the effort she'd expended, and she could feel the sweat sheeting down her body. But none of that mattered because Nic Fucking Demarco stood two feet in front of her, stabilizing the heavy bag.

"Don't let me stop you." Nic braced against the bag as if he expected her to pick up where she'd left off.

"Normally I wouldn't. But you do have a tendency to stop things right when they are getting fun." Jade grabbed her water bottle.

"Ouch." Nic stepped away from the bag and

motioned toward the sparring rings. Two were vacant. "How about you take your pound of flesh out of me while we are in the ring."

"You don't want to fight me." Jade chugged some water while keeping her eyes on Nic. Which wasn't hard because the man filled out his shorts. Jade's eyes traveled up from his prominent package to his tight abs and wide chest. She lifted an eyebrow at him when she noticed his smirk.

"Like what you see?" Nic crossed his arms, which flexed his biceps enticingly. Damn, the man was a freaking carnival ride of muscles. Too bad, because

she was never going to go back for seconds on that thrill ride. "I never denied I liked the wrapping. It was the gooey inside that bothered me." Jade finished her water while taking in Nic's reaction. To her surprise, he laughed.

Nic lifted his arms, pulling his t-shirt up and leaving an amazing view of his happy trail that disappeared inside his workout shorts. "I have news for you, women love this soft center. Leave it to me to find the one who didn't. No offense, doll, but you got the same line everyone else has heard. It was a line. Get over yourself." He dropped his arms before he grabbed his water bottle and ring kit.

Well, shit… that was unexpected. *Get over myself?* Hell, she hadn't heard that correctly. Couldn't have. Nope. But just in case. "Say what, now?"

"You marched out of my house like I'd proposed marriage, six kids, and a mortgage." Nic walked toward the sparring ring, and Jade grabbed her kit before she fell into step with him.

Well, she kinda had done that, but she wasn't going to admit it. "Whatever. Don't flatter yourself, DeMarco."

"I don't have to flatter myself. I'm fucking phenomenal. Ask anyone in my collection of little black books." Nic vaulted to the elevated ring and hopped over the top rope.

"Huh. You don't have self-esteem issues, do you?"

"When you're good, you're good." He huffed on his fingertips and brushed them against his tight t-shirt all while bouncing on his toes. "Get your ass in here and give me a workout, woman. Your reputation leads me to believe you can give me a run for my money." He stopped moving and winked at her.

"Yeah? Funny, that was what I heard about your reputation, super stud." Jade watched as he started to bounce on his toes again warming his body. He wasn't wearing a jock. His thick cock was clearly visible through the thin nylon of his workout shorts. She admired his optimism. Stupid, but optimistic. Yep, Nic was definitely a unicorn kinda guy.

"Which part? That I could give you a run for your money? I think I did. Twice, if I recall. Then you tucked tail and ran away. I thought you were tougher than that."

"Oh, I'm tough. Are you sure you want me to get into that ring with you? I don't take prisoners."

"Neither do I, little missy." Nic mimicked Jim Carrey when he spoke. The imitation was perfect down to the stupid facial mannerisms. He ran his fingers through his hair and smiled down at her.

Jade threw back her head and laughed. "Fuck you and the horse you rode in on."

"You doing horses now, too?" Nic lifted his fists into fighting position as he spoke.

Jade lifted herself onto the side of the ring. "Kinda have to; your dick isn't getting any of this."

Nic laughed as he wedged in his teeth protector. "You mean any more of that." He cracked his neck from side to side and beckoned her closer. "The winner should get a prize. If I win, I get another night. If you win, you get another night. No melty centers."

Jade assumed her ready stance and shook her head. "What makes you think you can win against me?"

"Persistence. I've been told all about your fancy fighting techniques, but I can take a beating and get back up. I'll wear you down sooner or later. This cop has mad skills."

Jade faked a left and dropped, sweeping Nic's legs out from under him. He hit the mat hard. Jade stood with her hands on her hips and waited. Nic rolled to his side and jumped up. "Cop, you may have mad skills, but they won't ever match mine."

Nic leaned forward and rested his hands on his knees. He nodded and drew a deep breath. Jade cursed and moved a second too late. She landed on her back with Nic on top of her. The bastard had tackled her. She arched, getting space between them and forced an elbow between his shoulder and her body. The other hand hooked around his back and grabbed the top of his shoulder. She faked a move pulling him away from her, and when he resisted, she moved with his momentum and rolled him onto his back. Her pointed elbow positioned at his throat. She pushed enough to let him know she could kill him. He tapped out, and she lifted away.

Nic rubbed his throat, hopped up and circled her. She stood her ground, ready for any other sneak attacks. "I'm sensing you don't play fair."

"Nope." Jade popped her 'p' and swiveled, so she was facing him as he circled her.

"Did you know you leave yourself open with that stance? You need to lower in your crouch and open your legs another six inches."

Jade blinked at the precise instruction. Her sensei had always told her that too, but she was comfortable. A flurry of movement came toward her and Jade reacted, blocking every strike. Damn it, Nic had been sandbagging. She fought furiously against his assault. He backed her into the ropes. She blocked, struck, thrust and blocked again in the span of two seconds. Nic's form was unbelievably good. He had to have studied under a phenomenal sensei for years. Jade saw her opening and kicked. The flash of pain in her knee drove her to the matt. Nic was over her in an instant, hovering, concern etched into the furrows of his brow.

"Are you okay? I forgot about your knee." He

carefully ran his hands down her thigh and manipulated her joint. He started to take off the brace.

"No, leave it on. I'm fine. It wasn't happy taking
all my weight and dealing with the torque of the
kick." Jade dropped back to the mat. "Fuck, you're
good."

"All the ladies say that."

"Asshat. How long have you been studying
Wing Chun?"

"Since I was a freshman in high school. Ma
made all of us take self-defense classes. I liked the
concepts. I had no idea you'd studied it. You threw
me with the punching bag routine."

Jade didn't move for several minutes enjoying
her rest on the mat. "Yeah, the art of Chi Sau that
Wing Chun teaches is great, but sometimes I just
got to beat the shit out of something."

"Oh, hell, I hear you. Not sure who would have
won that bout if your knee hadn't gone out. Guess
we'll have to call it a draw. We both win."

"Is that one or two nights then?" Jade rolled her
head and stared at the man sitting next to her. The
sheen of sweat accented the definition of his
muscles. Not that she noticed. Oh hell, who the
fuck was she trying to kid? She noticed, and she
fucking loved it.

"One for each of us." He tossed the answer out after seeming to consider it.

Jade held up a finger and pointed it at him. "No strings and no gooey centers?" She could really use an orgasm or twenty. Since Nic, she hadn't hooked up with anyone or called one of her acquaintances with benefits in the area. She refused to think about the reasons why.

"Guaranteed." He crossed his heart and held up three fingers.

"What is that?"

"Boy Scout's honor, I think. I promise not even the zombie apocalypse would make me get all mushy again."

Jade lifted to her elbows and stared at the man-child in front of her. "Hate to tell you this, Nic, but zombies aren't real."

Nic's eyes popped open, and his mouth dropped. Just as quickly his eyes narrowed, and he glared at her. "You don't know that."

Jade laughed at the stricken look on his face. "Yeah, I kinda do."

"Prove it."

"Prove what?"

"Prove zombies don't exist."

"What?"

"You can't, can you?"

"No, but that isn't an argument."

"Sure it is. The air you're breathing, can you see it?"

Jade blinked at him and shook her head. How the fuck did she get into a conversation about proving or disproving the existence of zombies?

"See, just because you can't see it, doesn't mean it's not real. Boom... lawyered." Nic lifted his hands into the air and made a god-awful noise mimicking a crowd cheering.

"You're broken." Jade dropped back onto the mat.

"Nope, strategically bent." Nic leaned over and kissed her.

"Right... whatever. Want to meet up tonight?" Jade sat up and cracked her neck.

"Tonight? Nah, I have this thing."

"A thing, huh?"

"Yep."

"Okay. Tomorrow night?" She didn't have any solid plans.

"Ummm..." Nic grimaced.

"Let me guess, you've got a thing." Jade raised an eyebrow at him.

"Yep. Family thing."

"Okay, you're given a pass on that one. Families can suck you into shit." Jade knew that for sure.

"Don't I know it."

"Saturday?"

"All yours."

"Fine. Text me with the deets." Jade stood and reached a hand down to Nic to help him up. He swatted away her hand and hopped up. Guess she was visiting the DeMarco playground at least two more times before she marked it off her 'to-do' list. Because Lord have mercy, she'd do DeMarco again and again. He needed a ball gag so he didn't say stupid shit, but she'd definitely do him.

"See you then." Nic slapped her on the ass before he spun and headed toward the men's locker room.

Jade reached around and rubbed the lingering sting of his hand on her butt cheek. A wicked smile spread across her face. Maybe a ball gag wasn't that far of a stretch.

CHAPTER 12

Nic waited outside the restaurant where he and Carla had agreed to meet. She was coming from somewhere around the United Nations, and since his mom's house was located on the West Side, they decided to meet in midtown in an up and coming neighborhood near the Garment District. One thing that he could say about this city was it never stopped re-inventing itself, and he loved the vibrancy and life that thrummed through the streets. He was lucky he had connections in the city, also known as his younger brother, because reservations at this place weren't easy to get. His brother Mario let him know in no uncertain terms that Nic owed him big time.

He recognized Carla as soon as she stepped out of the cab. She was a more mature version of the girl he dated. She stood maybe five feet tall and was petite to the point of being tiny. She was wearing her hair shorter than in high school, and her makeup and clothes were, as always, perfect. Nic smiled broadly and walked over to her.

"Carla, it is wonderful to see you." He bent down to hug his friend.

"Nico, you look so good! All grown up!" Her dark brown eyes sparkled with laughter.

"I wish I could say the same about you. Still a squirt, I see." They had a running, teasing dialog going back over the years.

"Hey, dynamite comes in small packages. You better watch out, or this squirt will take you out." She wagged her finger at him and arched an eyebrow in warning.

Nic couldn't help the laugh that erupted at her bravado. She was a hellion. A dainty, tiny, demon that would back up her sass with some outrageous act. She'd grown up on a tough block, and she could take care of herself back in the day. He wouldn't be surprised if the woman was carrying mace or a Taser. Hell, she probably had both in that designer purse. It was big enough to double as a gym bag.

"I promise to be on my best behavior." Nic extended his elbow and covered her hand when she took it. "It really is good to see you again."

"You too, Nico." She smiled up at him.

Nic felt a twinge of longing. Longing and desire, but not for Carla. He hadn't lied; it was good to see her again, but the chemistry he felt once upon a time for the girl he used to know wasn't there any longer. The feelings he had for the vixen he'd left at the gym this morning overrode any lingering memories of days gone by. He probably should have canceled the date with Carla and taken Jade out tonight, but he did want to catch up with her. She was one of his oldest friends.

The elevator took them to the top floor of the building. The table they were seated at boasted a fantastic view of the midtown skyline. Buildings familiar to both of them spired over the tops of smaller office buildings. The setting sun painted prisms of flashing lights across windows of the taller buildings, dotting the city with splashes of brilliance.

Carla pulled at the wine list the maître d'hôtel had given to him after the man had introduced their wait staff for the evening. The sommelier was at his elbow immediately to ask if he had any questions. Nic asked the sommelier to pair their dinner with the wines he felt were best. The man bowed and departed as quietly and quickly as he'd arrived. He was impressed with the service. It was on par with Justin's establishments, and they were world renowned for their service.

"So, Nico, tell me what you've been doing with your life." Carla lifted her eyes to him. "And don't leave anything out, because we are going to stay here until we are all caught up." She scrunched her nose at the wine selections and laid it back down at his elbow. "I want something with a kick. I've had a hell of a day. Would it be terribly uncouth of me to ask for a bourbon, water back, before dinner?"

Nic covered his astonishment. Carla drinking bourbon was something he didn't think he'd ever see. He lifted his hand, and one of the wait staff appeared at his elbow. "Two Pappy Van Winkles, neat, water back."

"The Twenty-Year Family Reserve, sir?" The young man asked.

"Of course."

"Very good, sir." The waiter turned away immediately.

"Pappy Van Winkle? You're joking, right? Is that a real bourbon?" Carla laughed aloud. The happy sound drew curious glances from nearby tables.

"Indeed it is. I actually found it when I was on the police force in DC, but the cost of a bottle was too steep for my paycheck. Fortunately, Mario gifted me a bottle one Christmas. Believe me, I was stingy as hell with the liquid gold and only had a small drink for special occasions, like when I closed a big case. Now that I can afford to order the best, I still prefer the Pappy over everything else." It had a sweetness to it that defied his limited vocabulary. "Perfection. Wait until you taste it."

"Your mom told my dad you work for Guardian Security now. That organization has intrigued me for a long time. What exactly do you do at the global bastion of private security?"

"I'm the Chief Operations Officer for the Domestic Security Division." Nic had used that line to get and hold the attention of many women. He would watch dollar signs light up their eyes. They were easy prey after that opening salvo. He lifted his glass of ice water to his lips.

Carla tilted her head at his words and then

squinted her eyes. "Bet that job title gets you fucked, a lot."

Nic choked. He couldn't breathe and his eyes clouded. Carla rose out of her chair and came over. She started pounding him on his back, which made one hell of a scene. Waiters appeared out of thin air, and there were so many people talking all at once, Nic couldn't understand anyone.

"Stop, I'm all right." He managed to croak out the words and draw a rough breath, coughing again, but not choking this time. The energized thrall of people around him faded away.

"Jesus, Carla, warn a man, will you?" Nic took another sip of his water raising his finger at his date when she opened her mouth to speak again. No, she could wait until he cleared his throat before she said something that would most likely send him into shell shock. Hell, he expected that type of response from Jade, but Carla? No. It was wrong, on all accounts. He put the glass down and regarded her.

"Sorry?" She pulled her bottom lip between her teeth and bit down trying to hide the smile that spread across her face. She failed miserably and started laughing at him. "You turned as red as Papa's marinara sauce."

"Yeah, hearing that from you was shocking, to say the least. What happened to the sweet girl I used to know?" Nic watched a million emotions flash across her face.

Finally, she pursed her lips and shook her head. "A lot actually. I got married to a wonderful man I met when I was in college. You would have loved him, Nico. Eric was my knight in shining armor. Not long after we were married, we had a baby. Little Anthony was perfect and looked just like his daddy." Carla swiped at a tear that threatened to fall. "Anyway, Eric lost his job when the economy nose-dived and the bottom fell out of the construction business. So, he stayed home with our son while I worked. Eric and Anthony had planned a surprise for me on my birthday. They were going to pick me up and take me to dinner. I was working second shift at the television station at the time, doing odd jobs and learning the ropes, but I'd gotten several on camera reporting spots with the evening news." Carla swallowed hard and blinked back the emotions she was fighting. "The cab they were in was T-boned by an uninsured, drunk driver. Eric and Anthony died. The doctors said it was instant. The cabbie lingered in a coma for five months before he passed away. The bastard that hit them was out on probation for his second offense DUI." She paused and took a healthy slug of her bourbon that the waiter had silently delivered while she was speaking, before she cleared her throat and continued, "I've changed. I used everything I had to make sure that bastard went to jail and stays there. I go every year to testify at his parole hearing. What he did... I've dedicated my life since then to making sure criminals don't get away with their crimes."

"How are you doing that?" Nic knew the woman was struggling to hang on to her emotions, so he diverted the conversation from her loss.

"Investigative reporting. I started small, worked on slumlord issues, instituted a Rub Out Crime campaign in the old neighborhoods. I've moved up to bigger things since then, and I've recently signed on with Channel One to do a series on national and international crimes. Oh my God, Nico, notorious crimes that would astound the average person are being swept under the carpet by governments and big business and the public rarely knows they happened."

Nic leaned back in his seat. The enthusiasm for her topic animated her features as she spoke. He nodded his head and smiled in the appropriate places but didn't interject much into the conversation. He knew very well the crimes that the nation's security industry kept from humanity. Working at Guardian had further opened his already wide-open eyes. He wondered if Carla had an inkling of what he and his company actually accomplished using the methodology she described.

"Congratulations on the job. I think you'll be amazing. Now I have to go search the internet for your news clips."

"As if. I'm nothing special, but the stories? The public needs to know what is happening. The blindfold that the world's governments and big businesses have put over the general public's eyes is reprehensible." She lifted her drink and took a sip. "So tell me, do you have a special woman in your life?"

He dropped his eyes as the image of Jade materialized in his brain. He shook his head to dislodge the unwanted remembrance of her soft skin and full lips. He glanced up at Carla and shook his head again before he took a drink of his Pappy. "Tough questions straight off the bat?" She'd always been direct. Now she was a steamroller.

"Investigative reporter, remember?" Carla

smirked at him and leaned back in the chair before she narrowed her eyes at him and smiled. "Oh, you can't fool me. I love you like a brother, Nico. We've always been friends. Kissing and feeling me up in high school does not negate that. There is some-one, isn't there? Someone special?" She leaned forward again, reached over, and grasped his free hand with hers.

Nic shrugged. "I guess I've had this growing idea that a relationship isn't the horror I'd always thought it would be, but I'm zero for two in that department. Well, actually, I struck out with the first one. She found a man about the time I decided I was interested in her. If I'm honest, I wanted that relationship for all the wrong reasons, and I'm pretty sure now we never would have clicked. Plus, I showed my... well, there is no other way to say it, I showed my ass on more than one instance. I'm claiming temporary insanity for those actions by the way. The other one? I have no idea what happened. It was supposed to be one night of no strings attached sex. I somehow managed to screw that up. We've agreed to try again, and keep it casual. The only thing is, the more I think about it, the more I know I no longer want casual. However, I don't have a snowball's chance in hell with that woman. She's the type that will never settle down."

"Bullshit." Carla leaned back and smiled at the surprise that had to be plastered all over his face.

"Excuse me?"

"This woman, the one that will never settle down? That's bullshit. Let me tell you a secret about women. One that will get me kicked out of the estrogen club if you tell a living soul that I told you. Every one of us is looking for that special soul that relieves the loneliness inside. The one who makes us complete. Man or woman, it is what everyone is programmed to find."

"Not her."

He finished his drink and thanked the fates for the waiter's excellent timing. The arrival of the appetizer course saved him from going down that road. Jade sure as hell wasn't willing, at least not with him, and he damn sure wasn't going to push his attentions on a woman who'd walked out on him. He had a second chance to spend time with her without strings and without feelings. He'd take it and pretend to be the man he used to be.

"So, Ma said something about Dante Capatoli going to jail?" Nic took a relieved breath when

Carla responded to his change of subject. He listened as Carla regaled him with what she knew.

Jade took Justin's hand as he helped her out of the limousine. Her brother's schedule had been insane and tonight was the only night he could spare to go out with her. Granted, he was taking her to a restaurant that he purchased majority shares in as a silent partner, but they were going to enjoy a meal and spend some quality time catching up. Finally. The man never stopped working, and his dedication to his businesses was kind of obsessive. Even Jason took time off for his family, and that man was a freaking workaholic. Justin's work ethic and lack of any type of life landed him on a whole different level of obsessed.

Jade wasn't much into the elegant dining scene. Hell, she'd be as happy going to a neighborhood diner for a greasy burger and an ice cold beer, but her brother's world revolved around the elite food service industry. The restaurant they were hitting up tonight was pretty freaking amazing. It was at the top of an old manufacturing plant situated in Midtown, outside the Garment District. The bottom three levels were shops and offices, and the remaining stories were in the process of renovation. The apartments would cost a pretty penny to buy, but with the way the neighborhood was revitalizing it would be an amazing place to live.

Jade accompanied Justin to a table with a magnificent view. The sun had set and the orange and gold hues of the evening were starting to fade into the light greys and blues of night. Lights in the surrounding buildings were slowly turning on, and the cityscape took on a sedate, lazy feel even though the thrum of the city pulsed below them.

"Do you own this building too?" She waited until the hovering staff had scurried off to get whatever Justin had ordered... in Italian... or was it French? She spoke some Spanish, but Justin had always had a way with languages. "What did you order us and was that Italian?"

Justin pulled his eyes from examining the comings and goings of the front of the house. "It was, and I know what you like, so relax, I didn't order you snails or caviar."

"That is so disgusting. Dude, like how do people eat those things? Snails look like snot someone hacked up and spit onto the sidewalk."

A snort from a nearby table caught her attention. The diners were an elderly man and woman. The woman cast her a look and turned her head away with a sneer of disgust. Jade opened her mouth to let the woman know exactly what she could do with the look and the attitude, but Justin placed a hand on her arm and squeezed gently. "For the love of all things important to me, Jade, please lower your voice and please, don't insult the matriarch of one of the wealthiest families in America."

Jade glared at the old farts again and clenched her jaw closed. It went against everything she was to shut up and say nothing. The last year undercover, she'd denied her instincts and forced herself to sit down, shut up, and color, but for Justin, she'd try to behave like an acceptable adult. She leaned over and hissed, "I wasn't talking too loud. I know how to conduct myself. That old bat was eavesdropping."

Justin rolled his eyes and leaned back as the wait staff arrived with an array of appetizers and wine. Jade popped a mushroom cap into her mouth, using her fingers to pick up the food. She focused on the old woman and smiled—openmouthed. The old bat shivered in disgust.

"Jade, please." Justin dropped his head into his hands and massaged his temples.

She chewed the food in her mouth and swallowed before she spoke because while she was making a point with the gray-haired Emily Post at the next table, her momma did not raise a heathen. Jade had obtained that status all on her own. "Oh, all right. Damn, you are wrapped way too tight, dude." Jade took a huge gulp of wine and swept the room. She grimaced at the taste of the wine. It was bitter and acidic. She'd much rather have a shot of tequila, but then again, this was Justin's world, and she was visiting.

"Hey, isn't that..." Jade lifted half-way out of her seat to see over some of the patrons. "... yep, that's Nic DeMarco." There was a sudden flurry of activity surrounding the table where Nic sat. Jade rubber-necked in that direction. The hubbub of motion faded away as rapidly as it had started. She grabbed the napkin off her lap where the waiter had laid it when they'd arrived. *Well, well, well. So that little piece of pretty is the reason I'm not having a DeMarco generated orgasm tonight, huh?* Maybe she'd been in error. Maybe Nic didn't have a gooey center, and the words he'd spoken when he was fucking her were just a line, like he'd said.

"Whatever is going on in that brain of yours, stop it." Justin's voice pulled her attention away from the cute little brunette sitting with Nic.

"What?" Jade hadn't done anything... yet.

"I don't know what you were thinking just then, but the look on your face reminded me of the times you'd take on both Joseph and Jason. You know, after they'd say something that pissed you off. You were planning something."

"Not fair. They baited me, and you know it." Jade returned her attention to the table in time to see the woman place her hand on Nic's arm. "I work with him. I thought I'd go over and say hi. It's the nice thing to do." She batted her lashes at her brother.

Justin squinted at her and shook his head slowly. "I know you, dear sister, and whatever it is that is brewing in your brain, I'm telling you now, you need to forget it. He's Jared's best friend, and if you mess around and ruin his night with his date, Jared will come unglued."

Jade made a loud raspberry sound and took a gander at the old bat. She winked at the old nag and laughed at the disgusted look she received in return. Jade turned her attention back to Justin. "Seriously, the man is a coworker. I'm going to go over and say hello. You can come with me if you don't think I'll mind my manners."

"There is no way I'd let you loose on the good people in this establishment without an escort."

"Don't you mean a leash?"

"If the chain fits..."

"Whatever. Come on." Justin lifted and offered her his hand. She rose and tugged her very short skirt down. She'd found the outfit in a quaint little Tribeca shop yesterday. It was a silk number that wrapped around her, hugging every curve. She fell in love with the array of reds that striped the dress. It was *hawt* and screamed Jade's name the second she saw it hanging on the wall.

They maneuvered through the tables and came up behind Nic. He was holding the woman's hand and leaning in, listening attentively. Of course, he was. He was a player. Jade knew that, but the sudden idea that she was next in line after this woman left a bitter taste in her mouth that had nothing to do with the horrible wine Justin had ordered.

The woman's eyes flashed up and held on them which drew Nic's attention. "Oh, hey! Justin and Jade!" Nic stood and extended a hand toward Justin. The men shook hands, and Nic's gaze tracked over her. He nodded giving her only a perfunctory acknowledgement before he turned back to his date. Well, fuck that was... weird?

"Carla, this is Justin King and his sister Jade. Justin owns several restaurants across the country and Jade works with me at Guardian."

"It is a pleasure to meet you, Mr. King. I must admit I do know who you are. I've been on a wait-list forever to get into Nido dell'Aquila.

"Please allow me to take care of that for you, Ms. Conti. I'm sorry that you've had to wait." Justin held onto her hand as he spoke.

Over Justin's outstretched arm, Jade blinked at Nic, who appeared as confused as Jade felt. "Justin... you know her?" Jade blurted, but hey, it was a legit question.

"Of course. Ms. Conti did a series of investigative interviews detailing the corruption within the transit authority in New York. I believe three people were arrested and a handful more lost their positions from the fallout. I must admit I'm a fan of your work. I appreciate the take no prisoners' mentality." Justin smiled at the smaller woman who lit up. Jade opened her mouth to speak as Nic reached into his pocket and pulled out his cell. He rolled his eyes and motioned toward the table.

"Would you join us, please? And excuse me, this won't take long."

Two additional chairs materialized out of thin air as waiters swooped in and added crystal and silver to the table top. Jade felt like she was watching a NASCAR pit stop. Hell, those guys had nothing on the wait staff of this restaurant.

"What?" Nic's exclamation of alarm turned every head in a ten foot radius. Jade noticed Nic's tense stance as he clasped the phone to his ear and plugged his other ear with his finger. He glanced up at her, his worried expression plastered all over his face.

"No. Don't touch anything. Are you alone?" Nic waited for a second and then continued, "Lock that fucking door. Go into your office. Lock that door too, and stay away from the windows. Call 911, Ma, and tell the cops. Yes, damn it, you need to do it. You can't screw around with this. I'll be there as soon as I can get there." Nic pushed his phone into his pocket.

"What's going on?"

"What happened?" Jade and Carla spoke at the same time.

Nic lifted a hand toward Jade, halting her words, and focused his attention on Carla.

Aaannnddd that little move is one you will pay for the next time we spar, either in the ring or in bed.

"Someone left a threat on Mom's doorstep. Probably one of the cases she's hearing. Carla, I'm sorry, but I need to go."

"If you will allow me, I'll ensure Ms. Conti gets home safely. Take my limo and send Paulo back after he drops you off. We'll finish dinner and wait for him here." Justin offered his help, and as far as Jade was concerned, his solution fucking rocked.

Jade stood and mentally jumped into the situation with both feet. "Let's go."

"No, thanks. I can handle this." Nic pushed in his chair and turned on his heel.

Unfazed, Jade fell into step beside him. "Fuck you very much, DeMarco. This is my specialty. I'm a PSO. You're a paper-pusher." They stopped at the elevator door, both of them looking at the display as it ticked off the floors. Thankfully, it was a dedicated system used only by the restaurant.

Jade stepped into the elevator as soon as it emptied and turned back toward Nic, giving him an expectant look. His eyes narrowed, and he strode into the confines of the lift. "I have more than enough experience to deal with this. There is no reason for you to get involved in my family's business."

"Damn. The cold coming off that shoulder would stop global warming." Jade didn't hide the sarcasm as she turned and faced him. "Seriously, is this because you're out with another woman? I mean, dude, we agreed on no strings. You do you, right? No skin off my nose." Jade turned to the front of the car and lifted her eyes to the rapidly descending numbers. The fact he was out tonight with another woman still shocked her, but hey... no strings.

"Of that, I have no doubt." The cornucopia of sound that blasted them from the street muffled Nic's words as the elevator doors opened.

Jade glared at him before she headed down the sidewalk toward the limo that pulled up to the curb. Justin's driver rounded the hood and opened the door for them. "Where to ma'am?" Jade motioned toward Nic who barked an address out to the driver as he got in beside her. She lowered the dividing screen and waited for the driver to merge into traffic before she spoke to him. "Please hurry, Paulo; it is essential we get there as quickly as possible."

"Yes, ma'am. I'll get you there right away."

. . .

Jade pushed the button to raise the privacy shield. The second the divider was up, she turned toward her quasi lover-slash-almost friend. "What the ever-loving-fuck, dude?"

Nic stared out the window and shook his head. He held up a hand and closed his eyes. Obviously, not in the mood to talk. Well, whatever. Two could play at that game. She was the queen of ignoring assholes. So what if this one happened to be sexy and, okay... obviously very worried about his mom?

They traveled for thirty minutes in thick silence before he spoke. "You don't need to be involved in my family's issues. You and I are a no strings attached deal. You meet my mother or help in this case, and presto, strings."

"Yeah? How so?" Jade couldn't wait to hear this one. She was going to be doing her job. Well, kinda, because she hadn't really been assigned to the case.

Nic turned to her. His eyes conveyed a fuck-ton of emotion. She looked away almost immediately, because whoa, she was so not expecting that.

He sighed and turned his attention back out the

window, speaking toward the lines of homes that stretched along the street. "Look, let's strip this to the bare bones, shall we? I don't want you around my family. You and I together are a problem. I don't want my mom to meet you, like you, or get wild notions about you and me being together. You play the field as much as I used to. If the tables were turned, you wouldn't introduce me to your family, and you know it. You wanted me without the soft center, so this is no soft center. I don't want you here."

"No, this is you being a dick and a stupid one on top of it. I tell you, Nic, it is a damn good thing you're pretty because when it comes to other things, you're seriously lacking. I am the best damn Personal Security Officer Guardian has on the books. I'm paid a fuck-ton of money to protect people like your mother, and I haven't lost a single primary to date. Not so much as a papercut on any of them. So let's cut the bullshit and tell me what the fuck is going on!"

Nic turned his entire body to face her. "Did you call me pretty?"

"Yeah, and stupid." She couldn't help pointing out that little fact.

"Why do I feel like my world has taken a trip

through a wormhole and I'm somehow in an alternate reality? One where the women in my life treat me like I used to treat them?" Nic pushed the hair off his forehead and leaned back into the corner of the seat. He drew a deep breath and shook his head. "Just take the car back to Justin. If I need help, I'll call. This isn't a Guardian issue. It is a DeMarco thing."

"Which makes it a Guardian issue. I don't understand why you are so set against me helping."

"NYPD will be there. My mom has had threats before. I don't know if this is more serious or if it is someone being stupid. Again, if I need help, I'll call in reinforcements." Nic looked at her and held her stare. She didn't believe a word he said, but he was correct. Guardian wasn't involved and inserting herself into his world could cause attachments she didn't want or need. She hated strings. Strings tied people up, made it impossible to leave, and inevitably ended up hurting or killing the people that originally embraced them.

"I think they made a movie about that once upon a time," Jade spoke as they turned into a plush neighborhood.

"What?" Nic pulled his attention from the floor where he was staring up to her.

"That alternate reality where the guy becomes the girl and gets to experience the bullshit most women deal with." Jade shrugged as if her knowing that wasn't a big deal.

"That sounds precariously close to a chick-flick. I thought we agreed the night we went out that we didn't like chick-flicks."

The smile she'd extracted from him was worth admitting she'd watched the horrible movie.

"Yeah, well, girls night at the King household is kinda mandatory if you are within a hundred mile radius. I'd rather get falling down drunk than watch some of the movies they've subjected me to, but I'm told that getting totally shitfaced around your mom is not a good idea."

"Yeah, who told you that?" Nic's expression seemed to be starting to relax.

"Well, my mom for one, and every one of my brothers. Assholes, all of them."

"Your brothers are not assholes."

"Did you grow up with them?"

"Well, no."

"Then you don't get a say on whether or not I think they are assholes. I love them, don't get me wrong, but they have this inner drive to be everything to everyone and steamroll over you when they think they know what's best for you."

"That doesn't make them assholes; it means they love you."

"Yeah, I get that they love me. I mean, why else would they put up with me, right? But it also means they think they need to run my life, which is so not happening. I'm a black belt in three disciplines of martial arts, I can shoot the center out of a quarter at one hundred yards, and I have taken each of them to the mat at least once. I don't need them to play 'daddy' for me. I had one of those."

Her gut sank at the thought of her father. It always did. Her life changed drastically after that night, as had the rest of her family, but the thing Jade carried with her, the anger at her father for lying... for dying... for leaving her, it was a real thing. She used the lesson she learned from her dad's death to forge her life—the one built without strings.

"Hey, you okay?"

Jade turned to look at Nic. She lifted an eyebrow and smiled. "I'm fucking excellent or have you forgotten already?"

Nic's gaze locked with hers. She silently begged him not to fuck up and get all gooey on her again.

She'd have to walk away, and as of this moment, she didn't really want to. What she did want was another go at Nicolas Fucking DeMarco. Heat filled her stare, and she licked her lips. Nic's eyes tracked the movement of her tongue. He blinked rapidly and cleared his throat.

"No, I didn't forget, and would you do me a favor and tamp down the seduction. I don't need to go to my mom's front door with a hard-on." He adjusted himself and laughter bubbled out of her.

"Big boy if you think my licking my lips is seductive, wait until our night together. I will blow your fucking mind and maybe other areas, too."

Nic studied his watch and then peered out the window. "We're almost to my mother's house. Let me deal with whatever is going on here. Meet me later tonight."

"Name the place and time." Jade lifted her arm to the back of the limo seat folding it to bring her fingertips to her lips. She flicked her tongue out to lick the tip of her index finger. Nic's eyes zeroed in on the action and Jade smiled when he had to adjust himself again.

"I'll text you when I'm done." Nic leaned over and took her mouth. He forced his tongue through her lips and dominated the kiss while fisting her hair at the back of her neck.

Fuck, she loved the way he twisted her hair to make her meet his kiss. There was something primitive and freeing when he held her immobile and added the slightest hint of pain. She sank into the embrace and allowed him to take what he wanted. She grasped the lapels of his jacket and pulled him closer. The warm smell of his natural musk accented by expensive cologne swirled around her, resurrecting decadent memories of their one night together.

He drew back and glanced out the window. It was then that Jade realized they'd stopped. There were three patrol cars and two unmarked vehicles lining the street in front of them. Yellow crime scene tape fluttered on the wrought iron railings of one of the porches. It wasn't difficult to see where Nic's mother lived.

"I'll text you later." Nic bent quickly and pressed his lips softly on hers before he turned and got out of the car. She reached up and touched the area where his stubble had sensitized her skin. The man could rev her engines. She had to give it to him. He was sexy and knew his way around a woman. Jade watched him identify himself to the officer keeping people out of the area and then bound up the stairs before he disappeared inside the house. She reached over and pressed the button that lowered the privacy shield.

"Paulo, would you please drop me off at Justin's apartment before going back to the restaurant to pick him up?"

"Yes, ma'am! Your wish is my desire."

Jade cocked her head and took in the sexy chauffeur. Maybe if she didn't have sex on a stick texting her tonight... Jade chuckled and hit the button for the privacy shield sending it up once again. Why play with amateurs when she had an expert?

CHAPTER 13

"Ma?" Nic bellowed as he pushed open the front door. He'd carefully stepped along the marked-off path allowing him into the house. The beheaded animal and the note that read, 'recuse yourself or die, bitch' was impossible to miss. No wonder his mother was upset. What a bloody mess. Literally.

"In here, Nico." His mom called to him from her study.

"What in the ever-loving fuck? You told me there was a threat. You didn't tell me about that!" Nic swung his arm behind him and pointed at the porch.

"Watch your language, young man." His mother

glared at him from where she sat opposite a suit, an NYPD detective no doubt.

"Sorry, Ma. How many active cases are you working on?"

"Why do you need to know that?" The question came from the detective, a middle-aged woman with grey streaks running through her dark brown hair. She stood and crossed her arms in front of her.

"Because I need to know." Nic drew a deep breath and faced off with the detective. "I'm sorry. I haven't introduced myself. Nic DeMarco, I'm Judge DeMarco's son and also the Chief Operations Officer for Guardian Security." He held out his hand.

The detective drew a short breath and exhaled in a huff before she took Nic's proffered hand. "Detective Sergeant Keller, NYPD. Until my superiors tell me otherwise, I'm assuming Guardian isn't taking over this case."

"You'll be hearing from your superiors by morning. Guardian most definitely will be assuming control."

Nic's mom held up a hand, stopping him from continuing. "Nico, I did not ask you up here to babysit me. I'm sure between the NYPD and the U.S. Marshals Service I'll be fine."

"Awesome, Ma. I'm glad you have faith in them, but I will be taking over and orchestrating your safety protocols while you aren't at the courthouse until I know who threatened you."

"We have a good idea who threatened her." Detective Keller pulled out her notebook and flipped back several pages. "We seized something the forensic techs believe is called a Piandao, a style of Chinese broadsword. Stroke of luck there, the tech only knew it because of a martial arts class he's taking, but Judge DeMarco indicated she was hearing a case involving a high ranking member of the Triad."

His mother lifted her gaze to him. *Shit.* The look of determination in her eyes forestalled any argument. No, she wouldn't recuse herself. Bettina DeMarco didn't run from threats, and that was one of the many reasons his mom was a fucking rock star.

"Ma, I need to make some phone calls. Detective Keller, as a professional courtesy, I'd appreciate a rundown on your impressions of the situation. I know not to ask for official documentation or access until we have jurisdiction. I won't put your career in jeopardy."

The detective's head snapped around, and she gave him a surprised look before she nodded. "It's rather refreshing having one of the big guns acknowledge what we do."

"I've been in your shoes. DCPD. Believe me; I understand the feeling when one of the suits shows up. I've had them look at me as if I were dog crap that someone stepped in. I'll never do that to the people who dedicate their lives to keeping this city safe."

"Huh." Detective Keller shook her head and flipped her notebook closed. "I don't know whether you're feeding me a line of BS or you're for real. I'm going to go against my better judgement and hope you're real. I need to follow up with forensics." She pulled out her card and handed it to Nic. "Call me in about two hours. I should have a solid grasp on the particulars of the case by that time, and any leads that Vice may have on the locals that may have participated. We have a Gangland Task Force that could provide some intel." The woman turned away from him and extended her hand toward his mother. "Ma'am, I'm sorry this happened to you. I appreciate your service."

"I appreciate your professionalism, Detective." His mother shook the woman's hand and escorted her to the front of the residence.

Nic sat down in one of the wingback chairs and pulled out his cell. He pressed and held #1. Jared's number popped up as his phone dialed his best friend.

"Vacations are supposed to be time away from the office. Did you miss me?" Jared sing-songed the question.

At any other time, he'd have said something inappropriate and sarcastic with a twist of demented on the side, but not now. Not tonight. "J, I need your help."

There was a moment's silence at the other end of the phone before Jared responded. "I've secured the line. What do you need?"

"My mom was threatened tonight. Someone decapitated a dog and left it on her porch along with a threat demanding she recuse herself. They found a Piandao at the scene. My mom is hearing a RICO case, and you get two guesses who it's against."

"The Triad." Jared didn't even hesitate.

"You got it in one," Nic confirmed his assumption.

"Oh… just fuck me now…"

"Can't do it, my man; your husband would get upset." The quip fell from his lips without him realizing it. The banter they shared was so easy and natural he couldn't have stopped it if he tried.

"Screw you, man."

"J, I love yah, but like I said…"

"Shut the fuck up. I'm looking at the caseload. It has quadrupled, and we are stacking up more referrals from other agencies. I'm trying to find someone who can run your mom's security detail and also find where I can shake out a good detective to work the case."

"Don't worry about that. I'm going to take a leave of absence. I'll handle it. I need this to be official. I need cooperation from the U.S. Marshals Service, specifically the Judicial Security Division."

Jared exhaled in one, long, drawn-out breath, before the man cleared his throat. "Dude, can we make a compromise? You do your normal job and take the lead on the investigation from up there. I'll find someone to work the PSO duties? I got to admit it brother, I'm drowning here."

Nic glanced toward his mother who was

talking with a uniformed officer. "Yeah, that will work. I'll take over my mom's office. Send me the equipment I need?" Someone needed to install secure phones and computers plus shielded connections.

"I'll get Jewell and Zane on the tech first thing in the morning. Hey, wait. I do have a PSO I could probably reach out and tap. She's in New York as we speak. Jade's supposed to be off, but if I know her, she'd be happy to step up and take the case until we can get someone else in."

Nic swallowed hard. Something in his gut told him he'd regret involving Jade, but it made sense to have her take over his mom's downtime security. She was damn good at her job and his mother's security outweighed his mixed up, emotional quandary about his supposed unemotional hook-up with Jared's sister. God, he needed a drink—or twenty.

"I'll call her. I saw her with Justin tonight at dinner." Nic purposely did not mention the fact that Jade had already offered her services. He closed his eyes at the double entendre.

"All right. Let me put the NYPD on notice. I'll also reach out to the Office of Protective Intelligence and Office of Protective Services within the

Marshals organization. We aren't going to be able to touch the security at the courthouses, but I'll put you in contact with the section chiefs so you can assure your mom's safety. When does this thing go to trial?"

Nic leaned back and shouted over his shoulder, "Ma! When do you start hearing motions on the RICO case?"

"Next week, Tuesday."

"Tuesday."

"Yeah, thanks for the busted eardrum, asshole."

"Sorry." Nic's mind raced with the minutiae that needed to be done to set up operations here and make sure Jade had everything she needed to protect his mother when she wasn't at the courthouse.

"No, you're not. Take a breath, Nic. Jade is one of the best we have. You'll both be there when your mom is outside the courthouse. The Marshals are damn good at protecting the judiciary. The Triad will strike at more vulnerable targets to try to fuck with the trial."

"Yeah, but only if they see a show of force and know we are on the scene. I'm going to give them that visual in a big way."

"Far be it from you to do anything with subtlety."

"That shit is overrated."

"So I've heard."

"Thanks, J."

"You got it. Go take care of your mom. I'll call Jason and get the ball rolling. Hopefully, you'll be set up with equipment and coms by Monday so I can dump some of this crap on my desk on you."

"I'll take whatever you give me, but J, I need to work this case, too. It's my family." Nic foresaw some serious late nights in his future, but he'd do what he needed to do to take care of his family.

"I'll keep as much here as I can. I get it, Nic. Family is everything."

Nic nodded, not caring if Jared couldn't see him.

"Stop tearing yourself up, DeMarco. There wasn't anything you could have done to prevent these assholes from threatening your mom. You're not a mind reader, and you can't see into the future."

"I'd give every last penny I have to be able to do that."

"Hell, wouldn't we all?" Jared's humorless laugh reached him, and he gave a small chuckle. "Call

Jade. She'll set up your mom's security... and Nic, she has one hell of a reputation, and she hides behind it, but Jade cares. She just doesn't let anyone see it."

"I've got no problem with her being in charge of mom's security."

"Huh... who said I was talking about your mom? Night."

Nic held the phone away from his ear and saw his features reflected in the black face of the disconnected phone. What the fuck did Jared know, and how the hell did he know it?

Nic noted the time on his watch and grimaced. He'd just hung up with the Chief of the Office of Protective Services. The Marshal had impressed him, and it took one hell of a lot for Nic to be impressed. Nic had established a relationship with the organization years earlier and was able to leverage a few favors to reach the top of the food chain at 2:00 a.m. His mother had gone to bed, but only after Nic had cleared her room, even though a patrolman had declared the house secure before leaving. Nic wasn't taking the smallest chance, and the fact his mother let him take over proved how shaken she was by the events of the evening.

He took out the card Detective Keller had given him and dialed her number.

"Keller."

"Detective, since you answered on the first ring, I'm assuming I didn't wake you."

"Ha, not getting any sleep for the foreseeable future. I got the official notification that you'll be taking the case. Got some new information in. I'm still processing it, but let me run down what I know and what evidence we have to substantiate it."

"Shoot." Nic grabbed a pen and pushed away several sheets of paper he'd taken notes on while talking to the Marshals office.

"Okay. The dog was already dead before it became a warning. My gut is telling me that animal was probably the victim of an illegal dog fighting operation. We are basing that assumption on the injuries sustained and state in which the animal died. The vet did a preliminary and said the injuries were similar to what he's seen from bait dogs. These bastards use the smaller animals to train the bigger ones to fight. It happens far too often. Believe me; we all want to catch the sons of bitches that are abusing those animals."

Nic closed his eyes and shook his head. After everyone had left tonight, both he and his mother had talked at length about the type of mentality it took to injure a helpless animal. Sick bastards. Give him five minutes alone with the son of a bitch who did that and he would teach the fucker a lesson he wouldn't soon forget.

"The weapon used to behead the dog had no usable prints. There were a few partials that smudged through the blood, but not enough to even try to match. The note was a computer generated font, Courier New, eighteen point, laser printer that has a dirty roller. It prints a ghost line every two and a half inches on the paper, the circumference of the printer wheel. We don't have a make on the printer yet."

"I'll take that information to my IT gods. They can work miracles. What else do you have?" Nic jotted a note down to send an email to Jewell before he stopped for the night.

"The paper was a generic bond, no discernable traits, and no prints, but I'm sure your forensics can go further than we can."

"Probably not, but we'll take a look at everything just in case." Nic never wanted to seem superior to the cops that were doing their damnedest to keep the streets safe. Been there, done that and got the condescension t-shirt.

"The GTF hasn't heard squat from the local faction of the Triad."

"Is that normal?" Nic made a note to himself.

"Nope, two days ago they were threatening a turf war with another gang over a drug trafficking corridor. All of a sudden every one of them has gone underground and radio silent. It is making the entire task force itchy as hell."

"That coincides with the RICO case being remanded back down to the District Court."

"Mmmm... yeah, fishier and fishier. Anyway, I'm assuming you'll run the traffic cameras in the area to see if you can find anything suspicious. I'm like number ten thousand on the waitlist as far as priority goes. Sorry, but the felony cases get top priority."

"As it should be, Detective. I'll make sure we leave no stone unturned."

"Roger that. Anyway, I'm writing up the reports, and they will be ready for youse guys in the morning." The detective's native New Jersey accent slipped out right before Nic heard a long yawn. "Damn, sorry. I'm getting too old to pull these all-nighters. Retirement is looking good right about now."

"I hear you. Thank you so much, Detective. It has been a pleasure." Nic disconnected the call and grabbed the charging cord off his mother's desk. He plugged in his phone and regarded the information in front of him. Grabbing the top sheet of paper, he started organizing his notes, typing them into his tablet. His phone rang, and he hit the button for the speaker on the secure landline and answered it without looking at the caller. "DeMarco."

"So are you generally against orgasms or is it orgasms with me that make you run for the hills?" Jade's sultry voice poured into his mind like a fresh breeze, sweeping out the staleness of the long night's events.

He swiveled in his chair and checked the hallway to confirm he was alone, but honestly he didn't expect anyone other than him to be up at 2:30 a.m. "Sorry. It appears the situation is a bit more tenuous than I had anticipated when you dropped me off." Nic leaned back in the leather office chair and closed his eyes. The Sahara had emptied one or two of its dunes under his eyelids again. Fucking desert.

"I heard."

Nic's eyes flew open. "From who?"

"Jared. He called about an hour ago. He assumed you would have contacted me by the time he called. Don't worry. I played it off as if you had. He's worked the logistics for my assignment, getting reciprocal authority for my concealed carry license, registering our case with the FBI, the U.S. Marshals Service and the NYPD, so we don't cross streams during your investigation. I've been doing research on the RICO case involving the Triad because most of it happened within the last year, so I was out of the loop."

"Good. I'll need you to get a tactical vehicle from the Guardian detachment here in New York. Cash in whatever favors you need to get one. I don't want my mom going to or from that courthouse in a vehicle that isn't hardened."

"Already working on it. I'll be there about eight. What's your mom's calendar like today? I was going to ask Jewell to hack it, but decided I should probably respect your mom's judginess and ask you."

"Judginess?" Nic chuckled at the absurdity of the word.

"Her honorness?"

"No."

"Her District Courtness?"

"Stop."

"Hey, does she wear like jeans and shit under her cloak?"

"Robes, not cloak, and probably a dress suit, minus the jacket." His mother worked hard and was a professional through and through.

"Robes? Really? I'd go naked except for one of those lace collars. Like Judge Judy. I bet that woman is stark naked under her robes." Jade chuckled at his groan.

"God, I can never watch that show again."

"Why were you watching it in the first place?" Jade laughed, bringing a smile to his face. "But for your information, that lace collar would be more than I'm wearing right now."

"Fuck, seriously?" Nic considered the wide open office door—open so he could hear if anything or anyone in the house made a noise.

"Yep. I'm lonely, too. My date stood me up." Jade's voice lowered and took on a suggestive tone that went straight to his cock.

"He did? I'm sure he had a good reason." Nic leaned back and adjusted his stiffening shaft.

"I'm sure he did, but I have it from a reliable source he should be done with work by now."

"The trip across town would take an hour." He read the time on his watch and shook his head. "He probably wouldn't have time to meet your needs before he had to leave again. Besides, I wouldn't leave her alone."

Jade made a purring noise. "I know you wouldn't, and I'd never ask you to do so. But it is a shame. You see, I've put a ban on self-gratification. Otherwise, I'd ask him to talk dirty to me. I'd be touching myself thinking of his hands on me." Jade made a delicious sound of pure desire.

"Maybe he can get me to lift that self-imposed ban. Tell me what he would do to me if he had me under him."

Nic pushed his palm against his dick, which had gone from interested to titanium rod in the length of time it took Jade to utter the last two sentences. He leaned over and put his elbows on his knees. The pressure on his cock felt horrible and fantastic all at the same time. It was everything he could do not to reach down and grasp himself. Fuck, that woman and her mouth. If it wasn't destroying him one way, it was killing him another. He vividly imagined the way her mouth could feel around his cock. Well, two could play at this game.

"I guess you'll have to wait to find out for sure, but I absolutely want you on my cock again. I want to watch you lose your mind and beg me to fuck you harder. Then I'd hold you in place while I worshiped your body, touching you and teasing you until you explode. As you try to catch your breath, I'd trail soft caresses over that super sensitive spot just inside your hip. I know I'd really like to..."

At the sound of a soft huff from behind him, Nic turned abruptly... and smashed his entire hand down on the button to end the call. Judge Bettina DeMarco stood with raised eyebrows and crossed arms in the office doorway. *Shit.* Suddenly, he was fourteen again explaining how five issues of *Playboy Magazine* got between the boxspring and the mattress of his bed. Embarrassment sent a rush of heat to his face. His phone rang immediately. Jade. Of course. Were he Jade, he'd be calling back for a multitude of reasons and not all of them having to do with premature withdrawal from phone sex. He held up a finger toward his mom and turned away from her to pick up the handset. "Hello?"

"Hello? What the fuck, dude? Are you okay?"

"Ah… yes. Fine, we can talk about that later."

"Later? One minute you're starring in a phone call that I'd hoped would turn X-Rated, and the next the line is dead. Wait…" Jade's laugh rang through the connection. "Who caught you? Your mom?"

"As I said we will discuss that at a later date." Nic glanced at his mother who had leaned against the doorjamb and now had a grin on her face. Great, both the women in his life were evil. Pure evil.

"Good night." He hung up the phone as the sound of Jade's laughter floated into the room. There was no doubt his mother had heard Jade's mirth before he'd disconnected.

"I didn't mean to interrupt what sounded like a fascinating call, but Carmine called me from California. He was livid. I guess Mario left a voice message and he'd just come back from a night of wining and dining one of their important clients. Anyway, I wanted to warn you that he was going to be calling."

As if by uttering the words, Nic's cell phone

vibrated. He looked at the face and held it up to show his mother.

"Don't let him upset you, dear. He means well."

"Right." Nic hit the side button to silence the call and threw the phone back down on the desk. There was no way he was dealing with Carmine's bullshit tonight. He needed sleep before he could face that drama.

"Sooo... the call I interrupted..."

"Ma, don't."

"Don't what? Is she special to you?"

"No Ma, she is someone looking for a good time, not a relationship."

"You didn't answer my question." Bettina DeMarco lifted from the door and moved into the room, dropping down in one of the chairs facing the desk.

"I did. She doesn't want a relationship; ipso facto she is not someone special."

"Objection, the witness failed once again to answer the question. Is she special to you?

"You are not hearing a case, Ma, and your ipso jure twist on the answer I gave does not constitute grounds for censure, nor does it compel me to answer your question." Nic and his brothers had grown up sparring in legalese with Bettina. He wasn't going to be bullied into admitting something that he didn't understand or for that matter want to address.

His phone rang again. Carmine. He glanced at his mother who shook her head.

"You might as well answer it and try to assure him that I am not at death's door." She got up and contemplated him. "Carmine's persistence saved you an interrogation. Count your lucky stars and remember that when you're talking to him. He means well."

Nic watched his mom leave and gladly accepted the call. He'd spend the next half hour calming down his obnoxious and major-league pigheaded brother if it saved him from a death of a thousand questions his mom was prepared to inflict upon him.

CHAPTER 14

Jade pulled up to the front of the home Nic entered last night. Yellow crime scene tape still fluttered from the bushes and wrought iron railings, and blood stained the stoop. She dealt with the NYPD cruiser posted across the street with a flash of her credentials. The officers seemed more than happy to release the scene to her once their dispatch confirmed Guardian was taking control of the judge's security. She knew as soon as the world woke, the innate curiosity of Judge DeMarco's neighbors would make her job a little more difficult, but that was to be expected.

Jade hadn't slept last night. First, she'd been waiting for Nic to text and then she'd been setting up the groundwork for her assignment. She'd inundated Jewell's team with requests. She added another as she stood on the front porch of Judge DeMarco's home. A profile of all the neighbors on this street. She'd also requested a document with photos detailing Judge DeMarco's coworkers, employees, and known associates. Jared had called her when she was driving over this morning. The Marshals wanted a meeting after Jade dropped Judge DeMarco at the courthouse. Her contact at the U.S. Marshals Service had indicated that security tripled in accordance with the higher security protocols. They created a clear zone, pushing parking further from the building. The defensive procedure kept suicide bombers from ramming cars laden with explosives into the building, but it also meant the cleared area made an excellent field of vision for snipers and lookouts. Thankfully, the Marshals were posting people on the rooftops. Jade pulled a Google Earth map of the courthouse and surrounding area to familiarize herself with the area. The path the judge would have to take to get into the facility may be well guarded, but that didn't stop Jade from requesting the blueprints of the building and details on the security for the judge.

She examined her clothes to make sure she was

presentable. She'd scrambled to find work clothes this morning because she hadn't brought any with her. Thank God for discount stores open twenty-four hours a day. The fit sucked, and there was absolutely no style to the cut, but they were serviceable for today at least. Dark wash jeans, a white tank top and a man's blazer that covered her weapons. Jade did a sweep of the street in front of the residence and drew a deep breath before she knocked on the door.

Nic opened it seconds later and walked out pushing her back two steps. Dark circles under his eyes and the wrinkled suit he wore gave her every indication that he hadn't slept last night, either. "We are not telling my mother anything about us. Are we clear?"

"Well good morning to you, too." Jade narrowed her eyes at the man. He obviously was in an ugly ass mood. Awesome.

"Are we clear?" Nic growled in a low voice.

"As crystal." The alpha male audacity of the man tripped a claymore in her mind, and all kinds of wicked images exploded across her imagination. Not that she'd use any of the ideas, but hey, fuck you very much, DeMarco. No, 'Good morning, thanks for helping me protect my family, sorry this event cut short your only time off in over a year.' Nope, momma's boy did not want to upset the applecart. Got it. Jade put her hands on her hips and stared the man dead in the eye.

He glared at her as if trying to read any ulterior motive in her answer or her expression. Finally, he nodded and opened the front door. Jade shifted into work mode immediately. She assessed the deadbolt and noted the balanced magnetic switches that activated the home's alarm system attached to the top of the door. The BMS switching system was effective but easily defeated. If she had a lock pick and magnet, she'd be in the house without tripping the alarm. An upgraded system run on fiber optics was a priority. She took out her phone and sent off a text. The windows toward the front of the street had BMS sensors and had ample lighting from the street. She needed the measurements of all the windows to order temporary ballistic shielding. Expensive as fuck, but necessary when the threat was from an organization like the Triad. She'd check the rest of the home while Judge DeMarco was at the courthouse. Jade followed Nic, taking in the flow of the home, the entrances to each room, and any possible exits that existed beyond the main entrance.

The smell of bacon and coffee beckoned her toward the kitchen. She paused in the doorway and examined the big bay window that overlooked a surprisingly long and lushly landscaped yard behind the home. There were rose bushes under the bay window. Crime prevention through environmental design. She'd taken several classes on using nature and manipulated design techniques to make a home or business an unlikely mark for criminals. Unfortunately, there were too many available entrances and exits to consider the beautiful old home safe. It would take a small army and cost a fortune, but by the time Judge DeMarco got home tonight, the house would be secure, and nobody would be pinning any epithets to the stoop. Motion activated cameras and pressure sensor plates on the stairs, under the windows and doors, and on the roof would ensure an immediate alert if anyone or anything decided to get close to the residence.

"Coffee?" Nic asked as they entered.

"No." Jade continued to work, taking in the back area of the residence, mentally ticking off things she needed to do and areas she needed to ensure were fortified, all while monitoring the judge and mitigating any issues the woman's schedule brought into the situation.

Jade felt the thrill of the case running through her veins. She lived for this shit. It felt amazing to focus on her primary job. The undercover gig had been a life experience, but she'd decided she'd decline any further such assignments. At least for the near future. Her mind clicked through a series of checklists as she moved toward the back door followed by Nic who greeted a mid-aged woman in the long hallway.

"Jade King, this is my mother, Bettina DeMarco. Ma, Jade has been assigned as your Personal Security Officer."

Jade finished her scan of the far corners of the yard. She turned around at the introduction, extending her hand. "Your Honor. It is a pleasure to meet you. I took the liberty of asking Nic for your schedule, and I understand you'll need to leave soon. Once I have you securely ensconced in your chambers and have talked to the U.S. Marshals assigned to you at the courthouse, your son and I will be meeting with the Marshals' directors, the FBI, and NYPD representatives, to go over a few precautionary plans."

She saw the respect grow in Judge DeMarco's

eyes as she spoke. Yeah, she got that a lot. Professionalism, knowledge, and skill overcame the instant assumption that a woman who looked like she did couldn't do this job. No, she didn't look like a bodyguard, but she was damn good at her job. It used to piss her off that she had to prove that fact repeatedly, but it didn't anymore.

"Well, all right. It is nice to meet you in person. I believe we talked last week? You answered my son's office phone?"

Jade let a smile crack through the professional veneer she'd plastered into place. "Yes, ma'am. He had an issue with one of his temps. I was able to help him out."

"I see." The judge's eyes flipped from her to Nic. He had his nose buried in his tablet and was taking a sip of his coffee. "Nicolas, did I raise you to have such poor manners? Offer this lady a cup of coffee and some breakfast."

Nic slowly raised his eyes from his tablet and motioned toward the coffee pot. "Jade is a big girl, Ma, and she isn't a guest. She's working. I offered her coffee, but if she wants something, I assure you she'll take it. She's pretty damn good at that actually."

Jade nodded her head and laughed. Nic

spouting a double entendre that his mother wouldn't understand was too funny. "Damn straight I will. I'm not bashful, ma'am, but I have had coffee and breakfast already this morning."

The judge gave her a sideways look before a sly smile spread across her face. Jade wasn't quite sure what brought the expression about, but she didn't really care. "Just let me know when you are ready to go. I'll leave first and check the vehicle to make sure nobody has messed with it. Nic will come out with you when I open the back door. That will be your signal to leave the house. Never, ever leave the building unless I open the back door of the vehicle. It has to be the back door facing the building where you are waiting for me. If I open any other door, that is a duress signal, and you are to get away from any doors or windows and lock yourself away. I don't care if it is a janitor's closet or a random office, just do it and do it without asking questions or wasting time, okay?"

"I got it. Back passenger door opens, I come out —anything else, I take cover and wait. Believe me, I'm not a hero, and I won't play with my security. Not after what has happened. I'll follow your instructions to the 't'. Let me get my jacket and briefcase, and I'll be ready to go."

Jade watched her make her way down the long hall and turn at the stairs. She spun on her heel and crossed the room before she took Nic's coffee cup from him and placed it on the counter. She placed her hands on his shoulders and leaned in for a kiss. "Good morning and thank you for the interesting phone call last night. Sometime in the next twenty-four hours, I would like to have that orgasm you keep promising me." Jade stepped back and picked up his coffee mug taking a sip. "Uggg. Should have known someone with a soft center would like it sweet." She set the cup down and turned to head down the hall.

Nic caught Jade's arm and spun her. His lips crushed against hers in a punishing kiss as his arms pinned hers against her sides. The kiss, or rather oral assault, was over before she'd been able to decide whether she enjoyed it or not.

"When it comes to the people I love, there is absolutely no give in me. Take your shots, but never doubt I would kill to protect those I love." Nic brushed past her and headed down the hall.

Jade wondered where the fuck that outburst came from and why Nic felt the need to drop it on her like a bomb. She shook her head and followed him down the hall. Damn good thing he was pretty, because he was harder than hell to understand.

The strain of the day was beginning to catch up to her. She'd had the alarm system revamped and put in a camera system that had a fiber optic, 360 degree surveillance, of the residence. The Marshals and NYPD had upped security at the courthouse due to the threat and the notoriety of the case. The FBI had been in on the briefings because everyone believed the threat was Triad based and the case was their collar. All the major networks were already requesting in-court coverage of the trial. Judge DeMarco had rejected all requests and had issued her intent to close the courtroom to the public. The woman was hell on wheels according to all accounts, and for that, Jade thanked her lucky stars. The judge had a spine and listened to directions. A combination she appreciated. It worked in their favor.

Jade had seen Nic twice after they returned to the residence. He'd locked himself in his mother's office and had been out of her way while she coordinated the work of Guardian's vetted contractors.

She had over an hour before she needed to return to the courthouse to retrieve Nic's mom. Judge DeMarco typically worked until seven every evening unless she was presiding over a case and then by all accounts, it could go much later. The breakdown of responsibilities between the agencies involved dictated Jade was responsible for the judge when she wasn't at the courthouse. The Marshals and Guardian had drawn specific lines to ensure there was no confusion as to who was on duty to ensure the judge's safety. Jade made another circuit of the house and consulted her phone, mentally ticking "completed" by each item on the extensive list of mandatory tasks she needed to finish today.

"You've managed a few miracles."

Nic's voice behind her shouldn't have startled her, but it did. She'd been lost in the minutiae of setting up security for his mother. "Yeah, Guardian has a great network in New York. I was able to pull in resources and contractors that I wouldn't have access to elsewhere."

"Are you done for the day?" Nic stepped further into the room. Exhaustion painted his face with dual black smudges under his eyes and deep furrows of his brow.

"Yeah, I still have several items that need to be addressed, but this house is now as safe, if not safer, than the courthouse." Jade peeked at the time on her phone. "I need to leave in an hour to get to the courthouse to pick up my primary."

"You mean my mother." Nic dropped onto one of the chairs in the living room.

"I mean my primary. She is my responsibility and my job." Jade sauntered over to him and straddled his lap putting her hands on his chest. "You still owe me an orgasm."

The man blinked at her as if she was speaking Greek. He looked around the room before he asked, "Now?" Nic's hands went to her waist and held her.

"I heard through the grapevine you were working here until this case is settled."

"True, what does that have to do with anything?" His hand ran up her side underneath the cheap, ill-fitting blazer she'd been wearing all day. Thank God Jewell was overnighting her clothes from Alexandria.

"Well, in case you didn't get the memo, I'm here for the duration." She leaned in and ran her nose along his neck to his jaw. God, the scent of him and his cologne, it did crazy things to her unsated lust for the man. She nipped his earlobe softly.

He ran his hand up her back and held her there. "I did get that memo." His hips lifted, pushing their bodies together.

She could feel his hard length beneath her. His other hand ran lower and cupped her ass, moving her hips down onto him. She inhaled a shuddering breath and whispered, "Your mom's security is in the hands of the U.S. Marshals Service once I get her to her office, and they'll watch over her until I pick her up. I wonder what I'll do with all that time off."

He pulled her away from his ear and found her lips. The delectable warmth and delicious taste of the man performed magic on her again. That special thing that disintegrated her brain's functions enough that she let him take charge and guide her even though that wasn't her normal response during a sexual situation. She could count on one hand the times she didn't take control of an intimate encounter. There had been three occasions; one while she was introducing herself to the BDSM scene—she enjoyed the experience but not enough to pursue the lifestyle—and the other two had been with this man. Jade melted against him letting him take what he wanted. Why did the man affect her like this? Better question, why did she care?

He pulled away, nipping at her bottom lip, allowing them to catch their breath and inhale a little sanity, too. Jade shrugged off her blazer exposing her shoulder holster, handcuffs, her utility knife, and shield. She let her hands travel under his suit jacket to where the exact same equipment lodged against his body. Contrary to her aggressive moves on Nic, she rarely hooked up with cops or fellow Guardian operatives. However, knowing that this man was her equal in every way melted her panties. Yep, she felt them ignite, boom, poof, sexual combustion at a cellular level. What was it about Nicolas Fucking DeMarco? Jade lifted away from him and slipped the knot of his tie loose as his hooded eyes watched her. She drew it out of his collar. "What would be wrong with a mutually beneficial arrangement? I come back from dropping her off in the morning, we have some mind-blowing sex, then I go to sleep for the day. You go to work, and everyone is happy. I bring her home, stand guard all night, take her to work in the morning, and we wash, rinse and repeat."

"You don't think it is a little unprofessional to be fucking my mom's security detail?" Nic tugged on the tie she held in her hands.

Jade stopped the slide of the silk through her fingers and shook her head. "I think it would be irresponsible to deny ourselves the opportunity. Your mom will be safe at work. You can schedule your appointments and virtual meetings around our time. Block it as gym time on your calendar. I promise I'll do my best to make sure you get all the cardio you can handle." She released the tie from her grip and started working the top button of his shirt.

His hand grabbed both of hers. Jade stilled her fingers and lifted her eyes to meet his. His gray gaze held hers unblinking. "That sounds awfully close to a relationship." He threaded the silk necktie around both of her wrists. Jade's heartbeat sped up when he made a half hitch securing her wrists, tying her hands.

"No, an arrangement for sex only." She watched his hands wrap the necktie around her wrists again and feed the long tail between them.

"I believe that is how most relationships start. It is an arrangement between people who are attracted to each other... for sex." He lifted off the chair throwing her off balance. Her hands bound together gave her no way to grasp onto his shoulders or anchor herself. His massive arms surrounded her and held her against him. Her legs dropped to the floor and she stood enfolded within the confines of his body. Nic nudged her chin, making her look up. He lowered his lips to hers and took possession of her. Jade sighed into the deep, probing kiss, allowing him the dominion he demanded. She felt the tie pull her hands down and to her side.

Nic lifted away from her. When he spoke, his words were low, intense and absolute. "If we do this, it will be sex on my terms. When I say and how I say. No exceptions." He tugged the tie lifting her arms slightly, putting a small amount of pressure on her right shoulder. Just enough that she knew he was serious.

Jade bent away from him and squinted at him as she processed what he'd stipulated. This wasn't what she'd envisioned. Every instinct inside her warned her to say no, to turn off whatever her lust for the man was inciting between them. He drew her back toward him and kissed her again. The arguments she'd been forming softened, and like mist, diffused. To allow someone to lead her in a dance she didn't know the steps to no longer seemed impossible—as long as that someone was Nic. *My terms.* The words echoed in her mind even as his lips continued their assault.

"When this is over, you can walk away, but until then, you agree to my terms." His fingers trailed from her jaw to her neck, down the side of her breast, brushing past her weapon and moving down her waist. His hand hovered there playing along the edge of her waistband. "Say yes."

His lips pressed against that spot again and she shivered. Saying yes wasn't what she wanted or needed. Was it? Jade focused on the movement of his lips against her neck. That talented tongue played her sensitive spots like Eddie Van Halen played the guitar. Too damn good. He sucked her earlobe into his mouth. His breath did crazy stupid things to her mind. She groaned against the assault as he left her ear and traveled down her neck again.

"Yes, damn it to hell and back, yes." She felt his lips spread in a smile against the column of her neck.

"First and most important term. Nobody but me. You are exclusive until this mission is done."

Nic's velvet timbered voice whispered against her flesh.

Jade nodded. Hell, she wouldn't have time to go out and hook up while on assignment anyway. Right? His hands traced her ribs. What did he say... exclusive? Yeah, okay. She could do that. "What else?" Jade damn near groaned the words as his hand traveled south and cupped her sex. She pushed into his hand, helping herself to the pressure she desperately needed.

"I'll tell you when I'm ready for you to know." He released his grasp on the tie that bound her hands and reached down, grabbing both her thighs, lifting her up. Jade looped her fastened hands over his neck and let him carry her to the office. It was one of the few rooms in the house without windows. He sat her down on the desk and laid her back while removing her arms from around his neck. The tie slithered from around her hands. He trailed the silk up her chest and pooled it at her neck. "We don't have time to make this last today. I'm going to take you hard and fast. Give you that orgasm you've been demanding."

Jade ran her hands up his muscled arms and grasped his shoulders as he unfastened her jeans and unceremoniously pulled them and her underwear down past her knees. He lifted and spun her face down over the desk, grabbing her hair and pulling her up in an arch to kiss him. She grabbed the edges of the desk for support, scattering the items on the desktop onto the hardwood floor. Jade heard him unzip and felt his hot cock brand her ass cheek. His hand remained tangled in her hair, pulling it enough to keep her back curved.

He leaned over her. "You can have this," He slapped her ass with his cock, "if you are on birth control, because baby, I don't have a condom."

Jade moaned. She hadn't been on birth control for over a year. Her undercover operation wasn't conducive to her getting to a pharmacy to refill her prescription, and she hadn't made it to the doctor yet. *Fuck, fuck, fuck!* "No, I'm not on anything."

"Too bad, sweetheart." Nic kissed her spine. His hands traveled down to palm her ass, kneading it with his hands.

Fuck! She whimpered in frustration and disappointment.

"Shhh… I got you." Nic lowered to his knees behind her and spread her folds giving him access to her sex. "Beautiful."

Jade arched off the desk when his tongue licked over her clit. One of his hands pushed her back down as he feasted on her body. Her legs shook in concert with his tongue and lips. Jade arched her back, begging for more. Nic's fingers finally entered her, his talented mouth stoking the fire as he filled her with three fingers. She rode his hand and pushed back to feel more of his mouth, lost to anything but the pursuit of her own pleasure. Her orgasm built like a leaded weight, blooming low and heavy with undeniable want.

"Nic, please." She grasped the edges of the desk in desperation. Her entire body shook with unfulfilled need. He moved away from her and kissed the inside of her thigh. Jade cried out in frustration.

"Shh... I'm not going to leave you hanging, sweetheart." He rose from his knees. His fingers shifted; and she gasped.

The sweet, intense pressure against her clit coupled with the motion and pressure of his fingers inside her sent her spiraling into a cyclone of sensations. Her orgasm ripped through her. Nic continued to work her body. She begged and pleaded for him to stop, for him to continue, for... something, anything... less... more. Her body struggled against his hand's demands. Her mind reached for the release he refused to let subside.

Jade bucked against him and peered back at him. Her breath caught at the sight of him stroking his cock while also pleasuring her.

His stare locked with hers and held her captive. "You need to come again, Jade. I want to feel the pulse of your release grip my fingers."

Jade pushed back against him, and his index finger slid over her clit at just the right angle. "Fuck yes! Just like that!" Jade pushed back again, and they found a rhythm of sensation that drove her over the edge. Her body clamped down around his fingers, and she screamed soundlessly against the fracturing of her mind and body. She felt his cock jerk and then the warmth of his cum on her lower back.

His staccato breath hit the back of her neck as he held himself off her and the desk. "Holy fuck." His words pulled a breathless chuckle from her.

"Not really, but close enough for government work." Jade loved the laughter her quip pulled from him. A ghost tremor from the fabulous sex shook her body. "Pretty boy, I suggest you make a trip to the drug store before tomorrow morning."

He slapped her ass, hard.

"Hey, what was that for?"

"First, quit calling me pretty and second, quit

being bossy." He reached for a box of tissues that perched precariously on the corner of the desk.

"First, it is a good thing you are pretty, Nic, because you are one high maintenance hook-up."

"Wrong. I'm no longer a hook-up." He took his time to wipe up his release from her and pulled down her shirt.

"Yeah, about that." Jade pulled her clothes back into position and fastened buttons and zippers keeping her fingers busy.

"Second thoughts?" Nic was pulling himself together.

"Actually, first coherent thoughts." Jade straightened her shoulder holster.

"Retracting your agreement?" He helped her to step over a stack of papers that scattered in a four-foot blast area around his desk.

"I'm not so sure I agreed to anything except being exclusive with you for the time being." Jade picked her handcuffs up off the floor and reattached them to her belt. She regarded the mess of paper, pens, pencils and at least five hundred paperclips that had scattered under and around the desk. Her cell phone chimed and she read the display. "I need to go get your mom." Jade smiled at him and motioned toward the mess. "I'll leave you with all this." The sleeve of her blazer peeked around the corner of the office door. They must have dragged it down the hall when Nic carried her from the family room. With a chuckle, she snagged it and began to put it on.

"Thank you, I didn't have anything else to do while you were gone." Nic smiled and ran his fingers through his hair and drew a deep breath. "We are exclusive during this case?"

Jade stopped with only one arm in her blazer and threw a glance back at him. Hadn't she already agreed to that? He leveled a blank stare at her. *Great, now we're playing poker. No worries dude, I'll learn your tells.* Jade chuckled ruefully. She didn't have time for this shit. She knew what she wanted, and she went after it. Usually. She was getting fucking whiplash being around this man, and while her body was still recovering from one aah-maz-ing, over-the-desk, non-fucking, she was beginning to regret the impulsiveness she succumbed to when she answered him earlier.

Jade shook her head as she put on the blazer and pulled her hair out of the back of the jacket. "I'm going to get your mom." Jade grabbed her keys and pocketed her cell phone before she headed for the door. She had work to do.

∽

Jade nodded at the Marshals posted outside Judge DeMarco's chambers. They would remain in position until she and the judge departed the courthouse. She knocked on the judge's door and waited.

"Come in."

At the muttered call, she slipped inside. "Ah, Jade. Is it time to leave already?" The judge removed her glasses and glanced at the grandfather clock on the far wall.

"I can wait if you're not finished, Your Honor." Jade clasped her hands and relaxed her stance.

"Well, no, everything else can wait, besides if we don't leave now, Carmine and Mario will beat us home."

Jade damn near jumped out of her skin. "Excuse me?"

"Carmine and Mario are coming over. We were supposed to go out to dinner tonight. Nicolas got us reservations at some nice place, but because of recent events that's definitely out."

"Obviously." Jade drew a deep breath and put her hands on her hips. "Ma'am, you probably should have called me and let me know your sons were coming for dinner. I need to know things like this in order to make sure your security encompasses anyone that comes to visit you."

"Oh, but they are my sons." Judge DeMarco said the words like that would magically erase any security concerns.

"Ma'am, let's look at this from the Triad's point of view. If they wanted to hurt you, who would they go after?"

The woman paled. "Sweet mother of God, have I put my boys in danger?"

"I can arrange to have them monitored, but in the future, if you are bringing anyone into your residence or interacting with them outside the courthouse, I'll need to know in advance." Jade pulled out her cell phone and started on the S.O.S. message to the Guardian office in Manhattan. She prayed they could rearrange assets to take on monitoring the two attorneys until she could pull assets from elsewhere. She knew the New York Office was ass deep in cases. They could ill afford to dedicate PSOs to a security detail that in all honesty would probably be classed as a precaution. Jade punched out an email to Jared and the agent in charge of the NY office. She courtesy copied Nic. Somehow, she didn't think he knew his brothers were coming to the residence tonight. He would have told her if he had. They both were concerned for his mother's safety, and bringing the brothers in would make matters more difficult. No, Nic would have told her. Regardless, if he didn't see the email, he'd figure it out when the alarm system went batshit crazy. She scanned the judge quickly and spoke as she continued to put out the fire the woman had set. "At dinner tonight, I'll brief them on specific personal security precautions to take. They will need to limit their exposure."

"Well, Mario won't have a problem with that, but Carmine may be a handful."

Jade glanced up from her phone. "Explain that, please."

"Well, you've known Nicolas for a while now, right?"

Jade nodded. She knew the man intimately, but she wasn't about to let his mother know.

"Nic is my middle child. He cares deeply about people receiving justice, and I'm so proud of the work he does at Guardian. There is a depth to that boy. He tries to hide that he has a heart with all the women that he 'dates.'"

She actually used air quotes on the word dates.

Jade suppressed a smile. Dating? Fucking more like it, but hey, his mom could call it whatever she wanted.

"That one is going to fall someday, and when he does it will be hard." Bettina DeMarco went to her closet and retrieved her purse and jacket. "Mario is my youngest. He's a charmer. The boy has never met a stranger, and you'd think he'd be the best in the courtroom out of the three, but no… he loves the paperwork. Contracts, that's his specialty. He's been dating the same woman for almost four years. If you ask me, they are too career oriented. She's a stockbroker, and he's building his law firm with Carmine. Those two, Mario and Bethany, they shouldn't be together. A mother knows these things. But Carmine? Well, he is my oldest. He took on the role of protector when my husband died." The woman made a cross over her chest when she mentioned her late husband. "Ask Carmine, and he'll tell you he has the answers to all the world's problems. Unfortunately, Carmine is an ass."

Jade's eyes popped at that statement and the judge chuckled. "What? I love him unconditionally. Unfortunately, one of those conditions requires I love an ass. Nicolas and Carmine have never gotten along. Oil and water, those two. That fact breaks my heart, but Nicolas has his own path to follow in this world, and he has never fallen into line with Carmine's vision for him. I have prayed and prayed about the conflict between those two. I don't know what caused the rift between them, but it is there."

Jade made a small noise indicating she heard the woman. Hell, she'd read the family background and Jewell had included all the personal skeletons they'd uncovered because Jade needed to know of any vulnerability that might affect the judge. Carmine and Mario had skeletons. Carmine's were the type the Triad could leverage, and that was something Jade wouldn't allow. She'd shut the man down, quickly and quietly. He'd agree and work with her, or his momma would find out some interesting facts about her son's sexual preferences. Damn good thing his kink was between consenting adults. Unfortunately, it was also information the Triad would use if they found out.

Jade escorted the judge out of her office and watched as she locked the door. She didn't know where to start with the dump truck of information about her sons that her primary had backed up and unloaded. She'd process it on the drive back to the residence. Maybe.

Jade left the judge in the Marshals' care and made her way to the vehicle. She inspected it thoroughly before she opened the back door. The Marshals escorted the judge out of the building to the vehicle and bundled her into the backseat, shutting her inside the protective cocoon of the SUV.

"See you tomorrow." Jade threw the comment out as she got into the driver's seat. The men both lifted a hand and headed back into the courthouse. Jade pulled away from the curb and merged into traffic.

"So, exactly how long have you known my son?" Jade flicked her eyes to the rearview mirror and shrugged. "He works with my brother Jared and took my brother Jason's place when Jason left Guardian during a hiatus... so, a few years now." She kept an eye on her six and maneuvered through traffic in a random pattern to try to draw out any tails she may have acquired, but none presented themselves.

"Have you dated him?"

Jade hadn't expected that question. She

searched the rearview mirror again. "Dated Nic? Nope." Jade popped the 'p' in the response.

"Huh. The way he looks at you when you aren't looking at him, I thought maybe…"

Jade shot a surprised glance to the back seat, but the judge wasn't looking at Jade. She was worrying her thumbnail and staring blindly out the side window. Jade shook the comment off. She couldn't be worried about Nic right now. She navigated the roads leading to the residence keeping an eye out for a tail which never appeared. Thank God. They pulled up to the residence and parked. Jade held up a hand when the judge reached for the door handle. The woman stopped immediately.

"Sorry, I was lost in thought. It was a reflex."

"It takes a while to get used to and remember all the security protocols. It will become second nature in short order." Jade pulled out her phone and checked the home's alarm system before she scrolled through the different camera views of the interior of the home. "Well, your sons are here." She held up the phone and showed the judge the picture of the three men sitting in the family room, all scrolling through their phones, none of them actively engaged in conversation.

"Did you install cameras in every room?"

"Yes, but only I have access to them, and I promise I will never violate your privacy. You agreed to monitoring when you brought us on board." Jade thought about the events in the office earlier today and reminded herself to scrub the server before Jewell's program backed up the digital files at midnight.

"I did, but I was assuming my bedroom wouldn't be part of that monitoring." The censure in the woman's voice washed over Jade.

Damn, the woman was good at the guilt thing— an art form that had to be a mom-issued talent. Maybe hormones changed a woman when they became a mother. She'd have to ask her mom the next time she talked to her.

Jade shrugged and put away the phone. "I understand how you feel. I know the security is an inconvenience. The question to ask yourself is who would you rather had access to your bedroom —Triad or me?"

Bettina cocked her head to the side and pursed her lips. "Have you ever considered a career in litigation?" Jade met her eyes in the mirror, and they both laughed at the judge's comment.

"You have the most uniquely beautiful laugh, Jade. I've never heard anyone laugh with such carefree and joyful abandon. I could recognize your laugh out of a crowd of a hundred."

"Well, I enjoy life, or I try to."

"A great way to look at things. Maybe it will rub off on my boys. Grumpy things, the lot of them, especially when I ask them when they are going to get married. I don't understand them sometimes."

"Ma'am, if you figure out the male species, would you let me know?"

"I promise, but if you figure them out first, you have to promise to call me."

"Deal." Jade's smile stayed on her face as she exited the vehicle ahead of her charge.

CHAPTER 15

Nic heard the door open. His eyes found Carmine. His brother looked up from his phone and stood, launching into the tirade Nic had already heard.

"Ma, what are you thinking? You need to recuse yourself from this case." The man's demand echoed down the hall.

Nic turned in his seat to watch his mother flay his older brother. She was so damn good at it. Carmine was a dick with a capital D, but unfortunately, in this case, he was right. That fact stuck like a fishbone in Nic's throat. He rarely agreed with Carmine, but in this instance, they were on the same page. Hell, the same paragraph and sentence. His mom needed to step away from this case. Let some other judge deal with the bullshit because Bettina DeMarco had presided over more than her fair share of difficult cases.

He could hear his mom's heels clicking on the hardwood floors as she walked down the hall toward the family room. "Carmine DeMarco could you let me get in the house before you start bellowing like a bull elk in full rut?"

Nic suppressed a smile, his mom didn't put up with her eldest son's shit.

"No, not this time. What the f..." The laser glare his mom shot toward Carmine had him back peddling quickly, and he managed not to drop the "F" bomb. "Seriously Ma, you need to recuse yourself. We are talking the Triad. They will kill you."

"No, they won't. Nicolas has taken care of my security when I'm not at the courthouse. I'm comfortable with the precautions that are in effect. Now, hush your mouth, because I'm not hearing any arguments or accepting any motions on the subject." She dropped her purse in the chair and took off her coat.

Nic saw the moment Carmine and Mario noticed Jade. She had trailed their mom into the room. Mario gave her a once over that left little doubt he liked what he saw. Carmine looked as if someone had slapped him. His face turned red, his eyes widened, and he raised his arm pointing at Jade. Oh fuck, this was going to be interesting.

"Who is that?"

Jade moved to the door and stepped to the left of the opening. She leaned back against the doorframe. Her vivid green eyes flashed around the room. She nodded briefly at Nic.

"That's my security officer, Jade King. Ms. King is amazing." Bettina walked over to the bar and lifted a decanter of red wine, motioning toward Mario in question.

"She is a 'she', Ma. Do you really think someone like her could protect you?" He spun on Nic, his face painted with rage. "You're supposed to be making sure Ma is safe, and you let your company assign a fucking model as protection? What the hell were you thinking?"

Carmine's outrage was nothing new, at least not to Nic. The man hated him and everything Guardian represented. Carmine was a defense attorney, and ever since Nicolas had joined the DCPD they'd been distant. Once Nicolas joined Guardian, it was as if he'd become the devil himself, at least in Carmine's eyes.

Nic glared at his brother, stood and walked to

the bar where his mom poured a glass of wine. Nic took the decanter and took over pouring the wine as he spoke. "I really don't think you want to get into this with me Carmine, and if you open your mouth again about the professionalism or capability of the people that Guardian employs, I may turn Ms. King loose on you. She could put you on the ground in less than five seconds. She's one of the best, if not the best, at Guardian and I would wager one of the best in the country. It's rather sexist of you to think otherwise isn't it?" Nic kept his back turned to his brother and flicked his glance at Jade. The woman was doing an awesome job of imitating a statue.

"Nico is right, Carmine. You owe Ms. King an apology. She's very good at her job."

"I'm not going to apologize. Why don't you have a protective detail from the U.S. Marshals or NYPD for Christ's sake?" Carmine stood in the middle of the room and raged.

Nic lifted another wine glass and poured a portion for Mario and then one for himself. Carmine could fucking fend for himself.

"Do you mind if I answer that question, Your Honor?" Jade's voice, low, sultry and sexy floated across the room.

Judge DeMarco lifted her hand and waved it toward Carmine, signaling go ahead as she tipped back the wine glass and took a huge gulp.

Jade straightened from the door and took slow, deliberate steps toward Carmine. She got into his personal space and took one deliberate step forward forcing the man back a step. She continued to put one foot in front of the other, backing his brother toward the corner of the room. Her voice was an inaudible whisper as she spoke to him, and whatever she was saying to his brother drained the blood from his face. He paled and nodded his head several times. Jade lifted her arm suddenly, and Carmine flinched. She smiled and pulled her hair to one side before dropping her arm casually. Oh, fuck, it was a thing of beauty to watch. She had Carmine terrified, handled, and willing to do exactly as she said, in less than twenty seconds.

Jade took off her jacket exposing her primary weapon, cuffs, badge, and her 911 Interceptor. She didn't have that knife on her when she'd left to pick up his mother. The thought of what she wasn't wearing when they'd last been in this house together sent a surge to his cock. Fuck, watching the woman intimidate his brother shouldn't be so fucking hot, but it was. Hotter than hell. He raked his eyes over her. She was amazing, and he'd bet this month's paycheck she had at least two other weapons somewhere on her person. Not that she'd need them. She was a lethal weapon all by herself. Jade turned on her heel with her jacket draped over her left arm, keeping her right available to pull whichever weapon she'd need.

"There was delivery for me from Guardian?" She smiled at Nic as if she hadn't handed a seasoned lawyer his hat and forced him to eat it.

"Couple of boxes. I put them upstairs in the guest bedroom."

Jade nodded and turned around to address the others in the room. "There are cameras and sensors surrounding the residence as well as ballistic shields in place. Don't answer the front door, or go near it for that matter. Nic or I will handle that. I'd hate anyone to come to harm on my watch. Your Honor, when your guests are ready to leave, I'll ensure their vehicles are secure before letting them out of the residence. If you need me, I'll be around." She spun and walked out of the room.

"What the heck did she say to you, man?"

Mario's face was a study of emotions, but shock seemed to override surprise and concern.

"Nothing. She, ah…" Carmine studied Nic as if weighing how much he should say. "… she's more than capable of taking care of Ma's security."

"I told you. Now, to the kitchen everyone. We have prep work to do. I'm thinking something simple like spaghetti. Carmine grab some of my homemade gravy out of the freezer and start defrosting it. Mario, you have meatball duty. We need to drop them into the sauce to cook them. Nico, you are on salad and bread. I'll go change. Carmine and I will make the pasta."

Nic watched Mario get up and head out to start the meatballs. Carmine held back and turned to Nic, grasping his arm, stopping him from following. "That woman is insane."

"Not true, we have her tested quarterly. It's a Guardian requirement. Although, now that you mention it, she may be off her meds." Nic shrugged off his brother's hand and followed Mario to the kitchen.

Dinner preparation was surprisingly cordial since Carmine's mouth wasn't running. Mario sat down next to him at the kitchen island while they waited. "So what is the story with the woman?"

"The woman?" Nic lifted his eyebrows at his brother. "She has a name, and if you value keeping your balls where they currently reside, I strongly suggest you drop your Carmine impersonation."

Mario chuckled and shook his head. "Yeah, Mom told me she thought there was something between the two of you."

"What? When?" Nic sure as hell did not need his mom on the scent of something that could never develop.

"When I was dropping the meatballs into the marinara. Not sure I see it. I mean, who'd want to fuck a woman who could kill you?"

I would. Nic took another sip of his second glass of wine. He wasn't going to respond to Mario's comment.

Mario chuckled and elbowed Nic, drawing his eyes to meet Mario's gaze. "Is she that good?"

"Where is your fianceé? Shouldn't she be here?" Nic regretted the jab when he watched Mario's teasing expression close off.

"Nah, she's working. Or has a meeting. Or is sleeping. Or doing yoga." Mario tossed back the rest of his wine and immediately reached for the decanter.

"Trouble?"

"Nah, we'd have to see each other for there to be trouble." Mario filled his glass and lifted the decanter toward Nic. He shook his head. Jade was on duty, but if shit hit the fan, he needed to be able to respond.

"Just a rough patch or...?" Nic left the question open ended.

Mario shrugged, and they both jumped when Carmine barked a string of cuss words that seemed to be directed at the pasta attachment he was struggling to put on the huge mixer.

"Fuck, that man is a heart attack waiting to happen."

Nic snorted a laugh at his little brother. "I hope he explodes on your watch."

Mario laughed and shook his head. "Believe it or not, he's not bad at the office."

"Huh. I don't believe it. Now, about you and Bethany?"

Mario shrugged. "We've both agreed the relationship isn't working. The sex is great when we do get together, but she has career goals and building the firm takes most of my time. We're getting together next weekend to figure out how to separate assets and go our own ways after four years, but for all intents and purposes, the relationship is done."

Nic put his arm around his brother's shoulders and pulled him in for a sideways hug. "Sorry man. It sucks."

"Unfortunately, the one who is going to be the most upset over this thing ending is Mom." They both laughed at the truth of Mario's statement.

"Shit, she'll double her efforts to marry me off." Nic jokingly pushed Mario away.

"You could do worse than the one upstairs." Mario absently watched Carmine and his mom work together to feed the pasta sheets through the press. "All fooling aside, she's hot. She can handle herself and this family. Dude, that's a keeper in anyone's book."

Nic chuckled and swiveled in his chair to look out the window. "Yeah, and Jade is as wild and independent as they come. She doesn't do relationships, and if she ever settles down, it would take a miracle of Old Testament proportions to keep her happy. Her brother is my best friend. I don't know, man."

"So you're telling me you're opposed to having fun with her until the marrying type comes along?"

Nic filled his lungs and then let them deflate slowly. He considered his brother and shrugged. *Why not be honest?* He knew Mario would keep his confidence. "Dude, I'm forty years old. I've watched all the people around me settle down and find happiness. I don't know, maybe they've infected me or something, but I'm over the random hook-ups."

"I never thought I'd hear those words from you." Mario swirled the wine in his glass before he spoke again. "So why not try to settle down with Jade?"

"Jade's fucking amazing, and if the opportunity ever presented itself, I'd be stupid not to make her mine, but she doesn't want a relationship, and honestly, that's what I do want. She's the type of woman I could see myself with long-term, but letting myself go down that path is insane." Mario nudged his elbow, but, lost in his thoughts, Nic didn't pay immediate attention. "I'm telling you, Mario, I'm fucking tired of playing the field. Meaningless sex with random hook-ups has lost its flavor. Sex is a biological catch and release now." Mario nudged his elbow again. "What?" His brother cleared his throat and motioned with his chin toward the door. Nic tossed a glance in that direction. *Fuck.* Jade stood inside the door and was well within hearing distance. *Wonderful.*

His mom's voice called from the other side of the kitchen, "Ah, Jade! Dinner will be in about ten minutes." Bettina held long strands of cut pasta up in the air. "I'll be dropping the pasta soon."

"Thanks, but no thanks. I ate before I picked you up. I'm doing my rounds." Jade turned and walked out of the room.

"Okay, there is plenty if you change your mind," Bettina called after her. Carmine let loose with another string of curse words. "Mario, come help Carmine disassemble the pasta attachment before he breaks it, please?" Bettina arranged her freshly cut pasta on a floured board as she spoke.

Nic leaned back in his chair and closed his eyes for a moment. He needed to end any idea of a real relationship with Jade. No matter how he twisted it, what they had wasn't a relationship. It was just sex. At least in her mind. He'd seen and heard the hesitancy when he asked if they were exclusive. If she had that much of a problem saying yes to being with one man, how could he ever hope to entice her to stay with him long term? Hell, maybe her hesitancy was because of him. God, what a stinking pile of shit. Life wasn't supposed to be this difficult. Undoubtedly, the sex with Jade was hot on a nuclear detonation level, hot enough to lay waste to his entire world, but it wasn't the sum of his attraction to her. Nic sighed and rolled his shoulders while looking down at his hands. The woman had gotten into his blood, and he was addicted to her taste, her body, and her laughter. The energy surrounding her fed him in ways that he didn't understand. He wanted more from her than just sex. The woman enthralled him, wrapping him in a hypnotic web that held him helpless and awaiting her mercy. Unfortunately, her mercy would never arrive. She would abandon the web and leave him to shrivel and die. He needed to end their games. Once the trial was over, he'd go back to DC, and she'd go on to another assignment. Back to business as usual. No harm, no foul.

Nic glanced up at the small camera in the corner of the room. He lowered his eyes and drew a deep breath before looking over at his family. Their laughter cut through his melancholy mood. He turned and peered back at the camera. Nic lowered his view to his watch. Eleven hours until he could speak with her privately.

CHAPTER 16

Jade unwrapped a protein bar and took a huge bite out of the chocolate covered sawdust. She washed the horrible taste down with a half bottle of room temperature water while she watched the family downstairs passing home-made pasta, tomato sauce, and meatballs around the table. It wasn't the first time she'd eaten a protein bar instead of joining her primary for dinner, and it wouldn't be the last.

Jade hadn't caught the entire conversation between Mario and Nic, but she'd heard enough. Nic wanted a relationship. A serious relationship and if what she heard was correct, he wanted it with her. But then again, he'd assumed he wanted that same kind of relationship with her sister

Jewell a few months back. Jade bounced her foot rapidly while she willed herself to reject the idea of a serious relationship.

What was it about the man that scrambled her brain so much that she sat here and contemplated changing her entire way of life? Her brain fired on all eight cylinders and listed the reasons for making it permanent with Nic before she could even think to stop it. *He's sexy as hell, fucking fantastic in bed, the best you've ever had. He gets your mentality; he understands your job. He knows you've played the field and made the circuit and still wants to be around you.* She shut down the mental diatribe and observed the dynamics of the family again. Carmine was back to his usual asshole self. He dominated the table. Mario and the judge visited with the blowhard, but Nic just watched. He'd barely touched his meal. Jade took a huge bite out of her supposedly chocolate flavored piece of clay brick and chewed it as fast as her jaw could power through it. Nic was upset. Those lines between his eyebrows were more prominent, enough that she could pick them out with the camera. Jade flicked her eyes toward her laptop. The screen split into six video streams: two cameras outside of the residence, which also covered the opposing sides of the building; a wide angle shot of the street in front of the residence; one from the rear of the yard watching the back of the home; one dedicated to the Guardian vehicle out front, and the last rotated through the images inside the home. Jade had the dining room called up on her phone and was able to monitor the family while still ensuring the security of the residence. This part of her job sucked feathered duck balls. The watching and waiting were boring as hell, but it was worth it if the primaries remained safe.

She lifted the cardboard flap of one of the boxes Jewell had sent her and pulled out her caffeine pills and a six-pack of energy drinks. God bless Jewell for her addiction to the highest-octane energy drink on the market. Until Jade got into a routine of sleeping during the day and staying awake at night, the energy drinks and caffeine pills would keep her alert. It was what it was. Not healthy, but then again if she fell asleep, the judge may not stay alive. That made any damage to her body from the combination in her hands well worth the price.

She watched as the family cleared the table and started washing up. She could tell it was a dance they'd done many times as each of them knew exactly what to do. She watched Nic roll up his sleeves and take off his watch before he filled the sink and started washing dishes. Mario dried while Carmine loaded the dishwasher and wiped down the table and countertops. Bettina DeMarco put the food into containers and placed them into the fridge. When they were finished, they headed into the family room. Jade switched cameras. Nic wasn't in the family room. She lurched toward her laptop. She caught him heading into the office. Keeping the family on the screen of her phone she propped it next to her laptop and froze one of the screens on the office frame. Nic walked through the space and raked his fingers through his hair. He walked over to the desk and pushed several pieces of paper off his tablet. Dropping down into the chair, he fired up his laptop and picked up the phone. The man was burning the candle at both ends. Not only was he coordinating Guardian's investigation of his mother's case, but also carrying his normal workload.

Jade's eyes flicked back to her primaries. Carmine appeared as if he was getting ready to go. Jade made a sweep of the exterior cameras, checked the sensors, and grabbed her blazer. Time to go to work.

Three hours later, with both the brothers gone, the house locked up tight, the judge in her room reading, and Nic elbow deep in paperwork, Jade slipped into the kitchen. She wasn't beyond rummaging through leftovers, because that protein bar was not cutting it. The light turned on, catching her holding a plastic container of pasta.

"I'll split that with you." Nic prowled into the kitchen and grabbed two plates out of the cupboard.

"Umm... okay, but I got to tell you, I'm hungry enough to eat this all by myself." Jade put the container down and grabbed the spoon that Nic handed her.

"There are enough leftovers in the freezer to feed an army. I promise you won't go hungry in this house." Nic slid equal portions of the pasta and meatballs onto each plate. He covered one and put it in the microwave before he spoke again. "Why didn't you eat dinner with us?"

"Wasn't feeling it." Jade shrugged away his question. He didn't need to know his words earlier tonight had hit her harder than a cannonball to the gut. She'd always described herself as a commit-ment-phobe, but hearing it come from Nic pulled the glitz and sass off the title and painted her for what she was—a woman who ran away from anything that would come close to a lasting relationship. Hell, she even kept her family at arm's length. Nobody really knew her. They only knew the persona she'd perfected. Granted, she had one hell of a lot of fun perfecting that image, but...

"Look, I was going to wait to do this until the morning, but you deserve to know the truth..."

Jade lifted a hand and stopped him. "I heard the truth tonight, and I've had some time to think about what you said." Jade pulled her hand through her hair and let her arm drop to her leg. She pushed out the words before she lost her nerve. "Look, if you promise to let me take this at my pace, I'm willing to... you know..." She waited for a reaction and when it didn't come she peered up at him. The confusion plainly displayed across his handsome face told her he had no clue what she was saying. "What's so hard to understand here? You said you were looking for a relationship with me right? I mean I don't know how to fucking do... that... but I'm willing to... you know..." She picked up the other plate and handed it to him when the microwaved beeped. Why in the hell was he looking at her as if she had three heads? She could change. He'd changed. Why couldn't she? It wasn't impossible. Was it?

"No, I don't know. You're willing to do what?" He stood there with the plate in his hands and confusion written all over his face.

Jade crossed her arms over her chest and stuck out her hip. Men. Men were so stupid sometimes. Damn, if Nic wasn't sex on a stick and pretty as hell, she'd walk away. How the hell did this guy manage to pass the bar and run a big part of a billion dollar company?

"Follow the bouncing ball, DeMarco. I'm willing to try."

"Try what?" Nic put the plate down and ran his hand through his hair, sending the thick bangs into total chaos.

Yep, sex on a stick. Albeit a dull stick sometimes. Jade scanned the kitchen for any possible eavesdroppers and then leaned in and hissed, "A relationship."

Nic blinked owlishly a couple times before a smile started to spread across his face. It faltered, and he directed a sharpened gaze at her. "That means exclusivity even when we are done with this assignment."

Jade narrowed her eyes and placed her index

finger on his chest, pushing a little harder than necessary. "I know that. Don't you think I know what being in a... What it entails?"

"You can't even say the word."

"Why do I have to? Is there a rule that says I have to label this thing?" She took a step to pass by him and slugged him on the shoulder. He grabbed her around the waist and then pinned her arms to her sides, nothing she couldn't break out of, but at this second in time, she was okay with his arms pulling her into his embrace.

"I'm a lawyer. We state facts and get acknowledgements. It's kinda our thing." He lowered his lips toward hers and stopped a hair's breadth away from her. "I like thinking of you as mine. Even though you are slightly violent."

His? Jade gasped right before Nic sealed his lips over hers. Her hand pulled out of the position he'd pinned it to and snaked up into his hair. She freed the other hand and pulled him down to her. Fuck it. If he was going to call her his, she sure as fuck was going to claim his ass and own it, too. Nic shifted and brought her closer against his body. There was no mistaking the hardness that pressed against her hip. She pulled away interspersing several small kisses as she broke the separation. "I have conditions."

"Too late, not stipulated before the agreement was brokered." Nic winked at her and kissed along her jaw ending up at that spot behind her ear that sent shudders of sensation through her body.

"Ah, no... Defense submits that the Plaintiff withheld exculpatory evidence and demands a re-examination of the terms of said agreement." Jade drew a deep breath and braced, forcing Nic's shoulders away. God, she really, really did not want to do that, but hey, she had the right to have a say since this was supposed to be a real relation-ship. Fifty-fifty and all that shit.

Nic loosened his hold on her and leaned against the counter bringing her to stand between his legs—his long, muscled, sexy as fuck legs. Jade fought a shiver of delight as it raced down her spine and pooled deep inside her.

"I thought you had conditions?"

Oh, yeah... conditions. "Yes. First, I do my job. You do yours. No crossing lines. I won't let you interfere with what I do. So you stay out of my shit, and I'll stay out of yours. Agreed?"

"Absolutely, unless it has to do with my mother's case and then we discuss it first." Nic bent and kissed her briefly. "Next condition."

"If this doesn't work out, we agree to walk away. No massive fights, no blow up. Got it?"

"I promise I will not blow up. I have tended to avoid confrontations with my past liaisons, so I don't anticipate changing my ways. Yet, I can't help but wonder why you would agree to a relationship if you already assume one of us will be walking away."

"No, counselor, I didn't say that. I said if this doesn't work we separate amicably." The more she thought about an idea of being with only one man the more panicked she got, but the thing that kept her from backing away from this agreement was Nicolas Fucking DeMarco. The man had somehow made his way under her skin. Continuous, distracting thoughts of him were festering right there... like a splinter. One she couldn't remove and irritating enough she couldn't forget it was there. Great, her relationship was like a fucking splinter—a sore, puss-filled... Jade shook her head.

Nic held her attention when no others had managed to do so. His quiet assurance that he was the best she'd ever had and his wicked sense of humor were the cornerstones for an attraction that was quite unlike anything she'd ever felt. Well, that and his fucking good looks and the molten hot sex.

"Okay, are you done?" Nic asked, and she nodded. Jade opened her mouth to speak, but he lifted a finger and put it on her lips. "My conditions are next."

Jade lifted an eyebrow. He wants to put conditions on a relationship that he asked for in the first place? She could hardly wait to hear what they were. She pulled away from his finger. "Sure, let's hear it. What constraints do you require on the relationship?" She leaned into him and couldn't resist putting her head on his shoulder and yawning. She needed another energy drink. It had been a long 24 hours.

"Your family and my mother don't know about this until we figure it out."

Jade popped her head off his shoulder and grabbed his biceps. "Oh, God! I concur. Telling the families would be monumentally stupid and open us up to a shit-ton of grief." The vivid picture his words prompted sent a jolt of adrenaline through her system. She was no longer tired. The thought of her family getting ahold of the fact that she was actually in a relationship put gooseflesh on her arms. No, just no. Her brothers would have a field day. She'd have to kill them. And probably her sisters, too... maybe even her mom. Nah, she couldn't do that to her mom, but her brothers and sisters? A real possibility. Getting your ass arrested for a serial murder of your entire family probably wasn't a good thing. There definitely wasn't enough money in her 'Bail Jade out of Jail' account for a murder spree.

"Right. Come on. Let's eat. Then I need to finish some work. I've told Jared I'll be working the night shift for the foreseeable future." Nic kissed her again, long and slow.

Jade tipped her head up and arched away from him, more than a little curious. "Why?"

"I figure Mom is as safe as possible at the courthouse. The transit time between the courthouse and home is when she is most vulnerable. I want to be available to back you up if necessary. Besides, when you take her to work in the morning, most of the people I need to get updates from are already at work. I can assign duties and responsibilities, get briefings and get one hell of a lot more done at night than I could with constant interruptions during the day. Jared and I have worked split shifts in the past when things got hot and heavy. It works out well for everyone."

Jade pulled her phone out of her back pocket. She peeked at the status of the alarm system and readouts of movements throughout the house. "Okay, food, then you and I both do what we get paid to do." She pushed up on her tiptoes and kissed him again. "I look forward to consummating this thing between us." Jade leaned against his hard cock and ground her hips against him.

"It's a relationship. And fuck, don't start something we can't finish." Nic grabbed her butt and hauled her even closer.

"Oh, I'll finish it, but not until your mother is under the protection of the U.S. Marshals Service."

CHAPTER 17

Nic collapsed and grabbed his chest as he rolled onto his back. His heart threatened to give out. He was forty years old, and this woman was going to kill him. Death by sex. Damn, what a way to go. "Oh man, I liked that. We need to do that again." Jade's breathless panting made him feel a little better. The woman had ridden him reverse cowgirl until his eyes crossed and he saw the heavens open up. God, could she ride, but he'd taken over because damn, the woman was a hunger he couldn't satisfy. He'd moved her to her hands and knees and finished with the hard fucking that they both loved. She was insatiable, and God help him, around her, so was he.

"Yeah, okay. But give me a couple minutes." Nic

pulled off the condom and tied it before he tossed it into the trash can. He flopped back down, rolling her toward him as he did. "Were there any problems at the courthouse this morning?" His mom was in the second week of the Triad trial. The US Marshals Service continued to impress Nic with the all-out effort they made to ensure his mother's safety while she was in court. The FBI had subtly increased its presence, but it was appreciated nonetheless. There were armed guards everywhere. The Triad would be idiots to try to breach security.

"Nope. I'm using different entrances and exits every day. Overall, the weakest point in our protection is when I exit the vehicle and go in to get her and then when she walks out at night with the Marshals. I know we have eyes on the vehicle from above, but that distance makes me a little wonky."

"Is there anything we could do to mitigate the issue?" Nic ran his hand down her spine. His fingers traveled over her soft skin sending small shivers through her. Aftershocks of great sex, she'd called it once.

"The New York office has two shadows on my tail going and coming from the courthouse. I have snipers on top of the building when I escort her in or out. The layers are effective and efficient. If this were my mom, I would know that I was doing everything I could to make sure she was safe." Jade trailed her fingertips through the hair on his chest. "Have there been any more leads from the FBI or NYPD?"

Nic shook his head. "No. The Triad contingency in the city has been silent." As in dead silent and that was concerning as fuck. "The Gangland Task Force is on pins and needles. The sergeant in charge of the group told me that he believes something big is brewing, but they have no solid intel to back up his supposition. Just the gut feelings of cops who've been doing the job forever."

Jade pushed away from him and rolled onto her stomach, rising up on her elbows. She pulled her bottom lip into her mouth and nodded her head as she stared at the headboard. She shot him a sideways glance. "Something big? Okay, so let's spitball. A grand gesture by a gang. Drive-by shooting maybe?"

"That, unfortunately, is an everyday thing." Nic put his arm under his head and stared at the ceiling. "But what about a full on assault? If they came en masse?"

Jade nodded, considering his words. "But against who? Your mom was the only one we know of that was threatened. The house is secure. The courthouse has more guns in it than a third-world country. The witnesses are in protective custody. Your mom said if the lawyers don't pull anything unexpected they should wrap up the arguments within two weeks and remand it to the jury. She sequestered the jury the moment they took their oath, so tampering with them is a moot point. That leaves a limited window for them to strike a blow at someone who would force a mistrial: the prosecutor or his team or hell, maybe even the defense's own team—anything that would force a mistrial, I guess."

"That would give them time to change the judge or find a way to manipulate a juror, maybe get a hung jury or even a not guilty judgement." Nic sat up and swung his legs over the side of the bed. He knew in his gut something ominous hung over this case, but he couldn't figure out what it was or where it would be coming from. He and Jade had run these scenarios repeatedly. There was nothing but supposition and a heaping helping of paranoia.

He reached back and smacked Jade on the ass.

"Get some sleep. I have a conference with Jason and Jared, so I'm up for a couple more hours."

"What is the conference about?" Jade stretched, pulling the sheet down and exposing her long, sexy back. Her ivory skin sang him a siren's song. Fuck, he'd never had a woman enthrall him like she did.

"Hey, DeMarco, close the mouth and eyes up here."

He tugged his eyes away from the sensuous dip of her back and up to her laughing face.

"That's it, big boy. Conference?"

Nic shook his head and smirked. "My business, not yours. No crossing lines, remember? Your condition."

Jade softened a burst of laughter and waved her hand at him. "Fine, go forth and push paper. I'm going to cuddle into these soft sheets and go to sleep." She pulled the sheet up over her shoulder and snuggled down into the pillow. "Don't forget to check the security feeds before you lock yourself in the office." Her words emerged muffled from the depths of the pillow.

"Stop working and go to sleep." Nic went into the guest room's ensuite and took a quick shower. He needed to clear the cobwebs before the meeting. They were discussing a case that needed a specialized skill set, and Nic wasn't exactly convinced that Jason's idea to meet those needs was going to work.

He checked the feeds after his shower and then headed downstairs. Nic made a single cup of coffee. He settled into his desk where he clicked open his browser and started to log back into Guardian's system.

The video conference icon was active. Nic clicked on it and brought up three screens. Jason, Jared, and Jacob were each in their own environment. When they noticed his log on, all three unmuted.

"Good morning. Nic, I know we are reaching into your evening hours, but we need to sort this case out so we can set the groundwork." Jason pulled a few sheets of paper toward him and then examined the computer video screen.

"Not a problem. I appreciate you letting me work the alternate schedule." Nic lifted his coffee cup and saluted the big guy.

"Whatever it takes." Jason's distracted words received three unanimous and immediate replies, "As long as it takes."

Nic sipped his coffee and relaxed in his chair. They hashed out the details of the case, with all four of the members brainstorming the best tactic for combining an overseas and domestic approach to prevent a known counterfeiter's seemingly miraculous jumps from continent to continent.

"No, I don't think he's using commercial aircraft. It has to be a private conveyance and the lag of times before he appears again..."

"Fuck! Did you see that? Turn on the news! Now!" Jacob's urgent interruption swung Nic's head to the television. He stood and grabbed the remote. It took several seconds before he understood what he was seeing. *No... no!*

He grabbed his phone and bolted out the office door toward the front of the house, screaming at the top of his lungs, "Jade! Jade! Wake the fuck up! The courthouse has been bombed!"

Jade stumbled down the stairs as he started up them. She had her weapons, shoes, and shirt in her hand. The woman had thrown on a sports bra and tugged her jeans on but left them unfastened.

"Let's go! You drive!" Jade lobbed him the keys as she spoke.

Nic caught the keyring, and they flew out of the front door. Jade slammed the front door shut and scurried into the passenger side as Nic threw the SUV into gear. He flipped on the SUV's emergency lights and siren. Her phone rang once before she answered it and put it on speaker. Her phone landed in a cup holder as Jason's voice came over the vehicle's Bluetooth speaker. "We are in contact with NYPD and the US Marshals' office. The explosion was in the southeast corner of the building."

Jade grabbed Nic's arm. "We don't know if court was in session."

Nic glanced at the digital clock. 10:30 a.m. Unless the court was in a recess... Fuck, his mother's chambers were with the other judges on the fourth floor on the north side of the building. He could only pray she was in her office. The courtrooms, clerk's offices, and meeting rooms were staggered throughout the facility. The massive devastation he saw on the brief glimpse of video footage meant the bomb was big enough to demolish one side of the cement and marble structure.

"First responder reports are coming in. Nic, the Marshals are trying to secure the scene, and they will give me an update as soon as they know anything." That was Jared's voice.

"J, do they know if my mom's court was in session?" Nic slammed on the brakes and took a corner on two wheels. He cast a quick glance at Jade. The momentum of the corner damn near ejected her out of her seat. Jade didn't say a word, but grabbed her shoe that had tumbled into the back seat. Stoic and unshakable, she continued to get dressed.

"Hold on. I've got the Marshals on line." Jason's gravelly voice answered.

Jade pulled on her shirt and shoulder holster. She clipped on her badge and handcuffs on the waistband of her jeans. Nic slammed his foot on the accelerator and jerked the wheel violently, steering the SUV over a curb, along a sidewalk, and back down past a car that refused to get out of the way.

"Dude, there could have been pedestrians." Jade reached for her seatbelt and strapped it on.

"There weren't." Nic pushed the vehicle to its limits, weaving in and out of traffic. Even with the urgency with which he was driving, it would take too long to get to the courthouse. "What are you hearing, J?" Nic knew his best friend wouldn't blow smoke up his ass.

"It doesn't look good. I'm waiting for Jason just like you, but the pictures being broadcast... the entire building has received damage. A few ambulances are on scene along with the first wave of fire and rescue. It's bad." Jared's voice seemed to echo in the cabin of the SUV. Jade pointed toward a vacant lane and Nic swerved into it and accelerated.

"Nic, you need to slow down, or you will kill us or someone else." Jade's calm voice floated from the passenger seat.

He peered down at the speedometer. Seventy in a forty zone. He drew a deep breath and lifted his foot slightly. She was right, but fuck, he needed to get to that courthouse.

"Nic, your mom's court was in session. According to the Marshal I spoke with, it was on the opposite side of the building. The U.S. Marshals Service cannot reach the men assigned to your mother's location. The floors above the level your mom's court was on have collapsed. Three courtrooms, all in session, are now unreachable. First responders can see some movement through the windows, and they are working on getting to that side of the building, but they are dealing with a gas main break and unstable debris at the front of the building first."

"Son of a bitch! We knew they were going to do something big. How the fuck did they get close

KRIS MICHAELS

enough to put a fucking bomb outside the building?" Nic slammed his fist against the steering
wheel and swore bitterly. He stared out the front
windshield and tried to get a grip on his runaway
emotions.

"I do know the U.S. Marshals Service has
checked the logs. There were no reports of anyone
outside the building for the last twenty-four
hours. Nothing immediately before the explosion
either. We don't know the bomb was located
outside the facility. It could have been inside or a
projectile." Jason's calm voice fed them the
information.

"Who is the on-scene commander and where is
the entry control point set up?" Jade asked as they
flew past cars and weaved through traffic.

"Your point of contact will be Captain Young,
NYFD. You can't get within two blocks right now.
They are expanding the cordon from five hundred
feet to three thousand, so you're going to have to
find someplace to ditch the truck soon. The gas
leak is endangering first responders and survivors.
Utilities are working on it..." Jewell's voice came
over the phone.

Until that moment, he hadn't realized Jason
had mobilized all available resources and Guardian

personnel in the DC Headquarters to deal with this disaster.

Nic floored the accelerator and drove like a bat flying straight out of hell. There were no more communications from Guardian Headquarters. He knew they had the phone on mute while they scrambled for information and rerouted resources in the area to help.

"Nic, over there. Pull off, and we can run over two blocks and up one." Jade pinpointed his attention to the spot she indicated up the road.

He slammed on the brakes and skidded to a stop before backing up and slamming diagonally into a parallel parking slot. Nic hit the ground running and felt, more than saw, Jade right beside him. As they rounded the corner, he saw billowing smoke in a thick, black, rolling cloud spread out above the buildings on each side of the street. The reality of the disaster pressed with a vice-like grip on his heart. Jade grabbed his arm and tugged, pulling him through an alley. They emerged, and both skidded to a stop. Chaos stretched out in front of them. Fire, rescue, ambulance, and police vehicles scattered in a random pattern among the pandemonium. The kaleidoscope of flashing lights was a momentary distraction from the devastation behind the vehicles. Over three quarters of the front of the building was missing. The gaping maw revealed partial courtrooms, offices, and hallways. Paper fluttered in the air, kept aloft by unseen currents. The pile of rubble that mounded at the base of the building contained enormous slabs of rebar reinforced concrete. The bomb had to have been massive. How did the Marshals guarding the premises miss an explosive device of this size?

"There!" Jade grabbed him again and directed his attention away from the utter ruin of the building.

Nic followed her pointing finger. She'd located the on-scene command center. It took far longer than it should have to reach the hub of activity. NYPD stopped them several times. Both of them flashed their badges to gain access. The impediments frustrated the fuck out of Nic. Once they arrived at the command post, Nic elbowed his way into a circle of men.

"Have you reached the courtrooms in the rear of the building?" Nic demanded as soon as he broke through.

The Fire Captain swung his attention toward Nic. "Who the fuck are you?"

"Nicolas DeMarco, Chief Operations Officer

for Guardian Security, this is my coworker, Jade King." They both held up their badges.

The captain shook his head. "We have two rescue units trying to clear the way. There is a passage that is partially clear, and they are using hydraulic lifts to try to stabilize the material."

"I need to get in there." Nic wasn't going to let anyone stop him. It was his responsibility to ensure his mother's safety, and he'd fucking failed. He had to make sure she was all right.

"No way. I'm not going to be responsible for your ass." The captain swung away from them and bellowed, "Where the fuck are my refilled air tanks? Someone find them and get them to my people. Now!" Nic grabbed Jade's arm and nodded toward the left. They worked their way through the crowd.

"I'm going in." Nic studied the area, looking for an access point.

"I figured. Look." She pointed toward a side entrance where first responders were entering and exiting the building.

"We need a way past the guards." Nic could hear the radio traffic. The NYPD and FDNY were in contact and not letting anyone into the area that didn't belong there. Nic slowly turned around looking for anything... Jade saw them the same time he did. They moved as one to a pallet of air tanks. He checked to make sure they were full before they both hefted two tanks each and headed toward the entry control point.

"Whoa! Wait up. Who are you?" An NYPD uniformed officer stopped their advance.

"Capt'n needs help to get the refilled air tanks in to his people." Jade shifted the tank on her shoulder and looked at the guy. "Call him."

The officer tipped the radio clipped to his epaulet and spoke into the mic. "Oscar 19, we have people bringing in refilled air tanks. Are they authorized?"

The static on the radio lasted less than a second before a bellowed reply shot back, "Let them pass!"

Nic led the way and handed off the full air tanks to the firefighter inside the door. Jade did the same. When the man's back was turned, they bolted up the stairway. Nic had been in the building only a handful of times, but he had a basic idea of where they needed to go. They ran up three flights before debris blocked their path. The door to the interior of the building was off its hinges, but they could hear voices. They maneuvered their way through the rubble and came up on a team working to remove the last portion of debris from a small passageway that led through the hallway.

"What the fuck are you doing up here?" one of the firefighters demanded when he saw them.

"Guardian Security. There are U.S. Marshals, FBI agents, and others in there. We need to determine the status of several people. The Capt'n cleared us in." Nic spun the lie and motioned toward the cleared path and the rescue crews that were now going into the area.

"Fine, but your asses are waiting here. I don't need you in my people's way." The man dismissed Nic without a second glance.

"Let them do their work, Nic. There is nothing we can do now but wait." Jade led him to the side of the hall, out of the way of the responders.

Nic leaned against the wall and then slid down it. Several tons of cement and iron rebar separated him from his mother. This disaster was his fault. He was the fucking point man on this investigation. He'd fucked up somehow. Missed something. There had to have been a clue, some intelligence that he'd discounted or overlooked. His mind reeled with guilt and despair. What had he missed?

Jade squatted on her heels facing him and blocking his view of the passageway. He moved.

She moved in front of him again, bringing his pissed off glare straight up to her face. She stared at him with a determination he'd rarely seen before. She spoke, low only for his ears, "There was nothing we could do to prevent this Nic, but there is plenty we can do to figure out who the fuck did it. Whatever happens inside that mess, we have a way to get even for what they've done. Get off your ass, and get your head on straight."

CHAPTER 18

The dust. Jade observed the dust that hovered around them. The first responders were doing triage. Radios squawked with words and terms she'd heard before. Nic stood resolutely beside her. While they waited, she fixated on the dust. It continued to layer itself on everything like a fine powder. It was easier to focus on the minutiae than the cosmic scale of fucked up that engulfed her.

Her heart hadn't stopped pounding. Adrenaline filled her immobile body. She wanted to scream in frustration. The second Nic bellowed her name this morning she'd been on high alert, but what she was feeling couldn't compare to the emotions that had to be tearing apart the man standing next to her. Jade shifted, leaning slightly into Nic, reminding him she was there for him.

She had no idea what she'd do if she were in his position. She couldn't comprehend the emotions that had to be playing through his mind. Didn't even want to try. She did know were she in his position, she'd want a way to settle the score. She'd want revenge. Jade put up shields and kept a distance from her family, but she loved them. The emotions that screamed through her mind now? Not even going to look at it. They were too raw, too tender to examine.

Jade pulled out her phone and glanced at it. There was a weak signal. Her fingers flew over the keyboard sending a text to Jewell telling Guardian where they were and what they were doing.

Several minutes later, a flurry of activity pulled both of them off the wall. Two responders carried out a person on a backboard. Jade recognized the man. He was one of the Marshals assigned to Nic's mom. The firefighters carefully transferred him to a waiting stretcher as a medic slid to his knees and started an assessment. A second Marshal exited, right arm bleeding and strapped to his chest. Jade recognized him immediately. She spoke to the man almost every night when they exchanged custody of Judge DeMarco. He noticed her and gestured with his good arm back toward the hole. "They are bringing her out. The FBI agents in the courtroom have secured the defendant. It's not good. Not good." The man staggered to a wall and leaned against it. He lifted his eyes toward them and shook his head slowly. "She's hurt bad."

Jade started forward, but Nic was past her in a second. The next person carried out was his mother. Jade grabbed him, stopping him and put herself between her lover and his mother. "Nic, wait. Let them work on her! Stay out of their way, for just a minute." She stood in front of him and wrapped her arms around him, turning her head so she could watch the paramedics work.

Blood painted Judge DeMarco's face. A thick layer of white dust also covered her, giving her a deathly, sallow appearance. Nic grabbed Jade's arms and squeezed, not to move her or get past, but almost as if the act could anchor him. Two medics scrambled, cutting her clothes from her body. As if in a coordinated explosion, their actions flew into hyper-speed.

"She needs to go. Now! She has internal bleeding."

The EMTs piled the equipment onto the stretcher with her and were heading out the door in seconds. Jade followed Nic down the stairs and to an ambulance. Nic flashed his badge and attempted to get into the back of the bus. "No room. Take the front seat!" shouted the medic working on his mom. Nic dropped off the back of the wagon and bolted to the side of the vehicle. He sent a worried expression to Jade.

She motioned for him to continue and yelled, "Text me which hospital they are taking her to. I'll meet you there."

Nic nodded and jumped in as the ambulance's siren started to wail. She watched the vehicle work its way through the cordon and then fly down the avenue.

Jade stood in the middle of the disaster. She swept her eyes over the scene, seeing but unable to come to grips with the incomprehensible evil that had brought down the building. The turbulent hum of activity dimmed as the magnitude of the entire situation settled upon her. She thought of the people who would never go home, and the families who would never hold their loved ones again; the first responders who worked to save lives and the mental and physical trauma they would endure during the rescue process. The totality of the malfeasance burned through her soul like acid—instant, unstoppable, and defacing. Jade surveyed the road where the ambulance had departed. Her heart bled for Nic. The man had done everything humanly possible to ensure his mother's safety and yet... She knew he blamed himself, or her, or both. He hadn't said it, but she knew. Just like she knew Nic meant more to her than a convenient hook-up. In the midst of the devastation surrounding her, the emotions she kept ignoring reared up and slapped her in the face. This time she didn't push the thoughts away. Maybe it was because of the horror she was witnessing, but whatever the reason, a flood of emotions swept her away.

Since her father died, she'd refused to let anyone close, but that hadn't stopped Nic. While she didn't know how to go forward with him, she knew she didn't want to go backward. Did she have the guts to let Nic in, to let him be her safety net? She'd been balancing alone on the tightrope of life for so damn long, she'd gotten fucking good at it. Jade stopped walking as a thought hit her. She honestly didn't need anyone to be there for her. But... maybe this time her mom's advice wasn't right. Maybe in this instance, she didn't need someone to keep her safe. Maybe this time, she was the one who would take care of Nic. The man was strong and could endure the fallout on his own, of that, there was no doubt. But now, he didn't have to go it alone, did he?

Jade turned, moving off the road to avoid an approaching fire truck. She kept her head down and walked out of the area heading toward the SUV they'd abandoned hours earlier. With each step, her path forward was clearer. It all made sense now. As long as she lived, she would protect Nic, because she cared for him. She didn't understand why, or for that matter how he'd come to mean so much to her, but he did. She'd lay down her life for him. Jade cleared the cordon and started to run.

If the disaster site had been chaotic, the scene that presented itself at the emergency room was unrestrained tumult. Jade tried three different nurses before she found one that could direct her to the person actually trying to process the multitude of patients into the facility. She waited her turn behind distraught family members. Several people were turned away because their loved one had not shown up at this hospital. "Next!" The man bellowed, almost breaking her eardrum.

"Judge Bettina DeMarco." Jade snapped the name.

"Family?" He flipped pages as he spoke.

"No, personal security." She pulled her badge from her belt and damn near stuck the thing up the man's nose. She was wearing a 45-caliber automatic on her shoulder for fuck's sake.

"Yeah, okay. Elevators to the sixth floor. Ask the nurses at the surgical unit. Next!"

Jade was on her way before she heard the person behind her speak. Crowds of people waited for the elevators. Instead of waiting, she pushed through the throng and headed for the stairs. The door banged on the cement wall as she flew past it and took the stairs two at a time. She exited at the sixth floor and took a second to get her bearings. About halfway down the hallway, there was a nurse's station. She headed there at a jog, dodging people who exited the rooms that lined the corridor. She stopped at the desk and waited while the nurse dealt with a husband searching for his wife. A loud voice echoed down the hall. Jade knew that voice. Fucking Carmine DeMarco. She sprinted down the hall and skidded to a stop at an alcove where Nic, Mario, and Carmine stood. Carmine's arm extended out, his finger pointed directly at Nic.

"This is your fucking fault! You were supposed to make sure this shit didn't happen!"

"How the fuck was he supposed to know someone was planting a bomb in the courthouse? Was he supposed to sweep the building? Do you think he would have seen what an entire contingent from the U.S. Marshals Service didn't? You're a fucking idiot!" Jade's snarled retort brought all three sets of eyes toward her.

"You! You were supposed to be this big, badass specialist! Where the fuck were you? Stupid fucking bitch..."

Jade would never know what else Carmine was going to say. Nic had him slammed against the wall, his forearm choking his brother. Carmine's face turned a deep red as he struggled to remove Nic's arm from his windpipe. Jade knew there was no way on God's green earth that was going to happen. Nic was fucking deadly, as his brother was learning—right now.

Nic pushed a little harder, forcing Carmine to stop thrashing against his hold. "You mother-fucker. You can accuse me of anything you want, but you will never say a word against Jade again. Mom was at the courthouse. Jade was off duty. That explosion was not my fault. It was not Jade's fault. The only responsible party is the bastards that planted the bomb, so take your rage and shove it up your ass."

Mario placed a hand on Nic's shoulder. "Hey, come on guys. Mom is in surgery fighting for her life. Don't do this. Not now."

Nic searched his younger brother's expression and then focused back on Carmine. He narrowed his eyes and shook his head. "We're done. Do you understand? I want nothing to do with you. Ever."

"Fine by me, you fucking worthless piece of shit," Carmine spit the words out.

Nic put his weight behind one more savage shove into his brother's neck before he released him. Carmine coughed, bending over to catch his breath. Rigid with barely restrained rage, Nic stepped away and leaned against the wall, his glare fixed on his older brother. Jade had five brothers and two sisters, and she'd never witnessed such a vicious display of anger and resentment between siblings. She walked to Nic after giving Carmine a dismissive look. Whatever was going on between the brothers would have to wait. "How is your mom?"

"She's in surgery. The ward nurse said it could be hours." Nic's eyes still shot daggers at his brother.

"Hey." Jade moved to stand in front of him and moved his chin to bring his eyes to hers. "Let's sit down. We can do a lot while we wait." Jade needed to get his mind off beating the ever-loving shit out of his brother. Besides distracting him, if they started working now, between the two of them, they could acquire intel, and work with their DC counterparts to try to figure this mess out. She lifted up on her toes and kissed Nic. Carmine's snort of disgust behind her didn't matter, but she threw the asshole the bird anyway. *Fucker.* Lowering slowly, she put her hand behind Nic's neck and pulled him down with her. "I'll be here every step of the way." Her voice lowered again. Her next words were meant only for Nic, "I'll be your protection in this storm, lover. Let go. You can drop the act. You're safe with me." She echoed the very words that had sent her running away from him that first night.

Nic straightened and searched her face with a desperation and depth of emotion that would normally terrify her and be the impetus for her to bolt. Not this time. This time she swallowed that fear, and let Nic see the truth of her words. She would be his refuge, protect this man with her life and keep him safe.

He nodded and closed his eyes, pulling her into him. She dropped her arms to his waist and held on to him as tightly as he was holding on to her. In the riot surrounding them, a cocoon of peace blossomed. Jade didn't know how long they stood there holding each other; what she did know was that Nic needed her strength, and she was going to give it to him. Her phone vibrated, breaking the moment.

Nic's arms loosened around her allowing her to grab the phone. "Yeah."

"Hey, any word on Nic's mom?" Jewell's voice came through the line.

"Surgery. What do you know?" Jade motioned toward a row of hard plastic seats on the opposite side of the room from Nic's dickwad brother. Nic moved to sit down, and she followed.

"I'll get the brothers on the line. Hang on."

Jade reached into her pocket and pulled out her earphones. She plugged it into the phone jack and handed one earpiece to Nic. "Jade? How's Nic?" Jared's concerned question boomed through her earbud. She thumbed the volume down while Nic answered.

"I'm here, J." Nic's non-answer carried more poignant emotion than any bullshit he could have lobbed.

"We are working this hard, man," Jared responded.

"I want in." There was no room for argument in his tone.

"I know." Jason's voice cut through the conversation. "I've asked Jacob to pull some specialized resources from overseas. They have a one-time permission to use their skills in the protection of your mom. Unfortunately, it will be at least twenty-four hours before they can reach the states. Once they are online, you can rest assured no one will get close to her."

"Thanks." Nic's hands shook. Jade reached out and threaded her fingers through his. She didn't know if it was rage or worry causing the man to vibrate as if he'd explode, she suspected it was a combination of both.

"What do we know?" Jade asked.

"We have a team inbound to work with the on-scene forces. The consensus is the bomb was inside the facility, but how it got there is unknown. Fifty-seven dead so far. The Mayor has held a press conference and called it an act of terrorism. The President hasn't come online to agree yet. My sources tell me he will within the hour. When that happens, we have more avenues available to us."

Jade knew he meant latitude in searching for and interrogating suspects involved in the bombing. The might of Guardian would rock the Triad. The limits and confines of the normal laws of the nation would not factor into the equation. A declaration of terrorism enabled the Patriot Act and unleashed all the unseen rules, agreements and operations that gave Guardian their well-deserved reputation. Criminals, terrorists, and extremists feared Guardian for a reason.

"Intel is sparse and probably will be until we can find the explosive device—if anything is left of the mechanism. I directed our team to confiscate the courthouse servers so Jewell can reconstruct the video feed. The Mayor has directed NYPD to cede any evidence they collect to us. We can process it faster. Technically, this is a joint operation, but we are the lead organization. It could be hours or days before we have anything to go on. Unfortunately, right now we need to wait." Jared's tone apologized for something he had no control over.

"So we do nothing?" Nicolas spat. His brothers' heads popped up. Jade held up her hand and shook her head, warning them to keep their mouths shut.

"No, you know better than that, man," Jared spoke, low and comforting. "Jewell is running through the traffic cameras. We are scouring them for anything out of the norm. NYPD is pulling in every member of the Triad they can find. They can hold the bastards for 24 hours, and once the President calls this domestic terrorism, we are taking over all interrogations. We will find out something."

Nic drew a huge breath and exhaled it before he spoke again. "Yeah, okay. I know you're doing everything you can. Thanks."

"You've got our direct focus on this case, Nic. When those fuckers decided to target your mom, they messed with our family. We will not rest until they pay." Jason's gravel laced voice rumbled over the phone.

"I appreciate that, Jason."

"You got it, man. We are going to get back to work. Call us with updates on your mom. Do you need anything?" Jared's question brought Jade's eyes to Nic's. He shook his head.

"Not right now. We'll be in touch." Jade replied for them both.

"Take care of our man, Pogo," Jason said before she heard the line click.

Nic pulled his earbud out of his ear. "Pogo?"

Jade shrugged the comment away. "A story for later." Her head tilted slightly toward where Carmine sat staring at them.

"What was that? Who were you talking to?" Carmine demanded from across the room.

"Guardian. We're working the situation." Jade didn't even look at the asshole when she spoke although she knew where he was at all times. He was an annoyance, and she wouldn't give him the courtesy of acknowledging him by looking at him.

They settled back into the chairs, and Jade still held Nic's hand. The contact grounded her and reminded her of the revelation she'd had earlier. She should probably let the man know about her epiphany but now wasn't the time. He had more than enough on his plate. She moved her arm, putting it under his and leaned against his shoulder. She felt him turn and then registered a soft kiss to the top of her head. She closed her eyes. Her brain raced through the events of the day. The horror, the shock, the revelations and the emotions all blended into a muddled replay that looped through her brain.

CHAPTER 19

Nic knew the instant Jade fell asleep. He lifted his arm and pulled her against him, shifting to get comfortable in the hard plastic bucket seats. She woke instantly. "Shhh... rest. One of us is going to need to be able to function." He whispered the comment to her, but Mario must have heard. He peered up and gave a wan smile. Carmine seemed entranced with the scene out the window.

Jade hummed and settled into his chest. He ran his thumb up and down her arm, needing the contact. She'd given him a shelter in the storm today. She'd also told him that she was doing it deliberately. He had no idea how far this affection between them would go, but right now he wasn't going to question it. He needed it, and he needed her.

He watched the shadows lengthen as afternoon encroached on evening. The clock against the wall became a torture device. Every minute that passed without word from the doctors amped up his anxiety. His mom had to survive. He didn't know if he could live with the thought that something he had or hadn't done led to the events of the day. His rational mind told him he'd done everything possible, but he wasn't thinking rationally. His worry and stress made it difficult to think of anything but revenge. He wanted blood. For the first time in his life, he wanted to go outside the laws that he loved and go rogue. The bastards that were responsible for this horrendous act needed to answer to a bullet, not to a jury of their peers. That thought should've repulsed him, but there was nothing the law could do to those bastards that a bullet wouldn't do faster. Fifty-seven lives at last count. He reminded himself he was fortunate to be here, waiting for word on his mom. There were so many families that didn't have this last shred of hope.

Nic heard the squeak of rubber soled shoes coming down to the alcove. The steps were determined and coming quickly. He nudged Jade, and she was awake and sitting up instantly. A man in scrubs stopped in front of them. "DeMarco family."

"That's me," Carmine responded and stood immediately.

Mario gave his brother a look of disgust. "That's all of us." He motioned toward Nic and Jade as he spoke.

The doctor nodded and smiled when he finally looked at Nic. Nic hadn't seen the man in a couple years, but knowing Driscol was operating on his mom lifted about ten pounds of worry off his shoulders. "Nic, good to see you again."

"Is she okay?" Nic shot past any pleasantries.

Driscol took a deep breath and planted his hands on his hips. "I'll give it to you straight. Your mom made it through the surgery. We removed her spleen, repaired a nick to her liver, and removed her gallbladder. We are concerned about crushing damage to her right kidney, but I've done what I could to repair it. I'm praying we won't have to go back in and remove it. Compared to the other injuries coming in, she's lucky. She did well through the procedure, but she is still in critical condition."

"Can I see her?" Carmine grabbed the doctor's arm. The surgeon flashed down at the hold

Carmine had on him. "She's in recovery. Once we get her settled in a room in ICU, we will let you in, one at a time, for a couple minutes each."

Carmine nodded and spun away heading back to his chair. The doctor turned toward Jade and Nic and lowered his voice. "Guardian contacted me when they overheard through radio traffic that the ambulance was bringing her here. We assembled the best team we could find. She has one hell of a long road ahead of her, but I have faith in the skills of the surgical team that operated on her. The next time you talk to Jared, tell him that he and Christian need to come up and visit my husband and me. It's been too long since we've seen them."

Nic nodded and extended his hand. "Thanks, Driscol. I'll let them know."

"Okay, sorry, but I've got to go. We have cases stacked up. I wanted to come out to talk with you personally." The man gave him a brief smile before he spun on his heel and speed walked back from where he'd come.

Jade and Mario turned to look at him, their expressions silently questioning how he knew the doctor. "Driscol's husband is the branch chief of Guardian here in New York."

"Ross Stapleton's married?" Jade asked.

"Yeah, they have been married about as long as Jared and Christian. When Jared came out, Ross felt it was safe enough for him to do the same thing. Those two have been together for a lot longer than that though."

"He sounded like Guardian pulled him in to operate on mom."

Mario crossed his arms and glowered at Carmine.

"Probably. He's the best. Guardian takes care of their own."

"Fuck you. If Guardian was so damn good, our mother wouldn't be laying in that bed."

"You're right asshole, she'd be dead." Mario's retort stopped Nic's angry reply. "Get over yourself and fucking swallow your pride. If Nic and Jade hadn't arranged for her security, she'd have been dead long before this happened." Mario turned his back on Carmine.

Nic leaned against the wall and waited. Jade left in search of a bathroom and coffee. He studied the second hand on the clock for what seemed like the five hundredth time this minute.

"Nic DeMarco?" A female voice brought him out of his inactive stupor.

KRIS MICHAELS

"Here." Nic lifted off the wall.

"Doctor Stapleton asked me to bring you up to ICU. Your mom is in a room, and we can let you see her for a few moments."

Jade walked in behind the woman with a tray of coffees. "If you would all follow me?"

Nic fell into step behind the nurse. Carmine elbowed his way up to her and demanded information. The nurse expertly deflected all his questions, which only seemed to infuriate the man further. When they reached the small waiting room, there were several other clusters of families sitting in the chairs. "Okay, one at a time, who's first?"

Carmine headed toward the door without comment or waiting. The nurse shook her head and followed him, swiping her badge to gain access to the ward.

"Why does he hate you?" Jade handed him a coffee. He took a sip of the hot liquid and shook his head. "Long story and I honestly don't want to get into it here." He peered down at her and pushed a small smile across his face.

She peered up at him and lifted onto her toes. They shared a brief kiss. He breathed her in as she pulled away.

"She'll be okay. She won't check out until all of

296

you are married, and she has a bunch of grandba-
bies." Jade leaned into him, and he held her,
reaching for the comfort she provided.

Nic held his mother's fragile hand in his. She
looked so much older now. The pallor of her skin
combined with the massive bruising and cuts that
littered her features accentuated her sixty plus
years. His resolve to catch whoever did this to her
grew into a fortress of intense hatred. He would
have his pound of flesh, and he'd make sure the
motherfuckers paid. A nurse cleared her throat
behind him signaling his time was up. Nic nodded
his understanding. He leaned over and kissed his
mom. "I'm going to catch the bastards. I love you,
Ma. Be strong."

He straightened and headed out of the ward
noticing two NYPD officers at the door. Jade was
waiting for him as he exited.

"For mom?"

"Yep, until a Guardian Detail can get here." She
fell into step with him. He didn't break stride as he
hit the door to the stairs. They exited in the emergency room that was still reeling from the impacts

of the explosion. Jade pointed to the SUV, and they moved with purposeful intent.

"Where to?" She pulled the keys out of her pocket.

"Branch headquarters. I want to know what they know." Jade jumped into the driver's seat, pulled out her phone, and was tapping away at the screen as she pulled into traffic. Nic let her drive. His mind was reeling, his thoughts so convoluted that he didn't give a shit she was texting while driving in New York City traffic. With his mother out of surgery, he could switch his focus to catching the bastards who'd planted the explosive device.

They entered the downtown office building after parking in a secure underground area. The process of getting through security had never been more infuriating, even though they were expedited into Ross Stapleton's office.

"Nic, Jade, come in. We are over here in the conference room." Ross turned on his heel and headed back to the epicenter of Guardian's New York response to the event. There were four video screens up and running. Two were playing feeds of what appeared to be a fast forward search of the surveillance footage from inside the courthouse.

"What is this?" Nic pointed to the screen.

"DC is running the videos. We are monitoring. CCS has been shifting through the last weeks' worth of video. What we are focusing on is this." Ross pointed to the screen at the far right of the room. Nic and Jade moved closer.

"What am I looking at, Ross?" Nic hoped like hell it was what he thought it was.

"This is a piece, the majority actually, of the explosive device. The building collapsed and folded like a deck of cards. The walls fell but are holding each other up at weird angles. The fire department, in an effort to keep the upper levels safe while they are evacuating, recovering the victims and clearing the building, started placing hydraulic lifts to hold the rubble up. They stumbled across this. We only have pictures right now, as you can see, the majority of the device seems to be surrounded by material. If that rubble shifts, it will bring down that section of the building. They are taking it slow and being very cautious. I don't know when we will get the physical evidence. If ever."

"If we can retrieve the device, we might be able to track the explosives or the maker." Jade acknowledged the hope that everyone else seemed to pin on the device.

Nic bounced his eyes toward the other screens that were still processing the security footage. "What have you gotten from the Marshals?"

Ross tossed down the remote for the video screen and made his way around the stacks of paperwork on the table. "We have sign in logs of all personnel going into and out of the facility after hours. My guys are running these to ground for the last seventy-two hours. The likelihood of the device being planted before that time would be slim. We will start there and work backward if need be. They are getting statements from all of their people, and we will be courtesy copied on all of them. NYPD is interviewing the survivors looking for anyone who was outside the facility before the bomb exploded. They've also been given permission to haul in every known Triad member they can find. The President declared this a domestic terrorist event. Thank God, because that unhandcuffed us."

"So we are dormant on responses until we get information from the ongoing investigation." Jade's statement put a nail in the conversation and hammered it closed. Succinct and to the point.

"Yeah. We are going after every possible avenue and working every angle, but until they recover that device and we start to get actionable intel, we are in stasis." Ross turned, looking at the detritus of the information and work they'd compiled to this point.

"Were you able to get the things I needed?" Nic blinked and damn near popped his neck whipping his head toward Jade. What had she requested? She hadn't said a damn thing to him the entire ride.

"Yeah. Downstairs. You'll be left alone." Ross turned back to the video screens.

"Great. Come on, Nic. We have work to do." Nic held up a hand. Whatever Jade had planned could wait for a second. "Driscol performed surgery on my mom today. I can't tell you how much it meant to me, personally, that he'd take on her case. I'd like to do something for him. Is there something I could get him? A pastime he enjoys or something that he'd appreciate?"

A smile spread across Ross' features. His eyes grew soft, and he visibly relaxed at the mention of his husband's name. "Yeah, he's into bonsai trees. We have about ten of them. He zones out and gets his Zen on when he does his manicure thing."

"Great. Please let him know how much it meant

to me." Nic knew the man's reputation, and he knew that his mom was under the best care possible.

"I will. I'll text or call as soon as we get anything." Ross turned back to the paperwork on the table and sat down.

Nic turned his attention to Jade. She crooked her finger beckoning him to follow. He put one foot in front of the other. He was braindead, and he was pissed off. He wanted to kill something. With each step he took away from Ross Stapleton's office, the need to lash out at the universe filled him. Jade hit the stairs, and they descended. She pulled up outside the fire door to the gym level. "We are going to go in, gear up and work out. You need to vent, and you can do it here, safely. It's either this or I'll go find Carmine, and you can beat the shit out of him."

An involuntary huff of laughter escaped. Jade understood what he needed. Nic rolled his shoulders. The tension of the day had formed a granite knot between his shoulder blades. "As much as I'd enjoy taking his ass down a few pegs, I think a heavy bag may be a better answer."

"Awesome. There should be workout clothes laid out for you in the locker room. I'll gear up, and after you work out some frustration on the bag, we'll spar. I want you completely exhausted so you can sleep. If you're anything like me, your mind is racing. You're pissed, and you want blood. I've found exhaustion and then oblivious sleep for four or five hours will take the edge off that."

He watched her as she strode toward the women's locker room and shook his head. Even with everything that was swirling around him, he could recognize the fact the woman was one in a million. He started disrobing as he walked to the locker room. Her words from earlier echoed through his mind. She was giving him a safe place to deal with the crisis. She understood the magnitude of the situation, not only for his family but for the city. He wondered how many women in the world would be able to walk down this road beside him. He unbuttoned his shirt and stopped midway. One. Exactly one woman would be able to walk beside him. His attention focused on the door to the gym. His heart shifted with that thought, locking the threads of feelings into ropes of reality. The wild, incorrigible, irreverent, and slightly insane woman had poured her essence around him when life threatened to break him apart. She'd kept him sane, given him an anchor and kept his focus where it needed to be and he... fuck, he loved her.

"Hey, get your ass out here, DeMarco! I'm going to wipe the mat with you!" Jade called from the gymnasium area.

Yeah, one in a million. Fuck. She'd run scared if she had a clue how much he cared for her. He threw on a Guardian t-shirt and hurried to finish changing. It wasn't as if he could act on this emotion. That was a worry for another day.

CHAPTER 20

J ade hurt in every muscle, joint, and bone in her body. Breathing took all her energy and standing was fucking hard. They'd taken turns letting out their frustration on the heavy bag. Holding it steady for Nic while he pounded out the rage he had bottled up inside him was a workout in and of itself. But, they both needed to work themselves to exhaustion, so she'd challenged him in the ring. Lord above, the man was fucking amazing. His stance was perfect and everything she threw at him, he countered and defended with a precision she'd not seen since her sensei had retired. She peered at the clock on the wall. Fuck, they'd been at it for almost an hour now.

Jade lifted a finger toward him, the universal

sign for him to give her a moment. She bent over in the middle of the ring. Her hair dripped sweat onto the blue mat making it darker. The light gray of her Guardian issued t-shirt and shorts had long since turned a dark sweat-soaked gray and clung to her like a second skin. She could feel rivulets of sweat dripping down the backs of her legs. To say she was through would be an understatement, but she wasn't going to quit until Nic was finished. Nope, it wasn't going to fucking happen. She lifted her head and looked at him. He was leaning against the top rope, staring at her.

"Going to call it?" His question sent a red cape flapping in front of her eyes.

"Hell no." She stood straight and dropped into her fighting stance bouncing on the balls of her feet. She was sucking wind right now because she didn't have the proper cardio conditioning after her year undercover, but she'd find the reserves... somewhere.

"Are you sure?" He lifted off the rope and took two steps toward her. "You're tired. You're going to make a mistake."

"Fuck you, DeMarco. Bring it." Jade knew he was right, but she'd never admit it.

"Such sweet words from my woman." Nic

bounced on his toes and shuffled side to side far easier than she could. Jade sneered at him. The asshole was showing off.

"Just as a point of clarification, this woman is going to kick your ass." She lunged forward and to the right, only to pivot, drop and sweep with her dominant leg. A move she had never shown Nic. She felt her calf connect with his legs and felt the mat bounce when his weight slammed down. The loud push of air from his lungs reminded her of an old bellows her mom and dad had for the fireplace when she was younger. A low-pitched tone over-rode the fast rush of air.

Jade pushed off on her anchor leg and vaulted over Nic landing with all her weight on his stomach. He curled up and groaned at the impact. "Whoops. I'm sorry, Nic. Am I too heavy for you?" She sat up and straddled him. She threw back her head and laughed with abandon at her success.

Jade felt the world rotate before she recognized the pin move that Nic employed. Her hair splatted against the mat and she wheezed a long "heee" as the air in her lungs fled upon contact with the mat. Nic appeared over her. "No. You're not too heavy. But we are done here for today. Neither one of us will be able to drive if we keep going." Nic dropped his weight on top of her covering her like a blanket.

"Get... off... not... driving... uggg... move!" Jade panted the response and pushed ineffectively at him. Nic lifted far enough that he could flip onto his back. Their legs tangled together as they looked up at the fluorescent lighting and black painted air ducts that crisscrossed the twenty-foot high ceiling.

"Asshole." Jade made a vain attempt at sending a backhand his way. It failed miserably.

"Fuck. Maybe we can get one of Ross' people to drive us. I'm not going to be able to lift my arms."

A little satisfaction settled in when she noted Nic was panting as much as she was. The asshole must have been putting on a front. Cocky bastard. They lay there for several long seconds, both panting and trying to recover.

Jade could finally spare some air for something other than staying alive. "I talked to Stapleton. We can use the apartment they keep for protective custody residents."

Nic rolled his head toward her, so she followed suit and looked at him. She chuckled at the physical exhaustion she witnessed. Nic was a solid mess, and Jade didn't doubt that she was a wreck, too. He licked his lips before he spoke. Her eyes followed the action because, damn, his lips were fucking sexy.

"Sweet. Where is it?"

"Where's what?" What were they talking about again? Her mind had launched into all the things those lips could do to her; she had no clue what the conversation was about.

"The apartment. The one we can use." Nic flopped his hand off his stomach, and it landed on top of hers. Their fingers threaded together in a natural movement.

"Oh. The tenth floor." She pointed toward the ceiling with the hand that wasn't linked with his.

"Fuck."

"Yeah, I didn't think about the walk back up." Jade tipped her head toward him again. "Wanna sleep here tonight?"

"We could, but I need a fucking shower." Nic wrinkled his nose and sniffed. "So do you."

"Bullshit, I smell like roses." Jade lifted her hand and waved it over her body motioning it toward Nic. "See, roses."

"Roses dipped in shit." He rolled up to a sitting position and pulled on their joined hands. "Come on. We'll support each other on the way up and share the shower. We might remain standing that way."

Jade sat up and leaned into him with her shoulder. "If you got any energy left after that workout, big boy, I'll do something to make sure we both have sweet dreams." She lifted her lips to his for a kiss but backed away almost immediately. "Damn, you do need a shower!" She popped to her feet as Nic lunged after her. The uncharacteristic squeal that emanated from her echoed through the empty gym. She laughed as he surged up and tried to grab her. "No way! Shower. First one to the apartment picks how the orgasms are going to happen."

She slid through the ropes and grabbed her cell, weapons and credential holder off the edge of the mat before she sprinted to the door. Although if the truth was told, it was more like a fast walk. Nic grabbed his cell, wallet, and weapon, and caught her before she hit the exit bar on the door. He pushed it down and opened it for her. "I don't suppose you thought about our clothes?" They both started the long haul up the ten flights of stairs to the apartment.

"Yep. They'll gather our clothes and any other belongings from the gym when I tell them we've cleared out. I asked Ross to send a runner to the house to get a new suit for you and a change of clothes for me."

"Is there anything you haven't thought about?" Nic's eyes shot to her.

She shrugged. "Jewell or one of her people is going to call the hospital every half hour. If there is any change, both of us will get a call. I asked that they stock the apartment with food and water."

Hell, Jason knew what she was trying to do to take care of Nic, and unless they recovered the detonation device, discovered something useful, or they got a massive break in the case, they wouldn't be bothered until morning.

"I have it covered." She glared at the painted numeral "1" on the door and groaned internally. "You can check in with Mario before we shower, but like I said, Guardian has the nurse's station on speed dial, and we will know if anything changes in your mom's condition. The same goes for the case."

Nic stopped on a landing between the second and third floor, pausing her progression with a hand to her forearm. "You did all of that on the drive from the hospital?"

She shook her head and motioned up the stairs. They plodded up as she answered. "I arranged the monitoring for your mom at the hospital when you were in ICU with her. I started lining up the apartment and things on the way here."

He stopped her again. She was two steps above him and looked down at him slightly. "Thank you." His eyes locked with hers and Jade pulled a sharp breath. The emotion that swirled in those eyes ran deep. Jade got what he was saying. She'd be hard pressed to acknowledge the acts of others if she was in his position. A smile tugged at the corner of her mouth. She wanted him in a position all right, but on the concrete stairs wasn't the one she was thinking about. Although…

Nic laughed. The warm, rich sound filled the stairwell. "I saw the exact moment you started thinking about sex." He pulled her in, kissing her hard and fast. He released her suddenly and grabbed her hand. "Let's see if we can do something about those thoughts." He yanked her arm as he took off up the stairs. Score! The man recovers quickly and has stamina!

Jade stepped out of the miniscule bathroom wrapped in one towel while drying her hair with another. Nic had decided to check in with his brother when they realized two people in the tiny bathroom was an invitation for an injury. He glanced over at her and did a double take. He winked and looked back down at the flooring as he spoke. From the sounds of his conversation, he was still talking to Mario. Jade dropped the towel she was using to dry her hair and retrieved a comb from the small vanity before she sat cross-legged on the bed working the teeth through the tangles. Nic finished his call, and the bed dipped next to her. "Ewww... no! Go shower!" Jade pushed him away from her laughing.

He pulled her towel off her and stood up. "I needed a towel." He stood staring at her, now naked on the bed.

"Shower." Jade pointed to the bathroom. He nodded, not moving other than the north south movement of his head.

"Nic, the sooner you shower, the sooner I promise you a mind-altering orgasm." She stretched out on the bed and flipped her wet hair behind her. The man's eyes traveled from her feet upwards. When his visual perusal reached her face, she lifted her fingertips to her mouth and licked them. His eyebrow lifted, and Jade lowered her fingers to her nipple. She circled the tip with her fingers and then pinched it slightly, allowing a gasp to float from her throat. Nic swallowed and shook himself out of his trance.

"Fuck, shower. Yeah... I'll be right back." He stripped his shirt off and dropped it on the floor. His shorts were off before he hit the bathroom door. Jade craned her neck to see that fantastic ass as he turned on the shower and jumped in without testing the water temperature. Brave man. She sat up and ran the comb through her hair quickly and efficiently. Just as she finished braiding her hair, the shower stopped. Nic emerged into the bedroom, dripping wet and heading her way.

Jade had never seen such a predatory look in his eyes before. It sent a thrill through her. She leaned back and attempted to push up toward the headboard. Nic pounced and grabbed her ankle pulling her down the bed and underneath him. He grabbed the other ankle and lifted it to his mouth, kissing the inside and slowly worked his way up to her knee. His fingers and tongue assaulted her skin in a delicate dance that awakened every nerve in her body. He repeated the cascade of sensation on her other leg. Jade's fists clenched at the bedspread under her. What he was doing wasn't typical for them. Jade knew that was her fault. Most of the time she'd demanded hard, fast sex. Sex where she didn't have time to think about the emotions that the intimacy produced. Now, things were different. Nic had deliberately slowed the pace, and Jade felt the swell of emotions flowing from him to her. The slow, deliberate possessiveness and tenderness that punctuated his caresses and kisses lifted the sexual act to a different level. Jade grasped his hand and pulled him down between her legs. The small drops of cold water that still clung to him did little to temper the fire that he'd ignited within her body. His hands worshiped her, his mouth explored her body and his eyes... his eyes expressed the depth of emotion he was feeling. Jade clung transfixed to the wellspring of validation in his gaze. She knew without saying the words that he cared for her on a level that neither of them had dared expose. The stone façade that she'd built around her heart crumbled silently with each emotion-laden kiss. Her well-crafted, honed defenses disintegrated with each look of need, longing, and perhaps even love. Jade couldn't put a label on what they were feeling. They were both too exposed, raw and vulnerable now to do anything other than experience the sensations and hold each other.

Their lovemaking became a gentler version of their past encounters—a shadow of the energy, but a blinding ray of hope and promise. When Nic entered her, she clung to his shoulders keeping them pressed together. Not because of the need to feel him so completely, although that was there, but because she didn't want him to see her cry. Big, full crocodile tears washed down her cheeks, taking with them the space and distance that she'd put between Nic and herself.

"Shhh... I've got you, babe. We're safe, together." Nic's words pierced through her own thoughts. His thumbs wiped away her tears and his lips sealed his promise. Jade's orgasm shattered through her. The electric current lit her core on fire in a thunderous clap of sensation. She arched against him, involuntarily tightening every muscle in her body as she climaxed. She felt him thrust deep inside her and release. He groaned against her neck, holding himself off her. Jade shivered. An involuntary reaction to the orgasm that was still sending jolts of electricity through her nerves. She collapsed, completely sated and emotionally drained. She turned her head and kissed his throat before reality smashed her bliss into a billion pieces. "Fuck! Did you use a condom?" Jade slapped Nic's shoulder. She'd never had unprotected sex before and she sure as hell wasn't on the pill. Her mind spiraled down a massive dark hole in less than a second.

Nic lifted his head. "Of course I did. Do you think I would have taken that decision away from you?"

Jade dropped her head and patted the shoulder she'd just assaulted. "I don't remember you putting one on."

"Thank you." Nic dropped and kissed her softly.

"Ummm... you're welcome?" She literally had no idea why he was thanking her. Unless it was the fucking amazing sex, and he did not have to thank her for that. Like ever.

"I'll take it as a compliment. You didn't notice me suiting up because I wrecked you with my awesome foreplay. I'll take it." Nic laughed and pulled out of her rolling onto his back and taking care of the condom.

"Hell, yeah. That was like a fifteen on a scale of one to ten." She tucked into his side when he lifted his arm for her.

"Thank you, for being there for me today." Nic's chest rumbled under her ear.

Jade yawned as her body relaxed against his warmth. "I don't think you have to thank me. I'm pretty sure that's what people in relationships are supposed to do, but since I've never been in one before, I may be wrong."

Nic's fingertips traveled in a lazy pattern over her arm. The small rhythmic action was hypnotic. Jade's eyes closed against her will to keep them open. She lifted her arm and draped it over his muscled stomach.

"I've never been in a relationship either. You matter to me. I've never felt this way before." His voice was low and soft.

Jade couldn't open her eyes. There wasn't enough energy left in her body. She managed to whisper, "I care about you too, Nic. It scares me how much I care." She slipped into that state of almost falling asleep, the perfect comfort before the restorative darkness enveloped her. Her last conscious thought was that maybe, just maybe what she felt was love.

CHAPTER 21

Nic woke to the sound of a cell phone vibrating. He flopped to his back and swatted his nightstand to grab it. Pain shot through his wrist. What the fuck?

"What?" Jade sprung up in the bed, her automatic in her hand, pointing it at the door. She was naked except for the sheet that pooled around her hips. Nic rubbed his wrist and tried to focus his eyes. "Nothing, I hit my wrist on the light." His phone vibrated again. He grabbed it and swiped the face.

"DeMarco." He blinked his attention back to Jade. She released her grip on her weapon engaging the safety before she scratched her cheek with the gun barrel. The woman was a hot mess.

"Nic, it's Jared. We got a call from the ICU. It's your mom."

Nic jumped from the bed. "What? Is she all right?"

"No, my brother. A pulmonary embolism took her about ten minutes ago. It was sudden and unexpected. I'm sorry. I didn't want you to find out from a stranger."

Nic fell back, sitting down hard on the mattress. She was gone. He'd lost one of the biggest presences in his life. He cleared his throat. "All right. I'll call Mario and Carmine." He pushed end on the call.

"Nic?" Jade's soft voice behind him jarred him.

He sent her a quick look. "Mom's gone. Pulmonary embolism."

"I'm so sorry…"

Nic held up his hand and shook his head. "I know. I get it, I do, but don't. Please don't. I can't handle sympathy right now. I need to make some phone calls, and I need to find the fuckers who did this. Just help me find those… Please, just… I need a fucking minute." All the helpless rage he felt blasted out at her with his explosion of words. He knew it wasn't fair, but God help him, he couldn't have stopped the onslaught if he'd tried. He pulled long hard breaths and stared at the floor in front of him. He heard her moving around the bedroom and then heard the bathroom door close. He swiped the face of his phone and dialed Mario. The phone rang twice before his little brother answered, "Hello?"

"Mario. She's gone. Ma died of a pulmonary embolism. I just got the call." Nic's voice cracked as he spoke.

"No," Mario whispered the word that kept repeating over and over in Nic's brain.

"When?"

"I got the call a minute ago."

"Carmine?"

"I'm calling him next."

"What do we do now?" Mario sounded as lost as he felt.

"We take care of Mom's arrangements. I'll meet you at the hospital. Then I find the fuckers who did this, and I take them out." Nic spoke with the venom he felt coursing through his veins. He would find out who ordered this, who committed the act, and all those in between. He'd take down the entire organization. They had no idea the wrath that would rain down on them.

"Okay." Mario's voice echoed the determination

in his. "Yeah. I'm heading there now. Nico, you got to promise me you'll find these fuckers. Find them and make them pay." Mario's voice faltered. Nic could hear the man's muffled sob. Tears filled his eyes, but he blinked them away. He'd grieve later. After he'd found the vengeance he craved. The line disconnected. Nic nodded and punched in Carmine's number.

"What?"

"Mom died. Pulmonary embolism. Call Mario. He needs you to take care of him."

"Motherfucker!" Carmine's venom spewed across the airspace. "You better find out who did this."

"Call Mario." Nic ended the call and looked around the room. The bathroom door was open, but Jade was nowhere to be seen. He looked out in the front room. His suit hung on the back of the door. He pulled the damn thing down. First things first. His mother's arrangements. Then he'd find and kill the bastards responsible.

Five hours later, Nic stalked into Guardian's New York offices. His head ached from suppressing the emotions he'd dealt with today. He arrived at the hospital first. A nurse walked him to the morgue in the basement of the facility. They allowed him to sit with his mom and say goodbye, but Nic had no idea how to do that. She'd been his only parent and his divining rod of right and wrong. He'd grown up with her at the center of his life, and now there was a huge gaping hole where she should still be. Larger than life, vibrant and filled with joy. Not the shell that was lying on the cold stainless steel table. When his brothers arrived, he let them lead as far as arrangements were concerned. They took over, and he stood back. Nic couldn't deal with the million small decisions about the funeral or his mom's last wishes. He steadfastly refused to face any of the emotions that were bottled up inside of him until he'd found the people responsible for her death. Nic glared at the slow ass elevator display as if by his will alone it would reach Stapleton's floor faster.

Ross met him as the door opened. He directed Nic to a small office off to the side and closed the door. "I'm sorry for your loss, Nic. Driscol wasn't at the hospital when she passed, but he told me there was nothing anyone could have done."

"Yeah, thanks. I get that. The staff at the

hospital did everything they could for my mom. The people responsible for this are the bastards who blew up the courthouse." Nic moved to open the door, but Ross put his hand on Nic's arm, stilling him.

"Jason called. He wants you to hold off on the case..." Ross stared him straight in the eyes as he said the words.

"Excuse me?" Nic could not have heard that correctly.

"He said he needed to ensure..."

"Ensure what? That I'm not going to kill the bastards that did this?" Nic clenched his teeth. "You know what, never mind. I need a phone. Now." He ground out the words.

"Okaaay... Let's just settle down, Nic. Jason and Jared should be here within the hour. There has been some movement on the device. Things are starting to shake loose. Listen, I can't get into the specifics yet because it is still highly speculative. My office is available to you until the big man arrives. He should be here anytime. They landed about thirty minutes ago."

Nic stared up at the ceiling trying to control his anger. How dare they try to pull him off this case? It was a slap in the fucking face. Every single King had been on the response team when Jade was in danger. His mother's murderer, hell the murderer of over sixty people was on the loose. Fucking fate owed him the right to go after the bastard. He lowered his eyes and glared at Stapleton. "Get out of my way."

"Nic, man. Please don't do this. I know you're hurting. I fucking get that this seems like bullshit, but Jason was explicit. You were not to get any information on the case until he arrived. He'd hoped to be here before you came back."

"Where's Jade?" He hadn't seen or heard from her since this morning.

"She's gone. Left this morning. She left a..."

Nic lost it. The idea that she'd bail on him at a time like this threw gasoline on a raging forest fire. "Get... the... fuck... out... of... my... way." Nic was so enraged his body shook. Jade was gone. Gone! Whatever fucked up version of a double standard Jason was employing wasn't going to stop him. He had contacts in the city. If the bastards wouldn't give him the information he needed, he'd find it another way. Nic shoved Ross out of the way, slammed open the stairway door, and pounded down the steps, past the security checkpoint. Four blocks away from the office building, lost among the throngs of New Yorkers hell bent on getting from point 'A' to point 'B,' his cell vibrated. He stopped and swiped the face but didn't say a word.

"Nic, man, what the fuck? Ross said you stormed out of here minutes before we arrived." Jared's voice came over the phone.

"You can't be serious? Aren't you supposed to be my best friend? What a fucking joke. Your sister bailed on me too."

"I am your friend. Wait, Jade did what?"

"You know what? Fuck you, man." Nic's grip on the phone tightened.

"What? Nic, this is not what you think. Jade is following a lead on the bomb maker. She left you a fucking note, which Ross tried to tell you about, but you wouldn't listen. Jason and I wanted to brief you on the case personally. Shit is moving hard and fast. We thought for sure we would be here before you arrived and asked Ross not to tell you anything so you wouldn't run off half-cocked. Like you just fucking did!"

Nic kept the phone to his ear and looked up at the small patch of blue sky he could see. He drew a deep breath and blew it out. Jared was still on the line, he could hear voices in the background. Thankfully, he was letting Nic wrestle with his thoughts. "Give me an hour." He needed to find a quiet corner and process. He owed that to himself, to his coworkers and to his friends.

"See you then, and Nic?" Jared's voice had returned to a normal volume, no longer shouting to get his attention.

"Yeah?" Nic dropped his eyes to street level and found a small bistro. He headed toward the establishment and prayed for a quiet corner and a cup of coffee that he could nurse while he pulled himself together.

"Things are moving fast. Take your hour and then get back here. We need you to be involved in what is going down."

Nic nodded and disconnected the line. His head ached, his eyes burned, and he felt... so fucking empty. He pushed open the door to the small bistro and headed to the farthest unoccupied table. The waiter appeared, and he ordered a coffee. Nic folded his hands in front of him and drew a deep breath. He'd been running on emotions since Jared had called this morning. Grief, anger, and frustration fueled his short-tempered outburst while he was in Ross' office. Nic shook his head and closed his eyes. He was better than that. His mother deserved better than what he'd displayed. At the sound of his coffee cup being set down at the table, he opened his eyes. The waiter asked if he needed anything else. Yeah, he needed the day to have never happened. Nic shook his head, handed the man a hundred dollar bill, and told him to keep the change. He hoped the tip would keep the waiter happy and him isolated.

Nic dropped his forehead into his hand and stared at the swirling steam as it lifted off the coffee. He'd lost his fucking mind. He was a cop and a damn good one. He knew how to handle stress. Hell, he'd lived inside a constant pressure cooker since taking the job at Guardian. Yet, he felt unanchored and adrift. He recalled the most recent conversation he'd had with his mom. She couldn't be gone. She was the steady, unshakable constant in his life. Nic huffed out a lungful of air. Yeah, she was a constant. A constant pest and a constant irritation. But she'd always given him her unconditional love, and he was lucky to have had her in his life. Man, was she ever involved in his life? The daily phone calls and the repeated questions asking when she was going to be a grandma. Lord, the woman could nag a dead horse into walking ten miles. Nic shook his head. He was going to miss that nosey busybody. A single tear fell to the white paper that covered the small wooden table. Nic watched the wetness absorb into the parchment.

His cell vibrated beside his coffee cup. He glanced at the face and then up at the window to the street. The evening had started to cast a cloak of darkness around the city. How long had he been sitting here? He got up and headed toward the door answering the phone as he strode out onto the busy street. "Hello?"

"Are you okay?" Jade's voice pulled at him through the airwaves.

"No." He couldn't come up with any other answer.

"Where are you?"

"Heading back to Ross' office. I needed time to…" What the fuck was it that he needed to do? Accept the fact that his mom was gone?

"You needed some time to yourself. I get that. Have you been briefed on what's going on?" He heard several male voices in the background.

"No, I left before Jason and Jared got there. Where are you?" He crossed the street with about a hundred other people and fought through the throng of homeward bound office workers going the other way. Getting anywhere when the office buildings let out for the evening reminded him of moving like a fish upstream.

"What? Yeah, okay, I'll be right there." Jade's comment was barely audible. She was clearly not talking to him when she spoke. "Nic, I've got to go. Get Jared and Jason to bring you up to speed. You need to be in on this." Jade hung up before he could say another word.

Nic crossed the street again and headed north. He could see the façade of the Guardian building and lengthened his stride.

Nic headed to Ross' office as soon as he processed through security. He had an apology to give. He caught Ross leaving the conference room. "Ross, I need to apologize."

"No, you don't, man. I can't imagine the shit you've been through today. We are solid. Get in there. The operation is building faster than we anticipated."

Nic dropped his hand on the man's shoulder and gave it a squeeze. He didn't deserve to be let off the hook for losing his shit, but today, he'd take it. He opened the door to the conference room, and every eye spun toward him.

Jared moved around the table and wrapped him in a bear hug. "I'm so sorry about your Mom. We

got you. You're family. When you hurt, we all hurt."
Nic let himself relax a bit.

He pulled out of the embrace and sucked a deep
breath. Breathing was hard today. It seemed like he
needed to remind himself to do it more often than
not. He nodded at Jared because the lump that
formed in his throat at Jared's words eliminated
the option of talking. He looked toward the
screens and then to Jason who was on the phone.

"What do you have?" He cleared his throat but
didn't repeat the words. Thank God, Jared
understood.

"A metric shit-ton of information and our
response. Some of this is going to be hard to take
in, but operationally, it is fucking brilliant. Jason's
strategy comes from so far out of left field that the
Triad will never know what happened. Sit down
over here. I'll get your tablet."

CHAPTER 22

J ade headed into the crammed conference room. The FBI, NYPD and the Marshals had formed an impromptu taskforce, and she was the sole Guardian representative. The two minutes she grabbed to call Nic had been the only free time they'd had all day. That didn't mean she hadn't thought about him. God, her heart bled for the man. That phone call this morning tore the scar tissue off her own ancient wounds. She knew what Nic was going through. The fact that he didn't want her around when he was going through it? That hurt a bit more than she wanted to admit.

Lieutenant Flowers from the NYPD Gangland Task Force spoke loudly, cutting through several side conversations that were going on. "Okay, we got word that the operation started by Guardian this morning has been given the official blessing. As of this minute, we are a federally recognized task force, and we have access to all of Guardian's nice new toys, the FBI's intel, and the Marshals' particular brand of crazy. Aren't we all just lucky motherfuckers?" The LT searched the room, and his eyes landed on her. "We have one of Guardian's finest with us today. The CEO of that organization indicated anything we needed we would have. It's about fucking time."

Jade cocked her eyebrow at the big man at the head of the table. He dropped a folder onto the table and leaned back against the wall mounted chalkboard. Jade had observed the men in the room for most of the day. Each of them was sharp, a few were complete assholes, but they all seemed to know what the fuck they were doing. She'd kept to herself, taking in the information and theories the men were tossing around. No one asked for her input although several had tried to hit on her. The icy stare of death she'd perfected over the years backed those assholes up and shut them down. She answered direct questions and worked damn hard to put the puzzle pieces together. There was so much information, or rather, misinforma-tion and supposition floating around the room, that she could gag on it.

"Kelso shut that fucking door." Flowers nodded to the door at the side of the room. The man reached back and slammed the door shut with a resounding thud. "Every last one of you mother-fuckers, take out your cell phones and turn them off."

"Say what?" One of the FBI agents popped off the question.

"What I'm going to say is that important. Turn your fucking cell off or get the fuck out. My Task Force, my rules."

Jade turned off her cell while she watched the Fibbies squirm. After an intense stare-down, they eventually turned off their phones. "Well now that we've measured each other's dicks, can we get started?" Lt Flowers drawled.

Jade chuckled, drawing all their eyes toward her. She lifted her hands and shook her head. "Y'all go ahead and whip them out anytime you want, but as for me, I want to know what the fuck is going on."

"Guardian has contained the information of Judge DeMarco's death. They still have her listed as stable. In fifteen minutes, an ambulance and guarded motorcade will take a patient from the hospital where she was treated to a private facility. Guardian has cleared the facility, and only law enforcement remains as 'staff.' As I speak, a press release about Judge DeMarco's condition and location is going out to all the press agencies. The goal is to draw the Triad into a trap."

"Yeah, that's nice, great thing Guardian has the resources, but there are so many holes in that plan, I need at least ten more fingers to plug the ones I see." That came from one of the Fibbies. Jade swung her head toward the man.

"So let's hear your objections." Flowers leaned back again. The relaxed tone of his voice didn't make it to the tense way the man held himself.

"We don't know the Triad actually tried to take out the judge. Anyone in that courthouse could have been the target." The man's ruddy red cheeks turned almost purple as he spoke.

"She was the only one with an active death threat against her. The other cases, while felonies, were not RICO cases. The Marshals that were in the courtroom indicated the bastard that was on trial made it a point to turn and look at the clock, turn back to Judge DeMarco, smile and then get under the fucking table seconds before the bomb blew."

"Granted, but that doesn't mean they will go after her again. They got what they wanted. They will have a mistrial." That came from an NYPD detective that Jade had been watching all day. He was a big guy. He had long brown hair, a beard, wore a black t-shirt with a pack of cigarettes in the pocket, jeans, black lace up combat boots and had a black leather jacket slung over his chair. Sexy and Dangerous.

"We have an informant who told us the Triad was making a statement. The explosion, even if it took out the defendant, was intended to kill Judge DeMarco. The real message is that woman dying." Flowers flopped open the folder.

"The informant suddenly showed up? That shit does not compute, LT. Why kill her? They could tie this up in the court system forever. They don't need to take her out." Sexy and dangerous leaned forward as he spoke.

"The informant is Carrillo's partner." The LT shot the detective a look.

The man leaned back and dropped his pen. "Jia confirmed the judge was the target?" The big guy's face went pale underneath his beard. His voice had an audible tremor.

"She did."

"When?"

"This morning."

"She's still alive." The bulky, bearded man dropped his eyes. Jade's mind made the leap. This Jia person was undercover, and there was a history. An unwanted thought floated through her mind. What would it have been like to have someone special waiting for her while she was undercover?

She studied the detective again before one of the Marshals she'd worked with on and off during Nic's mom's case spoke, "You know, Judge DeMarco stared that Triad scum in the face and told him she wasn't afraid of him or his minions. That was right before she started jury selection. It was only the lawyers and the defendant present with us. She point-blank told him that he was no different from any other man and he was not above the law. She dared him to prove her wrong." He turned his attention to Jade who blinked in surprise. They hadn't told her about Judge DeMarco taunting the asshole on trial. "It wasn't anything unusual for her. She was hell-fire and brimstone on that bench, and she wasn't going to be intimidated. I've worked in the court system for years. Judge DeMarco was the target. Guaranteed."

Jade cleared her throat, and all eyes swiveled her way. "Enough on the background. We understand your intel is credible. Why are we going on with the charade, and who is sitting on the two other DeMarco brothers? Mario won't be a problem, but the other, Carmine? Fuck, he'll blow this case out of the water."

"Why are you only concerned about two of the brothers? There are three." That came from the Fibbie again.

"Yeah, asshole, the third is our Chief Operations Officer for Domestic Operations. Guardian's Chief Executive Officer is briefing him on this operation right now. Nic DeMarco is tight, believe me, it is the brothers you need to babysit."

"We got Carmine in protective custody. You're right, the guy is a piece of work. Threatening lawsuits for unlawful detention. Hope like hell your company's money will pay for the settlement that asshole is wanting." The LT made the announcement before he pulled out three pieces of paper. "Enough with the banter. If the peanut gallery has no further objections, and I really don't give a fuck if you do, this is the op. Now pay attention."

Jade leaned back on the low table behind her and watched as the Lieutenant put the plan up on the board.

"As I said, Guardian relocated the medical staff. It is a ten-bed facility in a larger medical professional building. We've cleared the building, and no one is being permitted inside to work due to a water-main break. Don't know how Guardian did it, but there are actually city crews out there working on the water main."

Jade inspected the photo that the LT pinned to the board. She chuckled. Those weren't city workers. She'd bet her paycheck they were Guardian employees.

"The vulnerabilities of the structure are numerous. The rooftop, windows on the private facility level, the shared underground parking area, and of course there is always a chance of a suicide bomber, but with the heavy equipment blocking the front of the building that threat is a moot point. Single entities slipping through the electronic monitoring systems are the biggest vulnerability."

"So what the fuck? Are we keeping them out or

luring them in? I thought the plan was to trap them?" One of the Marshals popped his question into the LT's briefing.

"It is a smoke screen. Guardian is doing this so we can do what we are tasked with doing. Not our plan, not our operation. You are being briefed to make sure you know the totality of the situation. Guardian is monitoring the facility in the hopes of luring in whoever is getting paid to take out the judge, but that is secondary to keeping the bastards occupied."

"Wonderful, what the fuck are we going to do? Sit here with our thumbs up our asses?" The Fibbie spouted off again.

"You can go ahead and do that, Swanson. The rest of us are going to track down the fuckers that killed over sixty people yesterday." The LT gave the man a cold stare as he pulled another sheet from his folder.

"King, Swanson, Burns, you've got the detonation device. Burns, you're lead. Brief them on the way out."

"Marlow, Norris and Sylvester, you've got the explosives. Sylvester, you're lead. Get these fuckers and let Guardian worry about setting the mousetrap and smokescreen. We need to know who made the triggering device, where they got the explosives, and who placed it at the courthouse. Let's put these fuckers away for good. If either team gets a whiff of who placed the device, I know about it the instant you smell it. Got it?"

Jade stood along with the asshole Fibbie and Sexy and Dangerous. The detective grabbed his jacket and headed out the door without a backward glance. Fibbie followed, and Jade shut the door behind her.

"Where are we heading?" Fibbie fell into step with the detective, as did Jade.

"Guardian was able to reconstruct a mock-up of the detonation device. We've seen a triggering device like it before. Our explosive ordinance detail keeps a record of all the triggering devices they've found, or what was left of them. We believe one of the old school firebugs built it. Or he's taught someone his trade. Either way, LT pulled a golden ticket out of his ass and was able to hunt down a last known location right before we entered the briefing. We're paying him a visit."

Jade pulled her SUV's keys out of her pocket. "Here." She said as she tossed them to Burns.

He tossed them back at her. "I have an undercover vehicle."

"Yeah? Is it armor plated, bulletproof, and have a traveling arsenal in the back?" She tossed the keys up and caught them in midair.

"Can't say as it is. But I'm sure my Crown Vic will suffice."

"Fucking Guardian has all the nice toys." Swanson chuckled. "So you're a King? As in the founding family type of King?"

"That would be correct." They headed down the stairs and outside.

"Hell, no wonder we got strapped with you," Swanson muttered. "You'd think Guardian would at least send someone who knew the job. Not a fucking pin-up princess that we need to babysit. We need to hit this hard and fast, sweetheart. Maybe you should go back inside and wait. You know, where it is warm, and there are lights?"

"No shit." Burns spit out the agreement before Jade could comment.

"Excuse me?" Jade stopped and squared off on the men.

"Never mind sweets, don't worry, we won't let anything happen to you." Swanson made a move to pass her. She put her hand up, and he stopped.

Jade smiled sweetly at Swanson. The condescending piece of ass wipe. He didn't surprise her,

Burns on the other hand... she wouldn't have called that one. So she spun toward him and punched where she knew it would hurt. "Are you telling me, Detective Burns, that you don't believe a woman can do this job?"

Burns turned and stared straight through her. Anger, pain and something else lanced through his glare. "No, I'm telling you a woman shouldn't do this job."

Jade crossed her arms and settled her feet shoulder's width apart. "So Jia being undercover has tainted your view of females in law enforcement? Not my fault you don't trust her."

The man moved, but she was ready for his lunge. Jade caught his wrist, spun and slammed Burns into the wall, leveraging his arm high up on his back. She whispered next to his ear. "Now we can do this one of two ways, asshole. We can admit that women are capable of doing this fucking job, and you can say you're sorry, or I'll leave you strapped with that asshole over there, call in backup of my own, and leave you in the dust. Think about it rationally. If we take the Triad down, Jia will be able to come home. So how about you shelve your bullshit and let's go to work?" She upped the pressure on his arm, and he grimaced, slapping the side of the building.

"Fuck you."

"Uh uh. That wasn't an apology." She tweaked his arm a fraction of an inch higher. The man growled in frustration.

"Sorry, fuck you, bitch." Burns spit the words out. They dripped with poisonous hatred.

"Excellent choice. I'll get my own backup." Jade pushed him into the wall and spun away but kept him in her peripheral vision. She glared at Swanson as Burns rubbed his shoulder, his potent glare pinning her, still and hostile. "You know I have better ways of handling asshole government employees. Fibbies live for advancement, placement, and promotion, don't you? How well do you know Deputy Director Cole Davis? He's a very close friend. Bottle your fucking attitude and put a cork in it, Fibbie, or I'll make sure your record states you don't play well with others. Ever been to the field office up there by the Bering Sea?" Jade spun on her heel and headed toward the Guardian SUV. Her phone was on and palmed before she made it three steps.

"What's up, buttercup?" Jewell answered on the first ring.

"I need information. Last known address on the bomb maker the NYPD suspects made the device."

"Hang on." Jewell put her on hold. Jade keyed the fob and unlocked the SUV after she did a 360 looking for anything that didn't belong on, or under, the vehicle. It was a habit.

"Okay. Found it. Sending it to your phone. Weren't you supposed to be working with the task force on this?"

Jade heard the notification of the address reaching her phone. She mounted the cell to the dash of the truck. The vehicle's Bluetooth activated and put Jewell on speaker. Jade put the SUV into gear and spared a glance toward the assholes heading toward the detective's car.

"Yeah, that isn't working out so well. Hey? If I give you a license plate can you find out if the vehicle has LoJack?"

"Ummmm… yeah, I'd have to run it, find the VIN number and then cross reference it to the manufacturer's system. Why?"

"Take this number down and do that, would you? Off the books." Jade rattled off the plate number on the undercover vehicle that Burns and Swanson were getting into.

"Girl, what are you doing?" Jade could hear Jewell's keyboard working in the background.

"Striking a blow against misogynistic assholes for all women in law enforcement." Jade looked at the address and did a mental calculation. "Hey, do me another favor. Don't kill that engine for about five or ten minutes. I want them far enough away from the precinct that they won't be able to swap out cars."

"Oh, damn. You are really pissed aren't you?"

"Believe me, they deserve it."

"Well, then, by all means, consider this a done deal, and I'll keep it off the books. But you gotta know, I'm not okay with you going after this bomb dude alone."

"I'm not stupid, nor do I have a death wish. I'm not going alone. Talk to you later." Jade hit her navigation app and loaded the address Jewell had sent her. She'd head that way, but there was a phone call and a stop to make first.

CHAPTER 23

Nic looked down the street trying to pick out the Guardian SUV he and Jade had been using. The blur of headlights made the feat impossible. Jade had called almost twenty minutes ago and explained what she needed and why. He briefed Jared and left the man upstairs to deal with Jason's wrath.

Nic rolled his shoulders and lowered his head, trying to stretch the tight muscles of his neck and shoulders. Other than the stress induced body aches, he was numb. Thoughts swirled through his mind, jostling the information and tactics they were employing to take down the bastards that had bombed a federal courthouse. He drew a deep breath. The tightness in his chest constricted his ability to take in air. He'd talked to Mario minutes before Jade had called. His little brother's pain seeped across the phone's connection and amplified his own. God, he was fucking exhausted. Cognitive reasoning, strategic planning, hell, adding two plus two was more than he could manage right now. He put his hands in his pockets and lifted his head, gazing down the street once again. He'd pull his shit together, though. He needed to be on task when they found the bastard that created the trigger for the bomb.

Nic's eyes caught on a dark SUV traveling in the lane closest to the building. The blacked out passenger side window rolled down as it approached. The barrel of an assault pistol pointed out the window and the world slowed into a stop motion nightmare. The muzzle flash of the weapon registered as he lunged to his right, knocking the woman beside him to the ground. Glass fragments and chips of limestone and cement flew up around him. The woman under him crumpled. He kept his body over her, keeping her shielded from the bullets.

The weapon's reports silenced. Nic rolled with the woman cradled in one arm, his weapon drawn with his free hand. He aimed and emptied his clip into the rear of the dark blue Chevy. He memorized the last portion of the plate as it careened out of view. It was a mere fraction of a second after he emptied his weapon before all hell busted loose. Guardian personnel poured out of the office building. Nic sat up bringing the woman with him. She slumped into him. He pulled her close and hugged her, for no other reason than it felt right to try to give some comfort even though he knew the time for comfort had passed.

Nic watched the men deploy from the building with weapons drawn. Both Jason and Jared traveled with security teams. The Kings' security was the best of the best, and the men who protected them were loyal, fierce and deadly. They set up a cordon around him. The woman sagged. He tightened his grip on her to keep her up. Nic blinked to clear his vision. He took stock of the bullet holes, the men and women who were writhing on the sidewalk, and of those who were impossibly still.

Suddenly, Jared was beside him. He felt Jared grab his shoulders. His best friend's voice penetrated the eerie sense of disassociation that wrapped around him. "Nic, for God's sake, answer me!"

Nic blinked up at his friend. The worry and

concern on his face were all wrong. What had Jared asked? He couldn't be certain, so he relayed the information he knew, "It was a Mac 10." Nic brought his hand holding his weapon to his ear. "The report of the weapon was stifled or suppressed. Could be a Tek 9, but those fuckers are louder. Definitely an assault pistol by the shape. Didn't see the shooter. I got a partial on the plate and emptied a clip in the ass end of the Suburban. It was dark blue. Blacked out windows." Nic went to lower his hand and stopped with it held about shoulder level. Blood coated his hand, the white of his dress shirt appeared to be dipped in blood. He turned his head and examined the woman he held.

Nic swallowed hard and closed his eyes for a moment before he laid her down, slowly. Reality marched like a fucking brass band into the adrenaline-fueled explosion of clarity. Nic knew exactly what happened and when. He recalled the coppery scented tang of blood and knew the instant the woman died. The distinct and unforgettable odor of open wounds exposing internal organs filled his senses while he waited for his own death via a Triad bullet. Looking at the woman now, he felt... nothing. A bullet had blown off a large portion of her skull. Blood, brain matter and bone covered his face and clothes.

Several men converged on them at once, taking the woman from where she rested. He let Jared help him up. "You're not going out there. They declared fucking war."

Nic snapped his attention toward his best friend. "Bullshit. I am going with Jade to track down this bastard."

"Nic, get real. You've barely survived a fucking drive-by!"

One of the Guardians who was providing first aid stopped in front of Nic. "Are you injured?"

"No, blood from the victim." Nic pointed toward the woman. The man shoved a towel into his hand. Nic swiped at the sticky mess covering his face and hands.

A squeal of tires dropped everyone into firing positions with all weapons drawn. Nic hadn't reloaded, but his magazine hit the ground, and he inserted a fresh one by the time his knee hit the sidewalk. He drew a bead on the vehicle. Jade flew from the driver's side door and pounded around the front of the vehicle. Nic dropped his weapon as she slid to her knees and wrapped her arms around him. He could feel the impression of the weapon she had in her hand pressing against his back. "God damn it, DeMarco! It is a damn good thing you're pretty. Otherwise, I don't know if I could justify sticking around through all this shit." She pulled back and raked her eyes over him, assessing. "My God, are you hit?" The hand that wasn't holding her automatic moved his jacket and patted at his body.

He grabbed her hand and lifted it up to his mouth, placing a kiss on it. She stilled immediately. They locked eyes and time stood still. The emotion that passed between them sizzled. One hundred percent, over-charged, high-octane, and ready to explode. Not the sexual tension that usually bound them together, this was different. They couldn't deny this connection. A shuffle of feet beside him broke the moment. Nic shook his head to clear it before he chucked her under the chin. "I thought I asked you not to call me pretty?"

Jade choked out a half sob, half laugh. "Yeah, well you are, so get over it."

"When you two get done down there, with whatever the fuck is going on, we need to get inside." Jared's voice separated them further.

"So much for the families not knowing."

Nic shook his head at her whispered comment.

God, the woman was irreverent and impassioned and what the doctor fucking ordered. He needed her vibrancy and energy.

Jade jumped up and extended her free hand down to him. Fuck it. Nic grabbed her hand and allowed her to pull him up from his knees. "We've got to move. I have a head start on the fuckers from the task force, but if we don't hurry, the bastards they assigned to me will get to the last known location first. I want him, and I want the intel. We can get Guardian to relay any leads to Lieutenant Flowers and call in backup if necessary." Nic fell into step with her heading toward her vehicle.

Jared whistled sharply, bringing them both to a standstill. Nic looked back at his friend. Jared took off his suit jacket and threw it at Nic. He grabbed it out of the air and shrugged out of the blood soaked suit coat he wore and dropped it on the cement as he got into the vehicle. The new jacket covered the majority of the blood and bodily fluids his shirt had absorbed. Jade threw the vehicle into gear and forced her way into traffic.

"Whose blood is it?" Jade didn't look at him. She was transfixed on navigating through New York traffic.

"I don't know who she was. She was standing next to me when the shooting started. I pulled her down to try to get her out of harm's way."

"All the more reason to find these fuckers. Why in the hell would they do a drive-by on you?"

"As far as they know mom is alive and is in a secure facility. The one who is ordering this is unstable or is pissed and acting out."

Jade looked over at him. "Pissed people make mistakes. Let's hope for pissed. Unstable is crazy, and you can't get ahead of crazy."

"Fuck, don't I know it." Nic rifled through the glove box and pulled a first aid kit out. He grabbed the alcohol wipes out of it and tried to clean his face and hands. At best, his attempts were ineffective.

The drone of the GPS app on Jade's phone directed them through the city. "What intel do you have on the device maker?"

"Not much. Burns said it was an old school device. They matched the design with something one of the Explosive Ordinance guys had seen before. That's where we are heading. Give Jewell a call. She should have more on the maker by now."

Nic palmed his phone and placed the call.

"Holy horseshit, DeMarco! What the fuck was that? I watched the footage from the security monitors. We got the full license plate. You were right; it looked like a Mac 10. The slugs the guys are pulling out of the walls look like .45s, so that lines up."

Jade cut through Jewell's one-sided info dump, "Registered owner of the SUV?"

"A sixty-seven year old man from Yonkers. Stolen this afternoon."

"Fuck." Nic spat the word out. They couldn't fucking catch a break. "What information do you have on the device maker?"

"Oh yeah... hang on, I'll let Zane fill you in on that." Nic exchanged a confused look with Jade. Why in the hell would Zane brief them?

"Nic, when the name the NYPD provided was run through our database, we got a hit on an alias for one of our own assets." Zane's gritty voice filled the cabin area.

"You mean a member of Guardian built the bomb?" Nic's gut clenched.

"No. No, he is not Guardian, but we used his talents about two decades ago. NYPD has his alias. His real name is Montgomery Allen. He made the best remote trigger pieces in the business and was one of the good guys when Guardian was doing business with him."

"But he isn't now?" Jade asked as she came to a stop at a traffic light.

"No. He was on a government sponsored vacation upstate for ten years. Got out and disappeared. The FBI tied devices of his design to the bombing of those three financial institutions on Wall Street six years ago. Talking with a few contacts I have, we believe the Triad protected him while he was inside in return for the use of his abilities. Using that theory, we've been able to tentatively tie several previously unrelated incidents to Allen's designs and consequently the Triad. I'll have Jewell send you his picture. However, there is one flaw in our reasoning. The guy would be almost eighty now."

"So you think he took on an apprentice." It wasn't a question. If the Triad had protected him, the man could have taken on someone and taught him or her how to make the remote triggers.

"Most likely scenario."

"This last known address. How reliable is it?" Jade threw the question out.

"All things considered it probably isn't a valid address unless someone was feeding us the information for a reason." Jewell's voice came across the airwaves.

Nic scrutinized Jade. "It could be a trap." She considered him and nodded in agreement. "Jewell, we need to run down any known aliases Allen has used in the past. Dig into the Guardian archives. If he was using an alias when the NYPD tracked his last known, it could be a habit, and he may be using old aliases to fly under the radar. New identities aren't cheap, and the Triad wouldn't provide him an alias. They'd keep him under wraps, so if this guy is still alive and not a prisoner, he is using an alias. Also, check prison records. Who were Allen's cellmates? What known member of the Triad did he have contact with inside? Compare work details, lunch breaks and recreation hours. Is there any record of visitors for Allen? Family members or friends that the Triad could leverage? Pull up any bank accounts for Allen or known family members. Scour anything you can to see if we can substantiate the Triad is either forcing Allen to participate or paying him to do so."

"You got it, Nicster." Nic could hear furious typing in the background.

Zane came back on the line, "Be careful. This entire situation reeks. I'll brief Jason and Jared, and we will get you the information on Allen." The line went dead. Nic drew a deep breath and focused on the scene outside the window. They were rolling through what appeared to be a warehouse district —massive, sprawling compounds with inadequate lighting, fencing with gaping holes and graffiti splattered across limestone and brick. The area looked like a demilitarized zone. Jade pulled over and stopped. Nic inspected the GPS app and noticed they were about three blocks from the destination.

"We can come in from different sides. I'll take the west side. You take the east." Jade spoke as she opened the center console and took out two earpieces and small transmitters. Nic clipped the transmitter to his collar and put in the earpiece as she did the same.

They both exited the vehicle and headed toward the rear compartment. Jade opened the mobile weapon armory. They both grabbed ammo belts, extra magazines for their primary weapons, and clipped on pouches filled with 5.56. Nic unlocked the rifle rack and handed her an M-4 before he took one. They each chose an ankle holster and strapped on a smaller weapon. Jade pulled an Interceptor 911 and clipped the knife to her ammo belt. Nic shut the vehicle, and they locked and alarmed it.

Nic stood at the back of the vehicle and stared at the woman getting ready to walk into a potentially deadly encounter with him... beside him. Jade would stroll through the fires of hell and whistle as if she was on a day trip through the park. She was the antithesis of the women he'd dated in the past. Jade had flowed into the cracks and fissures of his life. She freely shared a strength that infused him with determination. He would be the man she could walk beside, not the player he'd been in the past. She deserved a man who understood her and stood with her, not in front of her. Jade looked up, questioning his stillness. He reached and tugged her into him. "Don't be a hero in there." He lowered his lips to hers and kissed her, hard and fast.

A wicked, evil smile spread across her face. God, the woman lit up from the inside and Nic could tell she lived for moments like this. Jade confirmed his suspicions when she reached up and pulled him down for an equally hot and fast kiss. "Don't worry about me, pretty boy. Just try to keep up."

CHAPTER 24

"Pretty boy?" Jared's humor-filled voice echoed in her earbud. "That is the second time in as many hours that my sister has called you pretty, my man. Don't suppose you'd want to tell us what is going on between the two of you, would you?"

"No, he wouldn't, and who is on this frequency?" Jade lifted her hand to Nic's chest and tapped it twice over his heart before she turned and headed out to her position at a slow jog.

"Jason."

"Jacob."

"Jewell and Zane."

Each of her siblings sounded off in turn. "And me, of course," Jared added.

"Nosey bunch of assholes aren't you? Stand

down, transitioning." Jade murmured as she slowed. She needed to be able to hear, so she requested the stand down on comms. She walked quietly to the corner of the building at the end of the block and listened. The noises of the night and the sounds of the city in the distance blended. There were no footsteps, scrapes of a boot against the pavement, or rocks kicked down the cement. Most importantly there was the continuance of ambient noise. Crickets chirped in unison and no animals silenced in alarm or warning. Jade peeked around the corner and took in the scene. After the building she was taking cover behind, she had a full block without cover.

"Jason, can we black out the neighborhood? I'm fucked if they have someone on the rooftop."

"One power outage coming up." Jason's voice rumbled in her ear.

"Nic, status?" Jade listened as Jared sent out the question.

"Clear. I'm covered to the back entrance. Three hundred more feet." Nic's hushed voice came over the comms.

"Stand down outside the facility. Do not enter." Jacob commanded.

"No shit, asshole. I don't feel like punching my

ticket today. Not a fucking rookie or an idiot." Nic muttered his reply.

"Don't be a jerk or I'll call your backup off." Jacob taunted.

"No, you won't. Your sister is with me." Jade could hear Nic breathing as he moved forward. "In a safe position. Standing by."

"I need five minutes. Jade, are you in a secure area?" Jason's voice made her jump. The man was too damn loud. Jade pushed back into the darkness and confirmed her safety.

"So what do we do for five minutes? I know! Let's play twenty questions!" Jewell's voice floated into her ear.

"Let's not." Jade and Nic said the same words at the same time.

"Oh, this is too good to be true." Jacob laughed for a moment. "Teams will be with you in less than ten minutes. Recommend standing by with the power outage until all personnel are in position."

"Acknowledged. Nic, do you see any movement?" Jared's voice chimed in.

"Standby." Jade counted to a slow ten before Nic's voice returned. "I have lights on in the facility. Bottom floor southeast corner. Unknown occupants."

"Copy that." Jared acknowledged the report.

"Soooo... how long have you two been dating?" Jewell's laughter broke the brief silence.

"Need to concentrate right now, and thank you very much, Jewell. I'll remember this." Jade hissed the words at Jewell and was rewarded with another laugh, this time it sounded like all her siblings laughing keyed the voice activated mic's they were wearing.

"That wasn't a denial," Jacob interjected.

"I have street cams up. Doing a sweep of the local area." Jewell interjected before she agreed with Jacob, "Nope, it wasn't a denial, but Jade doesn't date..."

"Lights out in six minutes. Status of your teams?" Jason's voice cut through Jewell's teasing tone.

"Thank fuck someone is concentrating on business," Nic chimed in.

"I am," Jason confirmed. "But I'd like to know what your intentions toward my sister are, DeMarco."

"Fuck you." Jade and Nic responded simultaneously, triggering another round of laughter.

"Teams are four minutes out." Jacob dropped the information.

"Traffic cams show no movement. There is no power at the facility to your left Jade. I recommend you take the team across the street to move forward. If there are emergency generators in the compound you are taking shelter behind, they may cut on and spotlight you." Zane's voice came over the comms. That was weird. As many operations as she'd done, it had always been a family member on the comms. Zane's sudden addition into the mix still surprised her. "Lights out in two minutes." Zane's voice again. Damn, she needed to get used to that.

"Teams arriving on scene," Jacob commented.

"Lights out in one minute." Adrenaline coursed through her veins at Zane's countdown.

"Teams deploying. Standby for arrival." Jacob reported the information. Jade would wait for them until the lights were out, then she was going in, the team could catch up. Of course, everyone on the comms would assume that bit of information, because, hello... she always did her own thing.

"Lights out in thirty seconds." Zane continued the countdown.

Jade heard the shuffle of footsteps behind her and waited until she could confirm the team's identity before she lifted from her crouched position and revealed herself. The team leader acknowledged her and called in that he was on scene.

"Ten, nine, eight..."

"In position." The second team radioed in. Jade released a breath she hadn't realized she'd been holding. Nic had backup. Ten pounds of tension slipped from her shoulders.

"... three... two... one."

The entire grid catapulted into darkness.

Jade moved out, trusting the team was right behind her. She crossed the street and sprinted down the block. The tactical belt and equipment made a minimum of noise, but the entire team running at the same time made a racket. Jade pulled up at the door to the warehouse.

"In position." She breathed the words through her comms.

"On three."

Jade listened to Zane count them down and took the high position as the door opened. The team leader took the low position. She cleared to the right and stood aside. The team had NVG's, and they were experts at urban warfare. Clearing buildings like these was what they did. She followed through listening to the two teams clearing the facility. A hum pulsed through the facility and lights flickered back on. The team lifted the NVG's, probably blinded by the unexpected return of electricity.

"Could have warned us." Nic's censure echoed her own thoughts.

"Not our doing. Some overachiever at the power company no doubt," Jewell responded.

They continued forward, but this time Jade was an active participant in the search. They split into two teams and cleared the west side of the building working toward Nic's team.

"In position." Nic's voice over her comms brought instant relief.

Jade said a prayer of thanks for the speed of the team assigned with her. The door that led into the next room was propped open about two inches. Instead of risking giving away their position, she reached up to her transmitter and clicked it twice, the established code for acknowledgement when silence was necessary.

Nic's voice floated to her. "On three."

Jade focused on the team leader, and he motioned low. She stood and leaned against the wall outside the door and listened as Nic counted down the entry. On his whispered "three", they exploded through the door at the same time as Nic's team entered at the rear of the room.

Two people sat at a workbench. Conventional wisdom would tell you they would jump at the explosion of movement, but they didn't. Jade drew down on them, as did Nic. The teams did their jobs and cleared the room. From opposite directions, they walked toward the two men. Jade noticed the bindings keeping them in the chairs. One was slouched forward. Blood coated his left side. The grey pallor of his skin told her the man was dead or close to it. The other man lifted his head. Montgomery Allen. Nic reached him first and pulled the gag from his mouth.

"Get out." The old man wheezed horrendously. "You have time, but you must go now. The detonator is simplistic. It runs on a timer. The timer is hardwired to the electricity in the building. The power outage gave you time, but it also activated the device. Go! Go now!"

"Cut the power again!" Jade pulled her knife out and cut the man's bindings.

"No! You must not! It has a failsafe. Another outage will trigger it immediately. Go, find them! They have four more remote detonators and C4."

Jade pulled the earbud out of her ear. The explosion of voices and yelled commands damn near deafened her.

The man reached for her arm. "I will only slow you down. Go."

Nic grabbed her by the arm and moved her out of the way. He bent and lifted the old man over his shoulder.

"Clear out! Follow Nic's team leader! Let's go!" Jade bellowed the command to her team before she ran after Nic and his team.

They sprinted through the halls, directly to the exit. Jade could hear sirens as soon as she emerged from the building. She wedged her earbud back in her ear as they ran. They raced across the street and took cover behind a sturdy brick building down the block. Nic bent slowly and controlled the elderly man's crumble to the sidewalk. Allen held his head in his hands, wheezing and coughing.

Jade bent down to talk to the man. "Do you know where…"

The percussion of the explosion pushed her to her hands and knees. She moved on instinct, covering the elderly person. Nic wrapped them both in his arms. A shower of bricks and mortar imploded to their left. The cover of the building they were leaning against prevented any of the debris from hitting them. Billowing cushions of smoke, dust, and dirt swirled around them.

"Report!" Jason's voice bellowed over the comms.

Jade listened to the team leaders rattling off information and details. An NYPD cruiser and an ambulance pulled up to the scene. Jade and Nic gave their M-4s and ammo belts to the team leaders to lock up. Jade listened to the back and forth between CCS and the teams. She moved out into the street and took in the remains of the building they had abandoned. A shiver ran up her spine. The specter of death surrounding them was strong. She glanced at Nic. He'd been brushed by death twice in the last twenty-four hours. First, his mother, then the random woman he'd tried to protect. She dropped her eyes to the old man. Would he be the third? God, she hoped not. They needed that man... alive. Jade returned her attention to Nic. As if he felt the weight of her stare, he turned his head and met her eyes. The emptiness in his spoke volumes.

Jade walked back to him and grabbed his hand as it dangled by his side. He squeezed her hand gently.

"We are taking him to County, it is the closest." The EMTs lifted the gurney into the back of the ambulance.

Nic and Jade moved as one.

"We're going with him." Nic's reply brokered no room for argument.

Montgomery Allen was their only lead, and they needed as much information as the man could provide. If he could provide it. The tinge of blood on the man's lips prevented her from assuming he'd be able to help.

Jade made a move to get into the back of the bus. Nic held her hand preventing her from moving. She stopped and took a hard look at the ambulance. It was the company that had taken his mom to the hospital. She got his hesitation to assume the same position as when they had transported his mom.

"Get in the back. I'll ride shotgun."

He nodded, squeezed her hand and moved to the back of the vehicle.

CHAPTER 25

Nic strode down the hall of the hospital. Thankfully it was a different facility than the one that had taken in his mother. Jade had 'acquired' a set of scrubs and a pair of old tennis shoes for him from the doctor's lounge. She'd also located a vacant room with a shower, and Nic took two minutes to wash the blood, brains and bone fragments along with the explosion's debris from his body. He carried his weapons, credentials, and cuffs under his arm, rolled up in his soiled clothes.

He turned the corner and saw Jade leaning against the wall outside Montgomery Allen's room. Two NYPD officers had accompanied Allen to radiology. Not that the man was a flight risk. The worry now was the Triad, or the injuries he'd sustained, would kill Allen before he could answer questions.

Nic took up the position with her, leaning against the wall. She peeked up from her phone giving him an appreciative once over. "Now, there's the pretty boy I know."

Nic chuckled despite the exhaustion he felt. "You're not going to stop calling me that, are you?"

"Naaahhh. I mean, it bothers you when I do it. A win for me. But seriously, all modesty aside, you must admit you are one pretty fucker, aren't you?" She elbowed him and smiled as she taunted.

"Yeah, yeah I am."

Jade threw back her head and laughed at his response. The sharp, happy sound reverberated down the hallway. A nurse popped her head out of the room across the hall and shushed Jade, throwing in a scathing look for good measure. Jade slapped her hand over her mouth and continued to laugh, albeit in a quieter fashion.

He shook his head and tried to stifle the smile that spread across his face. The woman was irreverent as hell.

After a moment to gain control of herself, Jade nudged him with her elbow again. "What's the game plan?"

"Question Allen. Go from there."

They stood in silence for several minutes until orderlies and a nurse wheeled Allen back into the room. The NYPD officers took up residence, one inside the room, one outside.

"Can we question him?" Nic asked the nurse while the men who wheeled in the bed locked the wheels into place and positioned the IV onto the stand next to the bed. The old man's skin color didn't look good. He was extremely pale with a bluish tint. Even though he was propped up, his breathing sounded harsh: a wet, rattle-like noise before the exhale and then a wheeze before the laborious inhale started again.

The nurse detached the portable oxygen and reattached the system to the one in the room. He situated the man's nasal cannula before he checked the drip on the IV. It was only after his patient was settled that he turned his attention to Nic and Jade. "He is sedated right now. The doctor will make her way down to talk with you after she gets a look at the pictures we took." The nurse opened a screen on the computer and started logging information.

Nic nodded at the NYPD officer that had settled in the one and only chair in the room. The cop had angled it so he could keep an eye on the patient, the door, and his partner.

Jade tipped her head toward the hallway. Nic followed her out and across the hall to a small waiting area. "Jewell wants us to call in."

Nic grabbed the ear bud Jade proffered him. He recalled the last time they'd shared her earphones for a call. God, it seemed like months ago, and yet only a handful of hours had passed. He didn't feel like the same man.

"All right sweets, we are here," Jade said as soon as Jewell picked up.

"Okay, so I'm supposed to update you and give you instructions. Update first. The NYPD has rounded up every known member of the Triad they could find. As a matter of fact, they have brought in all known associates and family members, too. So far nobody is saying squat, at least according to Lieutenant Flowers. He also had a few not so kind words to say about the way you ding-dong-ditched the two cops who were assigned to you."

"Figures, but I guarantee I won't lose any sleep over it." Jade shrugged as she spoke.

"Yeah, we didn't figure you would. Jason shut him down. Hard. Anyway, the C4 is part of a shipment scheduled for disposal. It was last logged in at Fort Myers EOD range. The Army is doing its thing. I'm monitoring the status, but I don't see the Army being forthcoming on how they lost a couple hundred pounds of major league boom-boom."

"No kidding." Nic could imagine the shit rolling downhill at that army base.

Jewell continued, "We are still looking into Allen's past and association with the Triad. Zack is running it to ground."

"Let me know as soon as you are ready to brief. What about the clinic?" Nic rubbed his eyes. Once again, all the sand of the Sahara seemed to have lodged itself between his eyelids and dry, itchy eyeballs.

"No movement or action. We have overlapping cameras, pressure sensors at all entrances, motion detectors and redundancies in place, but as of right now, no one has made an attempt to get into the facility. I see Allen's status is listed as stable but guarded. What did the doctor say?"

"Allen just got back from radiology. Not sure what's up yet. The doctor hasn't come down to speak with us yet."

"Correction. The doctor is here." A female voice across from them brought Nic's eyes up and a smile to his face. He pulled out the ear bud and stood before walking to the petite woman standing in the doorway. He wrapped her in a hug that she returned. She rubbed his shoulders. "I heard about your mom, and I called the hospital, but they said she was transferred?"

Nic pulled out of the hug. "Yeah, Guardian is taking care of... everything." Nic reached back to Jade and held out his hand to her. She arched an eyebrow at him but lifted out of the chair and came over. "Donna, this is Jade. Jade, my second cousin Donna Corzolli."

Jade extended her hand. "Pleased to meet you. Are you Mr. Allen's doctor?"

Nic drew a breath, thankful Jade had taken control of the conversation. He didn't want Donna to start asking questions about his mom that he couldn't answer.

"Yes, I am."

"When can we talk to him?" Jade peered up at Nic.

"He's heavily sedated right now. I don't know when he'll be cognizant enough to talk with you and, as his physician, I can honestly say I don't recommend any discussion that would prove strenuous."

"Why?" Nic folded his arms and leveled his gaze across the hall at the officer standing outside the door.

"Can't release that information to you. HIPAA laws." Donna shook her head. "I'd like to, but I can't."

Jade nodded. "Okay, I get that. If you were to guess, when would he be coming out of the sedation?"

"Not until morning. Not until visiting hours, I would guess." Donna glanced up at him. "Nico, does this man have something to do with what happened to Zia Bettina?"

Nic fixed his gaze on Jade and then nodded. Once.

Donna sighed and motioned them further into the room. She lowered her voice before she spoke, "He is terminal. End stage Emphysema. There isn't much left of his lungs. He won't be with us long. Come back tomorrow morning at ten. I'll stay after my shift to make sure he's comfortable when you talk to him, but Nico, I could lose my license for telling you this and for helping you talk to him."

"Don't worry, Donna. I promise we will protect

you and the information. Thank you." Nic pulled her into a hug again.

"Tell Zia Bettina that I love her, would you? I'll be over to see her as soon as she's released."

Nic swallowed the emotion that boiled up. He nodded. It was the only response he could manage.

"It was nice to meet you, and we'll see you soon." Jade shook Donna's hand again and watched her as she walked out of the small waiting area.

Jade dropped her head onto Nic's shoulder. "So how weird was it that I kinda wanted to rip her hair out? At least until you pulled out the cousin card."

Nic put his arm around Jade and pulled her into an embrace. He planted his chin on top of her head. "Really weird."

"I know, right? I mean, me? Jealous? What the actual fuck?"

Jade sounded so incredulous, he smiled despite himself. "One would almost assume we were in a relationship or something."

"I know, right?"

Nic felt her phone vibrate and sighed when she pulled away. He flashed a glance at the clock. They had five hours to wait until they could question Allen.

"Sooo... Jewell might have an idea we are seeing each other."

"No shit? What do you think gave her the first clue?" Nic blinked down at her, trying for sincerity, but there was no way he managed it.

"Ummm, I don't know. Could have been any number of things. But the fact remains she got us one room in the hotel across the street." She lifted the phone for him, and he read the text.

"God, I think I love your sister." Nic needed another shower, a bed and several hours of sleep, preferably with Jade tucked up next to him.

"Great, now I have to pull out Jewell's hair. This could get old, quick."

CHAPTER 26

J ade pushed Nic through the doorway. She could tell he was shutting down—physically, mentally, and emotionally. The stress he'd been under for the last twenty-four hours was enough to break the strongest people she knew, and she counted Nic among them. She dropped his bundle of clothes on the bedside table taking the time to remove his weapons, cell phone, credentials, wallet, and shield before she dropped the soiled mess into the garbage can.

Nic stood in the middle of the room, staring at the bathroom door. Jade walked up behind him and wrapped her arms around his waist.

"Come on, big boy. Shower time."

She pushed him forward and maneuvered them

into the bathroom. She watched him strip out of the hospital scrubs she'd liberated for him as she adjusted the water temperature. He walked into the shower as if he were in a trance. Jade laid her weapons on the vanity and quickly stripped out of her clothes.

The warm water rained down on them, and the white noise buffered them from the outside world. She picked up a bar of soap, ripped the protective cover off and lathered up Nic's back. She worked her fingers over his tense knotted muscles. He groaned and braced himself on the wall of the shower, dropping his head forward allowing the shower to sluice the suds down his back. Jade lowered and worked the tight muscles of his hamstrings and calves before standing and turning him to face her.

She put her hands on his shoulders and kneaded them with strong, sure pressure until the knots dissolved and his shoulders lowered. She washed his chest and abs and then dropped to her knees. His cock lay plump against his thigh, interested but not demanding. Jade washed his thighs and shins before placing the soap out of the way on the edge of the tile. She lifted her face into the shower stream and pushed her wet hair back away from her face. Nic's hand cupped her cheek. Jade opened her eyes and saw the need in his. She leaned forward and licked the swollen head of his cock, taking her time to roll her tongue around it before suckling it into her mouth. The muscles in Nic's thighs jumped when she pulled him in, and his legs trembled under her touch. Jade felt him thread his fingers through her wet hair.

This is what she knew he needed. Nic needed to feel some semblance of control, if only for a short time. His world had been shattered, and the elements of the disaster had beaten the man down, but he was strong, and he would endure. What she offered him tonight was a solace, a way to take back a modicum of normalcy. She grabbed the back of his thighs and pulled him to her, taking his cock to the back of her throat. When Nic pulled away, her eyes popped open and locked with his. She urged him forward again.

"Are you sure? I'm not strong enough to stop tonight. I need..."

Jade urged him forward again and hummed around his cock as it slid to the back of her throat. Nic grasped her hair and tipped her head back a bit further before he thrust forward again. Controlled and measured, he found his rhythm.

Jade sucked and swirled her tongue, encouraging him to take what he needed. One of his hands cupped her cheek, and she opened her eyes to gaze at the man above her.

She couldn't say what the sensation was, but a feeling swept over her, and at that moment in time she could swear Nic felt it, too. A connection so deep and pure she could feel his emotions as if they were her own. He pulled away and lifted her up. His mouth lowered and took hers in a kiss that was tender, soft and giving. Jade trembled when her palms smoothed over his pecs. Nic turned off the shower and drew a towel around her. Jade made a cursory attempt to dry off. Neither of them managed to do much more than drop the towels at the side of the bed. Nic grabbed a condom from his wallet before he dropped into bed beside her.

"Thank you." His eyes echoed the words and forced her to swallow hard.

She had no experience to fall back on. She didn't know how to understand the way she was feeling, and her uncertainty terrified her... her fear born of saying something or doing something that would make this precious... emotion... they shared break apart and fall away as if it had never been. Jade's hand trembled as she lifted it to his lips. He closed his eyes and kissed her palm as if the intensity of the moment was too strong for him, too.

"What is this?" She whispered the question to herself. Nic's eyes opened. He moved to settle between her legs, his torso over hers, and held himself up on his elbows as his eyes examined her face with the same intensity that she searched his.

"This is us." Nic bent down and softly caressed her lips with his before he slid his cheek against hers and kissed her jaw, her neck, and then her shoulder.

The contact sent rivulets of sensation through her. The connection they shared tonight was just as corporeal as the touch of his body against hers. Jade outlined the hills and valleys of his muscles with her fingertips as he held himself over her. He lifted to his knees and took the condom out of the package. Jade watched the muscles in his arms and chest roll with the movement. She followed his hand to his cock and literally licked her lips. He worked the condom down his shaft while staring at her. As he lowered, Jade ran her hands from his abdomen to his pecs, mapping the thick plates of muscle as they moved.

"Look at me." Nic's voice deepened. Her eyes rose from his chest where her hands explored. "I couldn't have made it through the day without you." His hips thrust forward filling her.

Jade lifted her hips encouraging him. Their eyes locked. "Tell me you feel this, too." This boiling tempest of emotion, the intensity of her feelings couldn't be one sided. God, she prayed it wasn't. She ran her hands up his shoulders and tangled them in his dark brown hair.

"My world has shattered into a million pieces. I can't explain how empty... how hollow I felt." Nic blinked, pushing back the emotion he refused to allow to fall. "Until you." He dropped his forehead to hers and whispered, "You're my sanity, my solace, and my beacon in the night." A single tear dropped from his eyes to her cheek. "God, yes, I feel it."

Jade choked back her own tears. He pulled her tight into his shoulder and stroked deep inside her. She embraced him as tightly as he held her. Jade came apart in his arms and held him as he shattered in hers. He rolled off her and disposed of the condom before he pulled her into him. Jade felt him drop into slumber mere minutes later and carefully pulled away, going into the bathroom to gather her things. She placed her weapons beside the bed and set the alarm on her phone after checking for any messages.

She pulled up the covers and slipped into bed again. Nic didn't even flinch at the movement. What was keeping her awake right now was the revelation that she cared for Nic with a depth and an emotional attachment she couldn't compre-hend. The intensity and urgency she felt was confusing and yet, breathtaking. A sigh eased from her lips and the tension in her body relaxed and allowed her to start to drift into sleep. The four-letter word that used to scare the shit out of her swirled around her mind. She was in love.

CHAPTER 27

Nic held the hospital door for Jade. Four hours of solid sleep had refreshed him, but the weight of the past few days still felt oppressive and unyielding. When Jade's alarm went off this morning, there had been no time to do the 'morning after' shuffle. Breakfast and a fresh set of clothing for each of them arrived at the same time. Jade said she assumed the wardrobe change was a present from Jewell, but knowing Jared the way he did, Nic wouldn't put it past his best friend to be watching out for them. Whoever sent the clothes, he appreciated it. They got dressed, ignored the food, and grabbed two cups of coffee before heading out.

Nic watched the stunning woman walking

beside him. They'd both agreed last night that something special had happened, yet it appeared neither one of them wanted to address it in the light of day. Nic sure as fuck didn't have the desire to pull out a fuck-ton of emotions and examine them, and knowing Jade, that was the last thing she would want either.

They rode up in a packed elevator and made their way to Allen's room. After flashing their badges and credentials, they entered the darkened room. Donna was present, and Allen was awake. Nic nodded at his cousin but addressed her patient.

"Mr. Montgomery Allen, I'm Nicolas DeMarco. This is Jade King. We're with Guardian Security, and we need to ask you some questions. Before I do that, I need to read you your rights."

The man nodded and lifted his finger beckoning them closer. "I waive my right to an attorney, and I talk to you because I choose to of my own free will. The doctor will be my witness. Come closer."

Nic rounded the foot of the bed and Jade went to the other side. "What can you tell me about who hired you to make the devices that brought down the courthouse?"

"I didn't make them. Johnnie, the man you found next to me last night, he made them." The wheezing rasp of breath morphed into a vicious wet cough. Allen coughed up a plug of blood and phlegm. He buried it in a Kleenex. It took several minutes for his breathing to return to normal.

Nic sought out Donna. She shook her head. "I spoke with him before you came. He agreed to talk to you. He knows he doesn't have much time."

"I know I'm dying. They can't hurt me any longer, but you have to promise me you'll take care of my granddaughter. They know where she lives. They said they would…" The coughing started up again, and Nic waited until the man stopped.

"We will protect your granddaughter." His eyes caught Donna's. "Do you have her name and address?"

"Let me check his records." She opened the computer on the nightstand and started working. "Yeah, she's listed as next of kin." Donna scribbled the address down on a prescription pad and tore it off.

Jade reached out and snagged it from her. She pulled out her cell and started texting, coordinating the protection effort and informing DC what was going on.

Allen dropped his head back and drew another wheezing breath. "Four more devices. I built them. Johnnie's failed. He didn't ensure the contacts were secure. The bomb beneath the north side of the courthouse didn't blow. Johnnie died for his failure."

"Who was forcing you to make the triggers? The Triad?"

Allen nodded. "They wanted Xie Jun to die in the explosion."

"Who wanted him dead? The Triad?" Nic was trying to follow.

Allen nodded. "If he is dead, the case goes away."

"Wait? They weren't targeting the judge?" Jade's eyes popped up and met Nic's when he asked the question.

"No. Xie Jun was the target. Orders came straight from China."

Jade stopped her furious texting and blinked up at Nic. "But that doesn't make sense. The under-cover cop, Jia something or other, told the GTF that your mom was the target."

"Jia Ru? She sits at the right hand of Yi Bao, the serpent's head. She is his niece. She feeds the

NYPD the information he wants them to have. They have many people in influential places."

"Where are they taking the detonation devices?" Nic's mind raced to keep up. If they weren't after his mom... what were they going to do with the explosives? Where was Xie Jun being held? Rikers Island?

"Are they going to blow up one of the facilities on Rikers?"

"No. The Tombs. They are going to kill Xie Jun. Yi Bao, the serpent's head, is here to witness his death. It is a matter of family honor."

"Family? Xie Jun is related to Yi Bao?" The serpent's head was only a rumored entity. Nic and Jared had chased the Triad down the rabbit hole many times. They'd never had names to go with the titles that were whispered with reverent voices.

"Xie Jun is his nephew."

"Jia's brother?"

"Half brother."

"Holy fucked up families," Jade mumbled as she continued to text.

If Nic had to guess, the woman was transcribing the entire conversation, word for word, and sending it to Guardian.

"But Xie Jun knew when the explosion would

happen." He remembered being briefed on that or had someone told him? Fuck it, it didn't matter how he knew it, but the man ducked under a fucking table. That much Nic remembered.

"Xie Jun was told the same thing as the cops. They were taking out the judge. He was told she would be shot, to duck out of the way. He wasn't supposed to live, but they needed him to be compliant."

"But what about the death threat and the drive-by last night?" Jade asked. She didn't lift her eyes from her phone and continued texting.

"Xie Jun still has loyal soldiers. He ordered the intimidation and the drive-by. The men who are still loyal to Xie Jun will also be eliminated."

"Men like you?" Nic asked.

"Yes." The man closed his eyes, his breathing heavy and wet.

"How are they getting into the tombs? Do they have someone on the staff?"

"No. They're under it." A violent episode of coughing shook the older man's body.

Donna wedged herself in, moving Nic out of the way. She hit the call button on the man's bed. She turned and spoke to Nic, "That's enough."

"Wait…" Allen held up a hand imploring them

to stop. Nic and Jade held their positions and waited for the man to rest a moment. "The devices trigger remotely. Cut the green wire first, then black, then white. Do not touch the red or it will detonate. Bao will have a remote trigger. He demanded I show him how to set and activate the timers."

The team of people who entered the room forced Nic and Jade to step away. They took refuge across the hall in the small waiting room.

Nic peered over Jade's shoulder at her phone. "What is DC saying?"

"They are alerting NYPD and the Manhattan Detention Complex staff."

The Tombs was actually a facility consisting of a north and south tower that were linked together by an elevated walkway. Nic could only imagine the number of people it would take to clear the sewers and tunnel system below the complex, even with the physical barriers that were erected to keep people out of the area below the prison.

"Jason is briefing the Mayor and bringing him up to speed on what Allen said about the Triad having people in high places. They're going to give Allen some time to rest, but every alphabet agency in the nation wants to talk with him.

Jason wants to run the show here even though the case is no longer in our jurisdiction. Since we have Allen's testimony that the Triad weren't after your mom, and it is Triad infighting, not domestic terrorism, our presence here is tenuous at best."

Nic stopped short and grabbed Jade's arm. "If the Mayor okays it, we can run the operation?"

"Well, yeah... but..."

He held up his hand and palmed his phone, pressing a contact button. "Carmine, you need to reach out to the Deputy Mayor."

Nic stared at Jade. Her eyes held his, and he shook his head as Carmine launched into a tirade. Nic interrupted him mid-sentence, "No, *this* is the way it is going to happen. If you want any justice for Mom's murder, get the Mayor to okay Guardian's involvement in the ongoing investigation."

"You've got fucking nerve, Nico. She is dead because you didn't do your fucking job." Carmine's voice boomed across the line.

"She is dead because the Triad blew up an entire courthouse, killing not only Mom but numerous other people. Call your Dom, and get this approved."

There was silence on the other end of the line. "That bitch told you."

"Jade? No, Carmine, I've known for years, and I've never told anyone. God, I don't care about your sexual preferences, but you are in a unique position to leverage your relationship. Get Guardian on this case. Get me permission to go after the bastard that planned and executed the bombing."

Nic waited, the silence broken only by Carmine's ragged breaths. "I can't guarantee anything."

"Get me in there. For Mom." Nic disconnected the phone call.

"We need to head to the Tombs. If we get approval, we need to be there and ready." Jade's quiet reply brought him back to the hospital room. "Call Jason and let him know Carmine is trying to up the pressure. I'll drive."

"Hey." Nic grabbed her arm as she started to move away. She stopped and looked up at him. "Whatever happens today, if we get the green light or not, thank you for everything you've done."

He watched as Jade swallowed hard and lowered her eyes. "I know Carmine blames you, but I'm the one who was supposed to ensure your mom was safe. I keep going over everything I set in place…"

"What? No, there was no way for either of us to know. Believe me, I get it. I've gone over everything, over and over again. I know you've done the same thing. If you could have changed anything, what would it have been?"

Jade looked up at him and shook her head. "I… I don't know."

"Exactly. We did everything we could to protect her."

"Maybe if I had been in the building with her…"

"You may have been killed, too." Nic pulled her into his arms. "No more second guessing ourselves."

"Easier said than done, but yeah… I know we did everything we could. It still hurts." She gave him one rib-cracking squeeze and stepped back.

At that moment, Nic realized Jade didn't need him to comfort her, but she'd accepted solace in his arms. That small concession was huge in so many ways. Jade was a lone she-wolf. She allowed him into her territory. She didn't need him to be there with her, but she allowed it, and that was a privilege very few received. Jade had a pack. She'd relentlessly attack anyone who went after those in her pack. The fact that they'd developed feelings for each other was huge, and he recognized it as something fucking special. The revelation didn't make her any less self-reliant or deadly. No, his little she-wolf did not need anyone. But, she wanted him. Nic smiled at his parallel. If the woman ever found out he compared her to a dog, he'd be toast.

"What?" She stared up at him. Her gaze roamed his face as if searching for what made him smile.

"Nothing. I just realized something. You're smart and beautiful. I got lucky."

"It took you this long to figure that out, DeMarco? Damn good thing you're pretty."

Nic dropped a fast kiss on her lips and motioned toward the door. "Damn good thing. You drive."

CHAPTER 28

Nic got the eerie feeling they'd done this before as Jade jacked the SUV into a partial parking space. The Tombs stood three blocks over, but the NYPD had barricaded the roadways, forcing them to sprint toward the facility. A long line of The Department of Corrections buses lined White Avenue.

"Fuck! Are they moving the prisoners? That could force Bao to speed up his plans," Jade said what they were both thinking.

They stopped to flash their badges and find out who was directing on-scene actions and then jogged over to the armored special weapons and tactics van.

"I don't give a flying fuck about the money, Mr.

Mayor. If you don't authorize more people, we are going to be facing a disaster that you don't want to deal with. We have 890 inmates and hundreds of staff in this facility, and we won't even count the people in surrounding buildings that will be killed if this building blows. I need more busses. Pull them off the transit lines if you have to, but get me transportation!" The NYPD officer slammed the phone down and let out a guttural sound of frustration.

"Sir, we are here from Guardian. We need to get underneath the structures." Nic and Jade both flashed their badges. "We have just interviewed the maker of the triggers. We can disarm them."

Tired eyes turned toward them. "The Mayor doesn't want you down there, but the Deputy Mayor told me to allow you two in. I don't know who is running the show up there, but I need all the help I can get down here. If I lose my job over this, you better be willing to hire me on staff." He pulled down a map from the shelving unit.

"Fucking guaranteed, you have a job, anytime." Nic would pay the man any amount of money to get down into the tunnels. A job for an honest cop that was trying to save lives? A no-fucking-brainer.

"Here." The man stabbed his finger at the sewer blueprints. "Enter here. I have a ten men team heading down there." He pulled a mic from the radio bank. "Hesston, are you underground yet?"

"Negative, Captain. We are still trying to pry loose the barricades." The captain swore bitterly and keyed the mic again. "I have two specialists coming your way. They will lead the search. Standby until they get there to enter." The captain grabbed the blueprints and shoved them toward Nic. "The intersection of Centre and Walker Streets. Don't make me fucking regret this."

Jade jumped out of the vehicle and spun to follow Nic. They ran down White Street and turned left on Centre, sprinting past businesses that should have been bustling with activity but were now vacant. As they approached the intersection, they saw several city crews waiting next to an open manhole cover.

Jade slid to a stop and let Nic go down the stairs first, flashing her badge at the workers.

"You won't get cell reception down there unless you're directly under a manhole cover, and even that isn't a guarantee."

"Got it. Get the fuck out of here. Clear out!" She watched the men scatter before she made quick work of the ladder leading into the bowels of the city.

The stench of the underground system reared up and slapped her with a viciousness that would have made her vomit if she'd eaten anything that morning. She flipped the flashlight on her phone and illuminated the concrete walkway for both her and Nic. The sound of voices led them to a huddle of men.

"I'm Nic DeMarco, this is Jade King. Your captain sent us down here to lead the search. I'm breaking us into four teams of three. Jade and you two will head here. He pointed to the west corner of the tunnels. I'll go here," he pointed to the east side. "You, what's your name?" He pointed at the man closest to him.

"Hesston."

"Hesston, you take two men and go here." Nic looked at another man who gave his name without prompting, "Mason."

"Mason, you take the last corner. Cells and radios probably won't work unless you are right under a manhole, even that isn't guaranteed." He eyeballed Jade, and she nodded. "We are looking for four devices. The C-4 would need to be substantial so look for a package taped to the wall or maybe on the ceiling. The triggering devices will be the way to disarm the bomb. Clear all the way to your assigned locations but keep your eyes open, nothing says they are placed strategically. As soon as you clear your area, report in to me. Get your cells out and give me your numbers. He added the numbers to his phone and sent out a text to each of them, including Jade. "We have a fuck-ton of territory to cover. If you find the device cut the green wire first, the black wire second and then the white. Don't touch the red."

"Red equals dead." Jade's voice pulled everyone's eyes to her. "What? I don't want to fucking blow up." She blinked back at them innocently, but she knew they'd all remember the comment.

Nic smiled at her, and she winked at him. "Get going."

Jade spun on her heel and took the lead. The men assigned with her used their flashlights to illuminate the tunnel. They continued down the tunnel as quietly as possible. She held up her hand, and the men held, instantly pushing their lights against their thighs. A sweep of a flashlight down the tunnel in front of them sent her heartbeat into overdrive. She rose and crept cautiously forward.

They moved almost soundlessly down the tunnel and stopped at a three way split in the passage.

The distinct sound of tape ripping off a roll echoed around them. A muttered phrase in some language, definitely not English, extinguished all sounds from her team and eliminated the glow of their flashlights which had illuminated the underground tunnel moments before. Jade prayed the men behind her would remain silent. She heard footsteps approaching. Reaching back, she placed her hand on the nearest man's arm and tapped him three times. Hopefully, he understood. She felt his body move and prayed he was relaying the instructions to the other man.

Jade listened as several people moved closer. They were coming from the right. She tapped the arm next to her once. She felt his hand reach down toward the flashlight. Thank God. She tapped him again and felt his muscles bunch under her arm. She heard a shoe scuff directly in front of her. That is where she would launch on three. Jade tapped the man's arm and pushed through her legs, lifting her arms to protect her head and neck. She closed her eyes, not wanting the flashlights to blind her. She connected with a warm body and threw her elbow. Two ear-blasting percussive blasts split the air. Jade rolled up and ducked into her ready position. The man she fought smiled and dropped, preparing himself to fight. She could sense life or death struggles happening around her, but she couldn't break her focus on the threat directly in front of her. An onslaught of fists, feet, knees, and elbows flew her way. Jade reacted on instinct. She pulled her weapon, but the bastard sent it flying in a move she'd never seen. Skill, training and some damn fine luck helped her to deflect all but one blow of the next flurry of fists, strikes, and kicks. She could feel the skin over her ribs burst with a sharp searing flare. Fucker. A warm drip told her the bastard had cut her. Jade deflected another round of blows, careful to block the bastard's right hand and the small knife he wielded. She dropped down and swept his legs. The fast son of a bitch was up before she could link another move. Jade could still hear furious struggles going on behind and beside her. The flashlights laid scattered on the walkway, abandoned but illuminating grotesque shadows on the tunnel wall. The bastard in front of her advanced again. The exact same movements. That was his fucking mistake. Jade sidestepped his attack and dropped, grabbing the flashlight. She swung the light hard and took out the bastard's knee.

Jade had to give the guy credit, he stayed standing, and he did not go on the defensive like a wounded animal. No, instead of protecting himself, he launched forward and hit her with a flying body tackle. His weight covered her, driving her into the ground. His fists pounded rapid punches against her ribs as soon as they landed. Jade kicked the knee she'd just shattered, slowing her attacker's onslaught. She reached to her ankle, but the bastard doubled up his fist and punched her in the face. Pinpoints of white light exploded behind her eyelids. Jade rolled up and tucked her arms to protect her ribs and head. She felt rather than saw the bastard struggle to his feet. Jade grabbed her ankle, released her holster's catch, and drew her secondary weapon. She palmed the grip of the automatic, which released the safety. Jade fired three rounds at center mass, which happened to be the fucker's chest, and then double-tapped the bastard between the eyes. She rolled and took aim at another bastard who was kicking the fuck out of one of her men. Two rounds later, all sounds of struggle silenced.

She saw one of the officers she'd been assigned

with moving. "You okay?" Jade asked, but her words seemed garbled even to her own ears. The fucker that she'd been fighting had one hell of a punch.

"I'll live. Cunningham is unconscious. You put down the fucker that took him out."

Jade closed her eyes and fought a wave of emotion. She didn't know the men she worked with, but losing a brother in arms would have gutted her. "Position him so his airway isn't obstructed. We can't take him with us. When we get word out about this, we'll send in the medics. Any other survivors?"

"Ahhh... give me a minute." She heard him move and closed her good eye, giving herself a second to assess her own injuries. The cut on her ribs was going to leave a scar, but it was a flesh wound. Her face felt like a fucking exploded watermelon, but she could see out of one eye, and she could think straight. Good enough to deal. "No. Just us."

"Need to disarm the bomb." Jade pushed up and sucked in a sharp breath. Fuck, she really needed to train more. This getting her ass kicked was new, and it sucked sweaty monkey balls.

Yeah, they were damn lucky to be alive, but

they wouldn't be for much longer if they didn't get to the bomb. She braced herself against the side of the wall and used her free hand to grab a second weapon and then the handle of the flashlight.

She waited for the officer to come back to where she was, because fuck no, she wasn't walking any further than she absolutely had to walk. Together, they checked on Cunningham. He had one hell of a lump on the side of his head, but he had a strong pulse, and he was breathing with deep, clear pulls of air filling his lungs. When he woke up, he'd have one hell of a headache; but unlike their three assailants, he would wake up.

Jade lifted away from the officer and ensured the Triad surrounding him were down and out. Three shot dead, and the fourth's neck had been broken. She bent down and turned over a body, just to make sure the man was dead. The groan the movement elicited from her echoed down the empty tunnel. She stood, waved toward the primary tunnel, and they headed out. Both had their weapons extended as they turned, searching for anyone who might still be waiting by the device. The passageway echoed in its emptiness. Thank God. Jade dropped her hand and limped to the device taped to the side of the tunnel. It was closer than she'd anticipated. She surveyed the detonator and then at her partner. "I need a small knife. That piece of shit had one." She motioned toward the tunnel where they'd come. Even if she had her Interceptor 911, the blade would have been too big to work on the small detonator.

"Here." A pair of manicure scissors appeared in front of her face. She turned and gave the guy a questioning stare.

"Don't ask."

"Oh, I'm going to ask, and then I'm pretty sure I'm going to laugh." Jade pulled the small dome cover off the device.

"Remember, red is dead." The guy's face was right next to hers. She rolled her eyes and nudged him away.

"Breathing room, brother."

The man nodded and gave her a few more inches of space. Jade snipped the wires in succession, green, black and then white. She bent them backward, so there was no chance of them contacting anything.

"Okay. Need to find a way to communicate and get Cunningham help." Jade pushed herself up and stared down the tunnel. She had no idea how far up the next manhole cover would be. "If we go back, we might miss another device. We don't know that they are spacing the things out. That was an assumption." Jade looked at her new partner. "I'm Jade, by the way."

"I say we go that way." He pointed down the tunnel away from where they started. "We can join up with Hesston's group. Name's Mickey."

Jade nodded and turned to head down the tunnel ahead of them. "We could get blown up, too."

"Never been blown up before." Mickey turned and motioned back toward where they'd made a stand. "I will admit you aren't half bad in a fight."

"That makes me only half-good? Hell, Mickey, I can promise I'm way better than that." Jade lifted the light and laughed at the man's shocked expression. Yeah, it was good to be alive.

CHAPTER 29

Nic held up his hand. According to the blueprints he'd examined before they started following the tunnel, the passage to the left would lead to the base of the south tower. It would continue and go under both buildings, following the same basic route as the elevated walkway that joined the towers. He paused and studied the tunnel where he'd told the others he would be going. He could go forward, but if he did, they wouldn't clear the smaller tunnel. Damage to the ground between the towers could destabilize both. Fuck, if he'd taken a few more minutes to plan the search he wouldn't have to make this command decision.

He sent a universal hand signal bringing the

men he was working with up to his position. Nic whispered, "This tunnel runs under the elevated walkway. It needs to be cleared, but we don't have the time to stop clearing the main passageways." They'd all heard echoing pops earlier. It was definitely gunfire, and if they heard it, anyone else in the passageways would have heard it, too. They needed to clear the tunnels, find the devices and deactivate them before Bao pushed that fucking trigger.

Nic motioned to the two men and then pointed to the main tunnel. He indicated he would take the secondary tunnel. Both of them hesitated, and Nic understood the hesitation. If he ran into trouble, he'd be by himself, but fuck, if they didn't clear the tunnel... Nic repeated the motion and waited. The men glanced at each other before they nodded and headed down the passageway.

Nic slid around the corner and worked his way along the smooth cement path. He held the flashlight against his chest with one hand and his weapon drawn in his other. He worked forward five steps at a time and illuminated the passage briefly with a sliver of light from his flashlight before he pushed the beam against his stomach again. Five steps, peek, five steps, peek. The pattern wasn't efficient, but it was a hell of a lot safer than illuminating the passageway and becoming an instant target. The sounds of the underground tunnel took on a familiarity. Nic had just taken his third step when he heard something. He pushed against the side of the tunnel and clicked the flashlight off. Dropping into a squat, he waited. There… a scrape… no, it sounded like something tearing. Nic peered at the pitch black in front of him. A sweep of light flitted, illuminating the tunnel in front of him for a fraction of a second. Fuck. How many were there? Nic lifted and tucked the flashlight into his waistband. His hand now free, he used it as a guide against the wall of the tunnel. Carefully and silently, he advanced his position. As he approached the junction of the tunnel, he heard hushed voices. The tearing sound echoed. Tape?

Nic drew a deep breath and let it out slowly. He stepped into the passageway. Four men. Three were working on the explosives mounted to the wall. Two working with the tape, the third holding a flashlight to illuminate the task. The fourth swept his light down the adjoining tunnels. He turned as Nic lifted his weapon. "Guardian Security. Drop your weapons…"

Nic lunged to his left as the first explosion of gunfire pitted the cement next to his face. He made it to the opening of the tunnel he'd come down as he returned fire. He heard one of the bastards scream before a rush of footsteps headed his way. Nic rolled onto his back and opened fire. He fired, emptied his weapon and reloaded. He rolled into the tunnel and immediately realized he was now in the crossfire of two shooters. He swiveled and took out the closest man, but it was too little, too late. The searing tug of bullets tore through his leg. Nic rolled and emptied his clip. The immediate silence that followed his weapon's last report seemed to mock the intensity of what had transpired. Slowly, small sounds made themselves known. The ragged sounds of his breathing almost drowned out a small moan from the man next to him. Pulling his flashlight from his waistband, he clicked it on. One, two... three dead. The fourth man's eyes were fixed on Nic. Blood seeped from his mouth and nose. Nic flashed his light to where the man's weapon laid. He reached for it and damn near fainted from the fucking pain in his leg. He crawled on his elbows to the weapon. Fuck, he was going to puke from the pain. Nic pushed himself to the wall and fought off unconsciousness. He had to defuse the detonation device. Grabbing the hem of his button-up, he pulled his shirt off and used the arms to wrap the material around his thigh and stem the bleeding. A flick of the flashlight told him the bleeding from his thigh wasn't going to kill him, but the bone poking out of his shin wasn't good. Fuck, fuck, fuck... he cast a beam of light around him. The filth was going to be his biggest problem with an open wound. Nic put the flashlight down and pulled off his t-shirt. He carefully covered the exposed bone and prayed that he could stay conscious long enough to get to the bomb. Wouldn't you know the motherfuckers got him in the thigh of one leg and the calf of the other? He couldn't put any pressure on his lower leg. He'd be lucky if the docs could put Humpty Dumpty back together again. Fuck. Nic closed his eyes and swallowed down the reality of his fucked up situation. His lower leg was shattered, and his thigh had a bullet in it. He was shaking like a fucking leaf and the cold he was feeling was probably shock. Hell, the device that was at eye level might have as well been at the summit of Mount Everest.

Nic eyed the detonation device. The fucker was taunting him, blinking its green light at him.

Motherfucker! Nic raked his shaking hands through his hair. Someone would be back for him... maybe. He slid his hand toward the device and bumped into something cold. He directed the flashlight toward the floor. A metal pipe. Nic examined the explosives. The detonator linked the top block of C4, not the bottom. Did he disrupt the assholes before they could extend the charge to all the explosives? Nic grabbed at the pipe and drew himself toward the device on his elbows dragging his injured legs behind him. Stopping only to dry heave because of a screaming torrent of pain, he managed to low-crawl the five feet. Covered in sweat, he shivered almost uncontrollably. Nic sat under the device and lifted the pipe. He worked at peeling the tape from the wall while taking frequent breaks to rest. Finally, he managed to peel the bottom strip of tape free. Nic pushed behind a brick of C4 and angled the pipe out. The weight of the cube peeled itself away from the wall and the tape. The block dropped, hitting him on the shoulder. Fuck, if he could get the rest off, when the device detonated, the damage would be minimal.

Nic worked prying three more nodes of explosives away. The top two had charges implanted with the red wire glaring at him. Red is dead. Jade ended up front and center in his mind's eye. Nic closed his eyes, exhausted. Jade's warning sounding loud and clear. He contemplated the device and then the tunnel he'd come from. If he made it to that corner, the second corridor might shield him from the worst of the explosion. If the explosion didn't cave the roof in on his head.

He took out his phone and studied it before he opened the text app. He thumbed the words in, careful to type what he needed to say and pushed send before he pocketed the phone. It may never get through, but he'd tried. Nic let his body fall onto the wet cement and flopped onto his belly. The jarring move blasted another torrent of pain through his lower limbs. He was so fucking tired. He reached forward and heaved himself up on his bloody elbows. He needed to try. He didn't want to die. He wanted time with Jade. Dying under a ton of rubble... hell, this couldn't be the end. Nic's arms gave out, and he dropped to the ground. He was so cold. The shivering was worse now. He lifted his head. The tunnel entrance was so close. Nic pushed up again. His teeth clenched against the pain. He held his breath and moved, dragging his body forward.

Jade tapped Mickey on the arm. The light from a manhole cover shone down like an answer to a prayer. She jogged forward, careful to clear the area ahead of her. Jade pulled out her phone and climbed the ladder. Text messages starting pinging as soon as she hit the third step. She read the group texts aloud to Mickey. "Hesston cleared his device."

"That's two," Mickey called up to her.

"Someone else... Rawlings said they cleared their device. Who the fuck is Rawlings? I thought that guy Mason had a team?" Jade lost her signal and stepped up the ladder as she typed her message.

"Rawlings was with your guy." Mickey's answer floated up to her.

Jade hit send. She looked down at Mickey's upturned face. "What?" Her phone vibrated. "Mason reports no devices found on his side."

"There is still one missing."

Jade gaped down the ladder at the cop. "Thank you, Captain Obvious."

Her phone vibrated again. Nic, finally. She opened the text.

>Unable to kill device. Small tunnel between

buildings. Not able to evacuate. Get everyone out. I loved you.

"Fuck! No!" Jade jumped down the ladder and grabbed Mickey by the arm. She slapped the phone into his hand. "Get up there and text everyone to get the fuck out. Tell the on-scene commander the device in the small tunnel between the towers is active." She grabbed his flashlight and spun around getting her bearings.

"Where are you going?" Mickey called after her.

"To find my fucking man!" Jade launched down the tunnel. Her lungs burned, and her heart pounded. She thought she knew where the tunnel Nic had mentioned was, but it was like a fucking labyrinth down here. She saw a defused device. Not the one she did with Mickey, and there were no dead bodies. Did that mean someone got out of the tunnel? Son of a bitch! Jade skidded to a stop at a junction. She closed her eyes and tried to draw the image of the tunnel system to mind and compare it to where she thought she was now.

She turned to her left and then to her right. She had no idea which way to turn. As she stepped to her right, a low rumbling thunder came from her left. The noise amplified and rolled, louder and louder. A blast of air, dust and small particles of debris pushed into the tunnel where she stood. Terror froze her to the spot she was standing for a moment. She jolted from its grip and started sprinting through the tunnel. Jade covered her mouth with her hand and blinked through the settling dust and dirt. The flashlight barely cut light a foot in front of her. She pulled her shirt off and wrapped it around her face. "Nic!" She screamed his name repeatedly as she advanced down the tunnel. Small blocks of concrete littered the walkway. They became larger as she moved forward.

She pointed toward the end of the tunnel. The debris formed a mound on the left hand side. Jade ran toward the junction, falling once. She skidded to a stop. The tunnel was blocked to her right. Huge pieces of concrete wedged in impossible shapes obliterating her passage. Jade dropped to her knees and screamed, "No!"

"Jade."

Her head whipped around at the sound of her name. Holy fuck! She swung her flashlight and saw an arm. Jade scrambled on her knees to the mound near the wall. Carefully she pulled the cement chunks away from his chest and a huge one off his shoulder.

"Nic, talk to me." Jade shook so bad she had trouble holding the flashlight. She placed her hand on his neck and felt for a pulse. Light and thready, but there.

"Nic, come on, babe. You need to talk to me. Help is on the way." At least she prayed it was.

"Cold."

"I know. Don't worry, I'll warm you up. I promise. Just keep talking to me, yeah?" She removed another slab of cement that pinned his hips.

"Love you."

Jade pushed the rest of the rubble off his legs and stifled a gasp. His leg below the knee twisted backward abnormally and appeared separated from his body.

"I love you, too. I'm going to put a tourniquet on your leg, okay?" Jade whipped off her belt and strapped it under his knee. She pulled the fucker as tight as she could and tightened it, even more, using the barrel of her weapon to spin the leather. "Nic, talk to me…"

He grunted something. Jade did a quick search and found the injury to his thigh that he'd wrapped himself. She lay down next to him and pulled his shivering form closer.

"Hey, stay with me, Nic. You need to keep talking, okay?" Tears streamed down her cheeks, but she didn't move to wipe them away. She wrapped her arms around Nic and rubbed his back trying to warm him.

"Tired."

"I know. So am I. When we get out of here, we're taking a vacation. You know what I mean?"

Nic didn't answer. She pulled back and found his pulse, barely there. Jade couldn't lose him. No, please, no... no... no... She moved her fingers, desperately searching for signs of life.

"Is anyone down here?"

Jade lifted her face and screamed, "Here! Hurry!" She lifted away from Nic and held her flashlight up, flagging it in the air.

Craning her neck, she watched the bouncing lights on FDNY helmets as they raced toward her. She cupped Nic's face in her palm. "Stay with me, Nic. Don't you fucking dare leave me."

CHAPTER 30

J ade smoothed the tented blanket over Nic's bed. After four weeks, the noise of the hospital faded into a mindless din in the background of her consciousness. The words of the intercom pierced through her wandering thoughts. "Paging Doctor Shaeffer, Doctor Shaeffer, please call extension four-zero." Jade snorted to herself and grabbed the remote for Nic's television. She didn't know who the fuck Doctor Shaeffer was, but the man... or woman... was in demand, like, all the fucking time. Jade turned on the TV and found the ballgame. She wasn't much of a football fan, but Jared had told her Nic was a devout fan.

Jade made her way back to Nic's side. She

hadn't left the hospital in four weeks. She ate, slept and showered here. Whatever strings Guardian had to pull, they pulled so she could stay with Nic. The fear of coming out to her family about her relationship with Nic never materialized. Or if it had, she'd missed the drama. Her focus was on Nic. She didn't fucking care if they approved or not. Nic's brother Mario was a constant visitor along with Jared and Christian. Carmine showed up once and only once. Fucker dared to make a scene. Jade sneered as she thought of the one-sided conversation she had with that asshole.

Jade ran her hand up and down Nic's arm. The doctors continued to caution her that he'd had serious blood loss and damage to his cognitive reasoning was a real possibility. If he woke up. No, he would wake up, because damn it, she wasn't going to let him escape their relationship that easy. They'd made a commitment to each other. Or she'd made a commitment to him. If he didn't like it, she'd make him change his mind. Didn't fucking matter.

Jade smoothed the tented material. Her man had lost his left leg from below the knee. He'd been shot in his thigh and had a broken clavicle and a crushed shoulder, but he was still alive. Nic had opened his eyes several times, but he'd never stayed awake or seemed to know that she was there. It didn't matter. She'd take care of Nic until the day she died.

He loved her. He told her that down there in that tunnel, and she believed him. She'd given him her heart and fuck the world if they thought she should give him up like yesterday's trash. She wasn't leaving his side even when they transferred him to that fucking 'rehab' facility. Bullshit. It was a nursing home. Well, she'd made other plans. She pulled all her money out of savings and was having her house renovated; complete with ramps, three-foot wide interior doors, PT room, and handicapped bathrooms with roll-in showers. Jacob and Jason were tagteaming the contractors to keep them in line. Her brothers had been pretty fucking wonderful through the aftermath.

Nic moaned and twitched. He did that more and more recently.

Jade leaned over him and dropped a kiss on his forehead. "Shhh... you're safe. I'm here."

His movements eased at her words. They would move Nic to her house when the work was complete. A full-time nursing staff and on-call doctor were already hired. Nic would have the best.

Jade pulled her chair up next to his bed and took his hand in hers. "I don't know what you see in this game. I mean, yeah, those guys have cute asses... well, most of them do. Some of those monsters that are on the front line... I'm not sure what they greased to get those britches on, babe, but no... just no. Oh hey, look. That guy clocked the hell out of that one. Why did they throw the flag? What is this? Ballet? It was a legal hit. Right?" She focused on Nic. His eyes flitted back and forth under his eyelids. "I know, right? Totes legal." Jade shook her head. "I don't know, sometimes you got to wonder. Oh, hey, did you see this commercial? I love it." She sang the jingle and squeezed his hand at the end.

Nic squeezed her hand in return. Jade jerked her gaze back to him. His eyes twitched under their lids.

The doctors told her that what she was feeling was his response to stimuli; it didn't necessarily mean anything. The first few times it happened, she was sure he was waking up, but over the last week, she'd started to accept the doctor's word. A loud burst of laughter sounded in the hall. Jade glanced up at the clock. Shift change. She knew all the nurses, now. Didn't like a few of them, and they for sure didn't like her. They had the gall to call her demanding. No shit. She was here to take care of her man, and fuck the world if they didn't like it.

Jade upped the sound and snorted as the intercom bleated for Doctor Shaeffer again. Jade mimicked the voice, "Calling Jack, Jack Daniels, you're wanted in room 313, stat!"

A snort from beside her damn near landed her on her ass. Jade grabbed the side rail of the bed to steady herself. Nic's eyes were open and oh... God... he was looking at her.

"Nic! Babe, can you hear me?"

His head moved up and down. He swallowed and tried to speak.

"Wait! No, no, no..." Jade reached for the call button and lit that bitch up like a Christmas tree.

She cupped his face with her hands and kissed his forehead before pulling back to look at those beautiful brown eyes. She was crying, she knew it, and she didn't give a flying fuck. "Hey DeMarco, it's a damn good thing you're pretty, yah know?"

His lips pulled up for a fraction of a second.

"You needed something, Ms. King?" A nurse peeked in the door.

Jade swung her attention to the woman. "He's awake and trying to talk." Jade held his hand to her chest and turned back. Nic's eyes had closed again. "No, he was awake, I promise."

The nurse came forward. "Remember, the doctors..."

"See!" Jade shrieked when Nic opened his eyes again. "Nic squeeze my hand if you understand me. She held his hand up where the nurse could see it. A slow, deliberate squeeze formed around her hand.

That got the condescending nurse's ass moving. Jade kissed his hand and leaned down to him. "You and me, we're going to be okay. I'm going to be beside you every fucking step of the way. You're stuck with me now. You got that, DeMarco?" His hand squeezed again before his eyes drifted shut.

Jade dropped into the chair beside his bed and put her head down on his arm. She held his hand. After twenty-eight days, she allowed all the doubt, fear, worry, and love she felt pour through her, and she sobbed for Nicolas Fucking DeMarco.

CHAPTER 31

Week 5 ANWU (After Nic Woke Up).

"This is complete and utter bullshit."
Jade marched from her den to the bedroom she
shared with Nic. She clasped her laptop to her
chest and tugged the strap of the teddy she was
wearing up over her shoulder.

"It isn't bullshit. You know I'm right. Just get
me my damn phone, and I'll call Jared to come
get me."

"Yeah? And where are you going to go?" Jade
stopped in the doorway.

"To New York!"

"Fuck you, DeMarco!" Jade stepped in and
slammed the door behind her. The concussion of

her anger reverberated through the walls of the house.

"Wouldn't that settle all of our problems?" Nic yelled back at her.

"Yeah, it might, but you're still a fucking asshole."

"I may be an asshole, but you need to step back. It's not like you're going to get any from me anyway." Nic folded his arms over his chest.

"Because you are fucking holding out on me! Like I fucking care about your God damn leg!"

"I don't need or want a pity fuck!"

Jade ground her teeth together. "A pity… you son of a bitch! You don't know how much I want to wind up and fucking knock this shit out of you."

"Whatever, just get me my fucking chair."

"No! God damn it, Nic, can't you understand that you are still so fucking sexy that I want you, like constantly?"

"Yeah. Right, because you get off on amputees?"

"Fuck. You are so aggravating! Look! You are more than your missing leg, asshat!" Jade threw the computer on the bed and lifted the lid. She tapped the screen. Typing furiously she pulled up a photographer's website before she clicked on the gallery. She plopped the computer down on Nic's lap before she climbed into bed and sat beside him. His body was rigid with anger.

"What the fuck is this?"

"This is proof. Stop being a prick for two seconds and look." She pointed toward the screen. A beautiful picture of a male model appeared on the screen. The nude, tattoo covered model looked back at them. The man was an amputee, and drool-worthy. "Read the fucking comments, DeMarco!" Jade tapped the bottom of the page. She let him read a few of the comments before she swiped her computer screen and brought another model up. She pointed at the comments. She felt Nic's anger subside and his body slowly relax beside her.

After the fifth or sixth picture, Jade lifted the computer off his lap and sat it on her nightstand. "I'm not the only one who can see past what life has done to these handsome men. Men just like you. I don't understand how you can think I see anything less than the man I fell in love with. You amaze me everyday. You're strong, and you face every fucking challenge head on. Every one except this one." She straddled Nic and ran her hands up his chest to rest on his shoulders. He wouldn't meet her eyes. Jade lowered her head, keeping her hands on his shoulders until their eyes met.

"I love you, DeMarco. Not your fucking foot. You are beautiful to me. I didn't sit beside you in the hospital for a month because I was going to leave you, and you sure as fuck are not going to push me away."

Nic shook his head and pulled his chin from her grip. "You deserve better."

"Like hell I do. I got exactly what I deserve, and that's you. Nic, would you leave me if I was the one who was hurt?"

"What? No!" His eyes shot back to her.

"Why in the hell do you think I'd leave you?"

"Because I can't even fucking walk!"

"Bullshit! I saw you in the PT room. They'll get the fit right on your prosthesis, and it will get easier."

Nic brought his hands up and scrubbed his face. "How can you still want me?"

Jade pulled his hands down and waited for him to look at her. "Because, you stupid man, you're my everything. Everything I have ever run away from, everything I've ever feared, everything I kept telling myself I didn't need. Is your rehab going to be hard? Damn straight. Am I going to kick your ass every step of the way to make sure you do what you need to do to get better? Fuck yes, and you got to know I'll enjoy that. Right?"

Nic fought it, but the smile won. He ran his hands up and down her arms. The sensation pulled a full body shudder from her. Fuck, she needed his touch, the touch he hadn't been willing to give her. "Yeah, you'll probably enjoy that."

"Fucking-A. But, what we both need, DeMarco is a little one-on-one time. The doctor cleared you. I want you inside me and fuck you if you think I'm taking no for an answer. Besides, I bought this damn thing for you, and you haven't even told me if you like it." Jade lifted both of the ribbon straps of her teddy and dropped them down her shoulders.

Nic picked at the ribbon on her arms. "I don't like it. In fact, I hate it. I think you need to take it off. It offends me."

"Yeah?" Jade lowered to kiss her man. For the first time since he woke up, the kiss moved past a platonic peck on the lips. His tongue swept over her lips asking for entry and Jade opened, letting her tongue dance against his. His hand snaked up into her hair, and he crushed her into his chest.

He pulled away. They both drew much needed air into their lungs.

"Fuck, babe."

Jade stood and dropped the expensive piece of deep green lace and ribbon to the floor. She ran her hand up her leg and hip and continued up to her breast.

"You want me? Then fucking take me, DeMarco."

Nic's arm shot out, grabbing her and drawing her down to him on the bed. Jade laughed as he rolled over on top of her. He settled his weight over her as she spread her legs inviting him into her. He kissed down her jaw to her neck and whispered against her neck. "You wait until I get you in that ring again. I'll take you down a few pegs."

Jade ran her hands through his hair and pulled him up so she could see him. The fire in his eyes replaced the desperation that had been living there for the last five weeks.

"DeMarco, I look forward to kicking your ass again. You name the place and time, and I'll be there."

Nic lowered his lips to hers and breathed, "With me, always."

EPILOGUE

Through the windows, Nic scanned the people milling inside the restaurant. Fuck, as much as he told Jade he was okay with the evening, he really wished he could forego making a grand entrance. Justin had set up the party for him. Hell, he closed one of his best steakhouses in DC for the night so the family, Gabriel, and his friends from Guardian could gather and relax. His eyes found Jade. She was talking to one of the team members providing security for the facility tonight. She raised her head and locked stares with him. The woman seemed to know the minute he turned his attention toward her. A smile split her face, and she excused herself, making her way to him.

"Are you sure you're ready for this?" Jade took his arm and glanced up at him.

For the last seven months, she had been his head cheerleader, chief ass-kicker, and immovable support system. She didn't hover, but she wasn't about to let him flounder either. They'd fought like cats and dogs and made love like there was no tomorrow. She was the yin to his yang. He laughed openly at that thought.

"What perverted thought just raced through your brain, DeMarco?" Jade narrowed her eyes at him and then let a smile spread across her face.

"Nothing." He bent down to kiss her and felt her hands brace against his chest. Ever since he'd advanced to his newest prosthetic, his balance had been off, particularly when he bent down. The feel of her hands on his chest steadied him. It wasn't something he told her to do, yet she did it instinctively. The woman was insane and irreverent, called him on every asshole thing he tried to get away with, but she loved him, and he was one lucky man.

"Yeah, right. Don't worry, I'll get it out of you later tonight." Jade pushed up and licked his bottom lip before she bit it. "I feel like taking a ride, baby."

Nic's dick twitched and plumped. "Evil woman." He swatted her on the ass, the resounding crack and subsequent squeal made him laugh.

"Dude, you know she can kill you, right?" Zane's gravelly voice came from behind them.

"Maybe, but I'm working on that." His first foray back into the sparring ring had been earlier this week. His center of balance and core muscles needed work, and he was training under a new sensei that Jade had found for them. The man worked out moves Nic could do within the limits of his prosthesis. He had one hell of a long way to go, but he'd get there eventually.

"No doubt." Zane extended his hand.

Nic grabbed it automatically. He and Zane had a solid truce going on. In his job running the administrative side of CCS, Zane had carved out an important and vital role for himself in the success of Guardian's expanding cyber-crimes branch.

"What are you doing out here?" Jade looked behind Zane. "Where's Jewell?"

"She's inside. I had to take care of something for Jason. Can I walk you in?"

"Sure." Nic moved forward. His gait was off, but his PT assured him he'd settle into the advanced engineering of his new lower leg and foot.

Zane pulled open the front door and let them go in first. A huge 'Welcome Back Nic' sign draped over the front of the dining area, and a cheer broke out when they walked inside.

"It is about time your ass comes back to work. Been milking that boo-boo for far too long, my brother!" Jared reached up and pulled him into a hug. Nic stumbled forward slightly, but his best friend held him steady. "I fucking missed you, man." Jared's muttered words were meant only for him.

Nic nodded and thumped the man on his back. "Yeah, I missed you, too." He lifted away. "Give me a month to catch up on the cases and then you and your husband can take off for a week or two and get reacquainted. I know you've been pulling some long-ass days lately."

"True, but nothing we haven't done before."

Jason and Faith moved forward, followed by Jacob and Tori. Christian caught up with his husband, and they linked hands. Zane put his arms around Jewell and pulled her into his chest.

Nic considered his circle of friends and shook his head. "I don't know how to tell you how grateful I am. Any other organization would have written me off, or put me out to pasture."

Jason snorted, almost choking on the drink he was sipping. "You've got to be fucking kidding me? You were worried about us letting you go? Dude, we need you. You were injured saving lives. There is no way we would have cut you loose."

"Yeah, who would save us in case of a zombie apocalypse?" Jared's taunt got everyone laughing.

Jason shook his head, "Dude, there is no such thing as zombies."

Nic's jaw dropped. "What the hell do you mean? Zombies are real! Tell them, babe, tell them!"

Jade leaned into him, buried her head in his neck, and shook with laughter.

"God, it will be good to get you back, you damn idiot." Jacob extended his hand.

Nic scowled but took his hand. "You guys will be saying you're sorry when the zombie apocalypse happens. Mark my words."

Jade stayed by Nic's side until the tension she felt in him all day ebbed away. Her man had been nervous about going back to work. He still had health issues. He was fighting to regain the strength he once had, and some days his injuries fought back. He'd waded through depression and come out on the other side.

Yes, Nic persevered, but he would not enter small confined areas any longer. If there wasn't a door or window and it was small like the little tunnel under the Tombs, Nic DeMarco wasn't setting foot near it. He was working with a shrink to overcome the events leading up to his injury and the aftermath. Jade had never met a stronger man and she would be with him every step of his recovery. She spied Jason in the corner of the dining room and excused herself to go talk to him.

"Have you heard anything on Bao?" Both she and Nic had been tracking the man's movements. Mostly rumors and supposition, but they would be patient, and they'd find the bastard.

"Nothing too much to report since the last time we talked." Jason glanced up from his phone. "How's your man holding up?"

"He's solid. He's started training again." Jade glanced back at Nic. He had regained some weight and muscle. His smile tonight was genuine, and it fucking rocked to see him happy.

"Mentally?" Jason folded his arms across his chest and looked down at her. Damn, she sometimes forgot how massive her brother was.

"He's in a good place now. We've talked a lot about what happened. Life is unpredictable, and there isn't always a pot of gold waiting at the end of the rainbow. Closure isn't always an option."

"But he did get his pot of gold, didn't he? He got you."

Jade threw back her head and laughed, drawing everyone's attention. She reached up and swatted Jason's shoulder. "Nah, dude, you got that all wrong. I won. I got a man I respect, one that can fuck my brains into mush, and there is never a dull moment. I won the fucking lottery." She damn near shouted the comment, and she could tell by the reaction of the people surrounding Nic that they heard what she'd said. Fuck it, she didn't care. Life was great, and so was Nicolas Fucking DeMarco.

Anubis rolled back, cloaking himself further in the shadows. He inspected the picture on his phone. He memorized every detail about Yi Bao. His handlers at Guardian had dropped the authorization into his lap less than an hour ago. The man he was looking at was coded and his days were numbered.

He surveyed the people gathered in the restaurant. The woman in red and the man with the limp kissed, to the amusement of everyone else in the room. Anubis used the distraction to move farther away from the gathering. He really shouldn't be inside, but the laughter had pulled him in. He'd sat in the dark and watched the people who could walk in the sunshine. Love, respect, and friendship wove around everyone in the room. Anubis took a deep, long breath. It was rare he could relax, but here, for the moment, he was safe.

Zane Reynolds gazed intently into the shadowed corners where Anubis had been only moments earlier. Perhaps a specter from his past life had brushed Zane's shoulder and caused him to examine the darkness and remember a man he'd called "brother". Anubis felt a sad, slow smile spread across his face. He doubted they'd ever meet again. His "brother" was free from the shackles of their once-shared profession. Zane Reynolds now lived in the light.

Anubis closed the door silently and slipped

away, unnoticed and unremarked. It was fitting he would remain unseen and in darkness, for he was an instrument of vengeance and the deliverer of justice. He dispatched death by an assassin's hand —silent, deadly, swift, and remorseless. Anubis, a shadow within the Guardian world, would once again become his nation's final play against a monstrosity.

To read the next in the King's of Guardian series, Justin's story, click here!

To Read Anubis' story Click here!

THE END

Kings of the Guardian Series

Jacob: Kings of the Guardian Book 1

Joseph: Kings of the Guardian Book 2

Adam: Kings of the Guardian Book 3

Jason: Kings of the Guardian Book 4

Jared: Kings of the Guardian Book 5

Jasmine: Kings of the Guardian Book 6

Chief: The Kings of Guardian Book 7

Jewell: Kings of the Guardian Book 8

Jade: Kings of the Guardian Book 9

Justin: Kings of the Guardian Book 10

Christmas with the Kings

Drake: Kings of the Guardian Book 11

Dixon: Kings of the Guardian Book 12

Passages: The Kings of Guardian Book 13

Promises: The Kings of Guardian Book 14

A Backwater Blessing: A Kings of Guardian Crossover
Novella

Montana Guardian: A Kings of Guardian Novella

Guardian Defenders Series

Gabriel

Maliki

John

Jeremiah

Guardian Security Shadow World

Anubis (Guardian Shadow World Book 1)

Asp (Guardian Shadow World Book 2)

Lycos (Guardian Shadow World Book 3)

Thanatos (Guardian Shadow World Book 4)

Tempest (Guardian Shadow World Book 5)

Smoke (Guardian Shadow World Book 6)

Reaper (Guardian Shadow World Book 7)

Hope City

Hope City - Brock

HOPE CITY - Brody- Book 3

Hope City - Ryker - Book 5

Hope City - Killian - Book 8

STAND ALONE NOVELS

SEAL Forever - Silver SEALs

A Heart's Desire - Stand Alone

Hot SEAL, Single Malt (SEALs in Paradise)

Hot SEAL, Savannah Nights (SEALs in Paradise)

ABOUT THE AUTHOR

USA Today and Amazon Bestselling Author, Kris Michaels is the alter ego of a happily married wife and mother. She writes romance, usually with characters from military and law enforcement backgrounds.

Made in the USA
Monee, IL
29 August 2021